PRAISE FOR BEVERLY JENKINS AND THE BLESSINGS NOVELS

"*Bring on the Blessings* is . . . a cheerful yet heartbreaking book about second chances."

—*Sacramento Book Review*

"Jenkins's dialogue crackles. . . ."

—*Publishers Weekly*

"This series is a winner."

—Examiner.com/Minneapolis

"*A Second Helping* is a must read. A fantastic story that is unforgettable."

—*Books2Mention Magazine*

"4½ stars. There is a beauty in Jenkins's storytelling that should be the standard by which to judge fiction writing."
—*RT Book Reviews* on *Something Old, Something New*

"Her stories are delicious and always leave behind both feelings of satisfaction and want . . . for her next novel."

—FreshFiction.com

A WISH
AND
A PRAYER

Also by Beverly Jenkins

A WISH
AND
A PRAYER

A BLESSINGS NOVEL

Beverly Jenkins

WILLIAM MORROW

An Imprint of HarperCollins*Publishers*

A WISH AND A PRAYER. Copyright © 2012 by Beverly Jenkins. All rights reserved. Printed in the United States of America. No part of this book may be used or reproduced in any manner whatsoever without written permission except in the case of brief quotations embodied in critical articles and reviews. For information address HarperCollins Publishers, 10 East 53rd Street, New York, NY 10022.

HarperCollins books may be purchased for educational, business, or sales promotional use. For information please write: Special Markets Department, HarperCollins Publishers, 10 East 53rd Street, New York, NY 10022.

Library of Congress Cataloging-in-Publication Data has been applied for.

ISBN 978-0-06-199080-9

12 13 14 15 16 OV/RRD 10 9 8 7 6 5 4 3 2 1

To my sister Arlene for her wishes and prayers

PROLOGUE

December
Florida

Bernadine Brown's vast wealth had gained her entrée to many top-notch places, but this was her first foray into the inner sanctum of NASA's sprawling Florida complex. A member of security ushered her into one of the offices, then withdrew silently, leaving her alone with the woman she'd come to see.

She was across the room and standing before a window covered by partially opened blinds. Her name was Dr. Margaret Winthrop, and she was one of the nation's foremost astrophysicists. Bernadine had been expecting a dowdy person in a lab coat. The reality was a tall, trim woman dressed in a fashionable black suit with assessing eyes set in a cocoa-brown face as beautiful as that of any supermodel.

She gestured Bernadine to a chair. "Have a seat, Ms. Brown, but I'm not sure whether I'm pleased to meet you or not."

Bernadine complied without taking offense at the honesty. "Thanks for agreeing to see me anyway. My apologies for intruding into your life."

"May I ask how you found me?"

"Your mother, Lenore Crenshaw, actually. She responded to the search Preston posted on the Internet. When we spoke, she told me where you worked."

"And people wonder why I dropped the Crenshaw name."

The bitterness in her voice was plain, and it gave Bernadine pause; Mrs. Crenshaw hadn't indicated that she and her daughter were estranged. Winthrop turned her back to the room, as if needing to put some distance between herself and whatever information Bernadine might be seeking.

"What's he like?" she asked.

Bernadine inwardly smiled, thinking about the fourteen-year-old affectionately known as Brain. "He's scary smart. Big heart. Dry wit. Wants to grow up to be Dr. Neil deGrasse Tyson."

Surprised eyes spun her way.

" 'The apple doesn't fall far from the tree,' " she quoted. "Preston's so intellectually gifted, we've had to bring in graduate students from the university's physics department to keep him challenged. When he gets older and has the opportunity to really exercise his mind, he's going to be a force."

Winthrop had refocused on the view through the blinds, and stood so still Bernadine wondered what she might be thinking.

"His father's name was Lawrence Mays. He was from Philly. Preston's named for Lawrence's grandfather. My parents didn't care for Lawrence or our relationship because he didn't have a pot to piss in, or a window to throw it out of, as my mother was so fond of saying."

Bernadine assumed the mother's intolerance was one of the reasons for the daughter's acrimonious attitude.

"But he was scary smart, too. Funny, witty, charming. The consummate gentleman. We met at MIT during our junior year. He was on scholarship."

"Do you know where I can reach him?"

"He died in a car accident two months before Preston was born. I was devastated. My mother said the death was a godsend."

Bernadine felt sorry for her. The resonating pain was palpable. "Did he have family?"

"Yes. His mother and father divorced when he was young, and his mom raised him and his sister alone. I met them once, but I didn't go to the funeral—my parents wouldn't allow it."

"Any idea if they're still alive, or where they might be?"

"No.

Bernadine shook her head at what this meant for Preston. She doubted Lawrence's family had been given any say in the decision to send him into foster care. She wondered if they even knew Preston existed. "Did his mother know about your pregnancy?"

"I'm sure she did, but if she tried to call after the funeral, my parents never told me."

She went silent for a short time, as if thinking back. "You have to understand; I wanted to keep the baby, but they were so opposed and I wasn't strong then. I was twenty years old—a sheltered little rich girl from Boston who'd always followed orders—but they kept hammering away at how an infant would mess up my career and keep me from finishing school, not to mention the stain on the great Crenshaw name, so I gave in and let them arrange for him to be taken away." Her voice trailed off to a whisper.

"I'm not here to judge you, Dr. Winthrop."

"I know. Maybe I'm trying to justify what happened in my own mind."

"Would you like to see a picture of him?"

"Yes." And she wiped away the tears pooled in the corners of her eyes.

Bernadine took out her phone and brought up a picture she'd taken of Preston, smiling and holding a clipboard during last year's August First festivities.

Winthrop walked over and eyed the image. "He looks a lot like Lawrence."

"He favors you, too." There was a strong resemblance in their eyes and in the shape of their jaws.

After studying his face a few seconds longer, she returned the phone. "Thank you."

"You're welcome. Are there any genetic health issues his foster parents need to know about?"

"No."

"Okay. Here's my card. If you ever feel the need to get in touch, my number's there."

She took the card, but shook her head. "I won't be barging back into his life, not after all this time. Is he happy?"

"Extremely, but reconnecting with you would make him even more so."

She didn't reply.

Bernadine told her sincerely, "Preston's a very special young man. If you change your mind, I know he'd love to meet you."

But she was back in front of the window again, seemingly staring out at the sunset. "Is there anything else, Ms. Brown? I'm meeting some of my colleagues for dinner."

Bernadine hadn't expected such an abrupt ending, but she

didn't hold it against her. The visit had obviously opened up lingering, unhealed wounds.

"No, but thank you again for your time. Would you like Preston to know we've spoken?"

"No, and I'd appreciate it if you wouldn't contact me again."

That was disappointing, but Bernadine let it go. "Thanks again for seeing me." Giving the back of the black suit one last glance, Bernadine rose and walked to the door.

"Ms. Brown?"

She stopped. "Yes?"

"My mother's poison. Don't let her worm her way into your lives. She only cares about herself."

Bernadine acknowledged the warning, and softly closed the door behind her.

Later, on the flight back to Kansas, Bernadine sat alone in the passenger compartment of her private jet and thought back on the meeting. Preston Mays was the only foster child in Henry Adams yet to make contact with a birth parent. After today's visit she wasn't sure he ever would, but stranger things had happened, so she said a prayer and vowed to keep an open mind.

CHAPTER
1

April
Henry Adams, Kansas

I f you don't open it, you're never going to know."
The unopened e-mail had been languishing in fourteen-year-old Preston May's in-box for more than a week, but as he and his best friend Amari July sat in Preston's bedroom in front of the computer monitor, Preston, aka Brain, was still unsure what he should do.

"Brain, didn't you want your birth family to contact you?"

"Yeah, but what if it's something bad?"

"Like maybe your family doesn't want contact, the way my birth mom didn't? Your grandmother could've told Ms. Bernadine that on the phone back in November."

Brain, ever the brain, replied, "Logically, I know you're right, but emotionally—that's another story. Tired of getting my feelings hurt."

"Understandable, but suppose it's something good?"

Preston sighed. Like Amari and the other kids in Henry Adams, he'd spent most of his life in foster care, living in a stream of homes that went from bad to worse until Ms. Bernadine swooped them up in her white jet and brought them to Kansas. Since then, life had been good. All the other kids had made contact with their birth parents in some way or another, and the experiences had gone from pretty cool, in Amari's case, to scary, in Crystal's, when she was kidnapped and held for ransom by her birth dad. Preston figured his encounter would be somewhere in between.

When he first began searching for his birth parents, he'd been confident about his ability to handle the results. Now he wasn't so sure. "But why would she wait so long to send this?"

Amari shrugged. "Maybe she's rich like Ms. Bernadine and spent the winter in France or someplace. Maybe she's been in the hospital. I don't know."

Preston didn't either.

Amari stood. "Look, I gotta go. Told my dad I'd meet him at the garage for lunch. Text me later if you want to play chess."

Preston nodded, but never took his eyes off the screen.

"Are you still trying to decide?" The question came from his foster mom, Mrs. Sheila Payne. She was standing in the doorway of his room. He couldn't have asked for a better parent. She understood him, supported him, and cared enough for him that he now thought of her as Mom. He never called her that to her face, because he didn't think it was right until he was officially adopted, but in his mind he was her son.

Her husband, Colonel Barrett Montgomery Payne, was a different story. He was a retired marine drill sergeant and a hard-ass. He and Preston had been making progress in their relationship, but the colonel was having issues with Preston's search for his biological parents, and their clashing led to them backing off each other, again. "Yeah, I am."

She walked up behind his chair and gently placed her hands on his shoulders. "You really should open it, son. It's the only way you'll know."

"Amari said the same thing, and you're both right, but—"

"Scared there might be drama?"

"Yeah. I've had enough of that in my life."

She squeezed his shoulders affectionately. "It's up to you, but the not knowing is adding its own drama. Might be best to read it and get it out of the way." She paused as if to let that sink in for a moment. "Lunch'll be ready in a few minutes."

"What're we having?"

"I'm not sure. The colonel's cooking."

His panicked face met her kind eyes. "But it's Saturday— aren't you supposed to cook today?"

"Barrett volunteered. It'll be okay. Promise." Giving him a supportive squeeze, she left him alone with his screen and his thoughts.

When he and the Paynes first came together as a foster family, everything ran on a tight, no-nonsense schedule. The household awakened at a precise time, Mrs. Payne served breakfast promptly at 7:00 A.M., and the rest of the day followed suit. But now she had a job as the Henry Adams VP of social affairs, and one of the first casualties had been what the colonel called household discipline. He and the colonel were now responsible for their own laundry and for cleaning up after themselves, and meals were no longer served at the exact same time each day. In fact, on the evenings Mrs. Payne worked late, the colonel was forced to cook dinner. Because of all the foster homes, Preston knew his way around a kitchen and didn't mind making himself the occasional grilled cheese sandwich. Plus he had a standing invitation for dinner at Amari's or Tamar's, so getting a good home-cooked meal wasn't a problem.

What was a problem for him was the colonel's inedible food. Out of respect, Preston always ate as much as he could, but the man couldn't cook, period. And now to find out that the colonel was in the kitchen fixing lunch made Preston sigh.

He got up however, washed his hands, and prayed he and Mrs. Payne didn't end up in the ER.

Taking his seat at the table, he nodded hello to the colonel, who was wearing a camo green apron tied around his waist that read "Marines Burn!" That the man burned food a lot made the words very apropos in their own sarcastic way, Preston thought.

The day's concoction looked to be rice mixed with a bunch of vegetables like broccoli, cauliflower, and tomatoes. The sight made Preston wish for lunch from the Dog and Cow instead. He glanced over at Mrs. Payne. She looked back at him. After taking a bite, she set her fork down on the edge of her plate.

"Barrett, what is this?"

"Just a little something I threw together. Healthy-looking, isn't it?"

"Have you tasted it?"

"Not yet, no."

She folded her arms across her chest in the way she'd taken to doing since getting her new job. The stance reminded Preston of how Amari's mom Lily looked when she caught Preston and Amari doing something dumb.

"Are you feeding us bad food on purpose?"

"What do you mean?"

"I've been married to you for almost thirty years, and I know you can cook better than this."

The way the colonel stuck out his jaw made Preston think Mrs. Payne was on to something.

"Forcing us to eat inedible food isn't going to make me quit my job to come home and run Camp Payne again, no matter how much you may want that. I've put up with these awful meals since the winter, hoping you'd get over yourself, but I'm done. No more awful food, Barrett Payne. You hear me?"

Preston wanted to leave the table and let the married couple work this out in private, but he didn't know how to do it without calling attention to himself. Although Mrs. Payne hadn't raised her voice, he could tell she was none too happy. To be truthful, if what she was saying was true, and he'd been eating all this bad food just because the colonel didn't want her to have a job, Preston was none too happy either.

She got to her feet. "I'm going over to my office and grab some files. I'll see you both later."

Preston wanted to protest at being left in the kitchen alone with the colonel, but she'd already made her tight-lipped exit.

In the silence that followed, the colonel met Preston's eye. "Guess I blew that."

"You think? Why are you trying to wreck her new life? You're supposed to be proud of her."

"I don't like the way things are changing."

"So you cook whack food? How's that supposed to help?" Preston realized he sounded just like Amari's mom. He wished she were there. If anybody could make the colonel get a clue, it was Ms. Lily.

But the colonel didn't have a response.

"I know I'm only fourteen, but maybe you need to talk to Reverend Paula."

The jaw hardened again.

"Or not." He got to his feet. "I'm going to hook up with Amari over at the garage. I'll text you when I'm on the way home." Not waiting for permission, Preston made his exit, too.

As he rode his bike into town, his stomach reminded him that he was still hungry, so he headed for the Dog.

It was lunchtime, and the place was packed. Mr. Mal July, affectionately known to Preston and the other kids as the OG, was on the cash register, and old-school music was pumping, as always.

"Hey, young gun."

The OG must have seen something in Preston's face, because he asked, "What's wrong?"

"The usual," Preston replied. "The colonel's being a dumbass again."

Mal shook his head with what appeared to be disappointment. "You'd think Doc Reg would've found a pill for that by now."

"I know."

"Well, things have a way of working out. You come for lunch? Be a few minutes before I can find you a place to sit. All the booths and tables are filled."

"That's okay. I'll do takeout. I'm going over to the garage. I can eat there."

"Sounds like a plan."

Preston gave the OG his order and went outside to sit on the bench by the door.

The construction workers had taken off for lunch, leaving their earthmovers and cement trucks and the rest of their equipment idle along Main Street. While he waited for his food to arrive, Preston nodded in silent greeting to some of the adults going inside, but mostly he thought about all the changes in his life. Three years ago, he'd been an overweight kid with braids and asthma, struggling to breathe in an environment that didn't care if he lived or died. He'd had no friends, and had been forced to hide his brain power to keep the bullies from using him as a punching bag every day after school.

Now he was in Henry Adams, and happier than he'd ever thought possible. He had friends, family, and people who cared and considered him special. He even had a mom who'd gone from being a meek little lady mouse to the VP of social affairs. He was real proud of her, even if the colonel wasn't. And now he'd been contacted by his birth family. He turned his mind to that. All his life he'd wondered who his real family might be, and why he'd wound up on the garbage heap of foster care. He'd imagined all kinds of scenarios, from having been stolen from the hospital as an infant by some psycho to having been given up because he wasn't wanted. The latter held the most pain, and the reason he hadn't opened his e-mail. He didn't want to learn that he'd been discarded like an old Game Boy, but as everyone kept reminding him, he'd never know the truth if he didn't read the message sent by his biological grandmother, a woman named Lenore Crenshaw.

He pondered that for a moment. Was Crenshaw his real last name? Why had he been contacted by her and not his biological mom? Was she dead? And what about his dad? Did this Crenshaw lady know who he was, where he was?

There were a gazillion questions yelling in his head, but he had no answers.

The OG walked out and handed him a big white bag with his lunch inside. "You want to talk, I'm here," he said, sounding sincere.

"I know. Thanks."

And as Preston rode off, he was thankful. All the kids in town knew they could talk to the OG about anything. Mal always gave good advice or offered words that made them feel better, but in this case none of that solved Preston's problems. The only way out was to read the e-mail, so he had to man up.

CHAPTER
2

Inside the Dog and Cow, the place was packed as usual. The six red leather booths along the far wall were full, as were the six booths on the back wall and the six that lined the windows that looked out onto Main Street. There were a few empty chairs at the ten small tables in the center of the room, but they wouldn't be unoccupied for long.

When the Dog wasn't serving breakfast, lunch, and dinner, seven days a week, it was holding town meetings, wedding receptions, and birthday parties. Henry Adams was a small town, population maybe sixty, and if you sat in the diner long enough, you had the chance to see just about everybody around.

Jack James, the town's lone schoolteacher, was sipping coffee in a booth by the window. He and his teenage son Eli had been residents for a year now, and in that time the Dog had helped him learn who was who—like the owner, Malachi July, former veterinarian, Vietnam vet, and recovering alcoholic. The drinking part of his life accounted for the diner's head-scratching name.

Mal was standing next to a booth on the far side of the room, flirting no doubt with his lady love, Bernadine Brown, town owner, miracle worker, and all-around force of nature whose hand and bank account spun Henry Adams's world. She'd purchased the town off eBay three years ago, and because of her TLC it had gone from having one foot in the grave to standing tall and strutting around with its chest poked out.

Seated in the booth with her were school superintendent Marie Jefferson and Marie's BFF, Genevieve Curry. Last fall, Genevieve had broken her hand decking her ex-husband Riley in an altercation that served as the talk of the town for months, but she'd healed up well. Too bad the same couldn't be said for Riley, the town's former mayor. She'd broken his nose, and folks swore he hadn't looked the same since.

Jack had yet to be formerly introduced to Curry, but he knew the man wasn't well liked. According to the gossip, Riley was currently holed up on the town's outskirts in an expensive double-wide trailer he'd shared with his girlfriend, Texas millionairess Eustasia Pennymaker, until he'd gotten on her nerves so much that she'd packed up her bucks and her beloved sow, Chocolate, and two-stepped it back to her ranch outside Laredo. Word was, Riley was preparing for the big court battle involving his six-hundred-pound hog Cletus, who three years ago had sat on a man and killed him. The county wanted the hog put down, but Riley swore Cletus acted in self-defense. Apparently he loved the hog more than he had his wife Genevieve, which was one of the reasons she'd socked him.

Another reason Jack liked hanging out at the Dog was the fancy red jukebox that played all oldies, all the time. Currently, Diana Ross and the Supremes were cooing "Come See

About Me," and heads and shoulders all over the room were keeping time.

But the number-one reason Jack came to the Dog whenever he had a free moment was to watch the diner's manager, Rochelle Dancer, work the room. The locals called her Rocky, but he didn't think a woman with her beauty should have a name evoking Sylvester Stallone or any other pugilist, so he preferred to call her Rochelle.

When the Supremes finished singing, the jukebox played the opening strains of "Sun Goddess" by Ramsey Lewis, a selection Jack thought quite apropos. Ms. Dancer was indeed a goddess, even if she did act like a pissed-off one most of the time. He was pretty sure he was in love with her. Why her? He didn't know. She rarely spoke to him, refused to go out with him, and did her best to let him know that the planet would be a better place if he weren't on it. However, the moment he laid eyes on her a year ago, his heart had opened up for the first time since the death of his wife Eva, and the light that poured in was blinding. Something had happened with Rochelle, too, and that seemed to piss her off all the more.

In many ways, he was having fun watching her deny what they both knew, but getting her to own up to it was going to be about as easy as summiting Mount Everest without oxygen.

She was still working the room, along with her crack staff of college students dressed all in black. She topped off coffee cups and checked on every customer at every table except his, probably hoping if she ignored him long enough, he'd get up and leave, but it was a sunny Saturday afternoon, and there was nowhere he needed to be. If he wanted to sit in the booth and drink coffee until she closed the place at midnight, he could.

The Dog was all about good food and service, though, and

he knew her devotion to duty wouldn't let her ignore him for long. Sure enough, she made her way over to his booth.

"Why are you still here?" she whispered crossly. His empty plates had been taken away thirty minutes ago.

"I like the coffee." He raised his half-empty cup for more.

"Your bladder should be tar by now." She poured from the carafe in her hand.

She was five foot six, and so gorgeous he'd seen men walk into the Dog's walls after getting their first look at her. Luckily for him, he'd been sitting down on the day they met.

"So when are you going to go out with me?"

"Why do you keep asking me that?"

"Because you keep saying no and won't give me a reason. Is it my race?"

"You being White has nothing to do with it."

"Then what does?"

She sighed aloud and looked away for a beat. When she finally looked him in the eyes again, she said, "I'm scared, Jack. Just scared, okay?"

"Of what?" That she'd actually addressed him by his given name made the sunny morning even more so.

"Of things going well between us for a while, and then you wind up wearing my underwear."

"What?"

"Never mind." She walked away.

Her underwear?

While Jack sat there, trying to make sense out of that, Mal walked up.

"Why're you looking so confused?"

"Rochelle said she won't go out with me because I might wind up wearing her underwear?"

Jack swore Mal almost smiled.

"Any idea what that means?" Jack asked.

"You'll have to ask her. Not my place."

"There's actually a story tied to whatever this underwear thing is about?"

"You'll have to talk to Rock."

Jack could see her delivering a tray loaded up with full plates over to a bunch of construction workers crowded into a booth up front.

Mal's voice brought his attention back around. "A lot of pain went into making that thick hide of hers, Jack. Just keep that in mind."

"I will."

"Patience isn't one of her strong suits."

"I've noticed."

"We're all rooting for you, even though we still think you've got a snowball's chance in hell."

"Good to know."

They spent a minute more talking about the next meeting of Dads Inc., the local father's support group, before Mal moved on to chat with Bing Shepard and his crew from the Black Farmers Association at a booth in the back. Bing was a World War II vet, and his war experiences were going to be a part of the upcoming week's history lesson for Jack's students.

Jack went back to sipping coffee and wishing he knew the details of the underwear story. This sense of not knowing the whole picture was nothing new. For such a small town, the secrets were legion, and it seemed everyone had them—even his students. Mal and 99 percent of the locals had grown up in Henry Adams, but Jack had grown up in Boston, and had been living and teaching in L.A. when he was hired to be the teacher. After losing his wife, Eva, to cancer, he'd had to raise their teenage son, Eli, alone. The idea of teaching in a small town had been appealing; he'd imagined a slower pace and the kind of environment where Eli could shed his grief-fueled anger. Nothing could have prepared either of them for Henry Adams, though. If someone had told Jack he'd find heaven in a small historic Black township on the flat plains of Kansas, he'd've asked them to take a drug test. Because of the elders like Tamar July, and others like town owner Bernadine Brown, Jack's last nine months had been the sweetest, wildest ride he'd ever taken. If it was left up to him, he'd spend the rest of his life within the town's loving confines—which might be just long enough to convince the Dog's resident goddess to go out with him.

A grim Rocky barreled through the door that led into the kitchen. Assistant chef Siz looked up from the potatoes he was peeling.

"Jack still out there?"

She could swear he was smiling, and that earned him a glare, but he knew her well enough now that her Medusa stare no longer turned him into stone.

He glanced back. "Why don't you just go out with the guy?"

Another glare.

"Okay. Shutting up and going back to my potatoes."

"Thank you. If anybody needs me, I'll be in the office."

In the office, Rocky sat down in the chair in front of her desk and powered on her laptop. She had vendor orders to review and pay. She was determined not to think about Jack

James, but his good-looking face kept shimmering in her mind's eye. Cursing softly, she ran her hands over her eyes. *What are you doing, Rock?* Truthfully, she didn't know.

No matter how hard she pushed him away, he wouldn't move. Instead, he lingered in her brain like an old-school outlaw propped against a post waiting for high noon, and she was so tired of staring him down it was keeping her awake at night. She bounced her forehead on the edge of the keyboard. Everybody in town kept saying, "Just go out with him," but they didn't understand how scared she was of having her heart run over.

None of the romantic relationships she'd had in her adult life had ever worked out. When she and Bob Lee became man and wife, the first few months were okay—until the day she walked in on him modeling her underwear in front of their bedroom mirror, and that was that.

Now Jack. Although she refused to admit it, parts of her liked him a lot, and wanted to know if he was as nice as he seemed, but in her world nice always morphed into scary. Better to keep her feelings under lock and key—that way they didn't end up roadkill.

Riley Curry had to make three trips out to his old white truck to bring in all the books and DVDs he'd borrowed from the library. Once he had everything transported, he made himself comfortable on the living room sofa. Putting on the reading glasses he'd picked up at the dollar store in Franklin, he spent the next thirty minutes leafing through the enormous law books he'd borrowed before sadly coming to the conclusion that he couldn't make heads or tails out of the words on the pages. Even worse, none of the books offered any strategies pertinent to defending a hog in a court of law, let alone in a life-or-death case.

Finding Cletus good legal representation hadn't become an issue until Eustasia ran out last fall, taking her checkbook with her, but now, with Social Security as Riley's only income, hiring a fancy lawyer was out. He'd hoped the library books would be able to teach him how to save Cletus from a dose of lethal injection, courtesy of the county vet, but it didn't look that way.

He closed the books. He didn't know what he'd do if the county prevailed. Clay Dobbs had sold Cletus to Riley five years ago as a piglet, and they'd been as inseparable as father and son ever since. According to what Eustasia had found on the Internet before running out on him, hogs could live as long as fifteen years, some sites even said twenty-five. Cletus wouldn't live to be six if Riley didn't come up with a way to free him. He was the only family Riley had, and had proven to be a hundred times more loyal than Eustasia and that damned ex-wife of his, Genevieve. Thinking about Genny made his nose and eye socket throb. The doc said the bones were healed up from her sucker punch, but Riley wasn't so sure.

Putting Genevieve out of his mind, he refocused on Cletus and the plight they both faced. Since the law books hadn't helped, he decided to go with his second plan of attack and learn the ways of lawyering from one of the best. Walking over to the TV, he put in the first DVD and settled down to watch two years of back-to-back episodes of *Perry Mason*.

CHAPTER
3

Over at the Marie Jefferson Academy, Crystal let herself into the building with her key and took a moment to relock the door. Even though Henry Adams was out in the middle of nowhere and there wasn't any crime, no sense in tempting fate. She'd already been kidnapped once in her life, and she didn't want to go through that again.

Although it was Saturday afternoon, she'd come to school to work on a project. One of the biggest and most prestigious art museums in L.A. was holding a nationwide search for high school art students, called Young American Artists. It was kind of a strange name for a competition, but no more than *American Idol*, and besides, the name wasn't her concern. The top two winners would be given their own five-day show. Scholarship money was also one of the prizes, but she'd already decided that if she won, she'd turn it down. She wouldn't feel right accepting the scholarship, not with Ms. Bernadine as her new mom. As far as Crystal could tell, the only person with more money was probably God.

The school's interior was quiet enough for Crystal to hear her own footsteps. Making her way, she stopped for a moment at the big wall-mounted aquarium to check on the fish. The multicolored guppies and cichlids looked good, as did the small gauges that measured the temperature and water quality. When the school opened last year, Mr. James had invited a lady from an aquarium company to visit and teach Crys and the other kids the ins and outs of proper maintenance. Mr. James then paired everybody up, and each week a different team was assigned aquarium duty. Amari and Preston were the first pair in the rotation, and all the fish died because neither of them had checked the temperature gauge. The two knuckleheads had looked so contrite that Mr. James apparently hadn't had the heart to yell at them, but Crystal had, and no one forgot after that.

With her fish check done, Crystal proceeded down the hall to the art room. She loved to draw and paint. Growing up in foster care, she hadn't had the opportunity to pursue her passion, but after Ms. Bernadine came into her life, the sky became the limit. She had all the supplies an artist could imagine, and she really wanted to win the competition so she could show Ms. Bernadine that all the money and time she'd invested had been well spent; not that Ms. Bernadine cared about the cash, she just wanted Crystal to be happy, and Crystal was the happiest teenager on earth, as long as she didn't count the two new girls who'd enrolled in Ms. Marie's academy last winter. Their names were Megan Tripp and Samantha Dickens. They were from Franklin, the next town over, and were as snooty as they were clueless. They were forever staring down their noses at Crystal like she was supposed to be impressed that Samantha's father owned two McDonald's and Megan's father was an optometrist. They didn't treat the other Henry Adams kids any better, except for Eli. Him they swarmed around like ants on a dropped ice cream cone, but he never paid them any attention, so Crystal let him live. The jury was still out on them, though.

Putting them out of her mind, Crystal took the draping off her nearly finished triptych and evaluated it critically. She called the three canvases *Life*. The first one represented her childhood. It was an abstract filled with darkness and wild colors and splashes of red to represent how bleak and dangerous life had been for her in those days. The second represented the present. It was a watercolor portraying one of the beautiful fountains she'd seen in Barcelona last year. She painted it in the Impressionist style of Monet, to relay how dreamy and shimmery her new world had become. The third canvas was blank. She wanted it to represent her future, one she hoped would be filled with art, success, and travel. The medium would be oil, but she was still trying to get what she had in her head onto the canvas, which is why she'd come to the school on a Saturday afternoon. It was nice and quiet, and she could think and pace and talk to herself without a bunch of people staring. She could have worked on the project at home in the room that she'd turned into a small studio, but she didn't want Ms. Bernadine to see the completed work until all three parts were done.

Her phone buzzed. She read the text message. "@ door. Let me n." She sighed. It was Eli. So much for working alone.

She let him in.

"When do you think I'll get my own key?"

"Never, because you keep asking for one."

"I'm a responsible person."

Crystal relocked the door and had nothing to say about him being Mr. Responsible. "I thought you were going to hang out in Franklin."

"Changed my mind. Thought you might want company." He checked her face. "No?"

Eli had to be the finest White boy she'd ever been around—dark hair, dark eyes, tall—but he'd come to town acting like a brat, and she'd wanted to smack him upside his head every time she saw him. When the adults in Henry Adams let him know they didn't tolerate bratty kids, he'd cleaned up his act and turned into an okay person. Lately, she got the impression that he wanted to hit on her, but wasn't sure how. That was okay—she was way more interested in Diego July. She'd met him last Thanksgiving when the Oklahoma Julys came to town for Trent and Lily's wedding. He'd even tried to kiss her. Although Diego was only a few years older, he made Eli seem like a baby in comparison.

Eli accompanied her back to the art room. "How're your pieces coming?"

"Okay, I guess. Still trying to figure out the last one."

Eli was an artist, too—a sculptor. He stopped in front of her two finished canvases. After a few moments of silent evaluation, he said, "They're really good."

Crystal wasn't sure how much of the assessment was tied to his feelings for her, but she told him, "Thanks."

"Do you want to catch a movie tonight?"

The only movie theater was in Franklin. "Who else is going?"

"Just us."

"Is this like a date?"

He gave her a shrug. "Yeah. Sure."

"No."

"Why not?"

"Because I'm not dating you, Eli. We're friends."

"But you'd go out with that Diego guy."

"Maybe."

"Because he rides a motorcycle? Amari says he never even finished high school."

"So."

"So? You want a man dumber than you?"

He had a point, but Crystal wasn't about to admit it. "I'm not dating you. And I came over here to work, so is there anything else?"

"No."

"Then bye. I'll see you later."

He walked out.

She sighed. Boys.

On Monday morning, Bernadine Brown arrived at her office well ahead of her executive assistant and town administrator Lily Fontaine July. Because of the long hours Bernadine kept, many people joked that she didn't sleep. She did, though; in spite of Henry Adams's small-town status, there was enough going on every day to fill up three days in a normal place, so a good night's sleep was required to stay on top of things and not lose her mind.

Getting in early gave her a moment to catch her breath, say her prayers, and look over the day's agenda so she could hit the ground running when the building opened for business. The residents called the town's administrative offices the Power Plant because it was the seat of power. Nothing happened without her input or approval. Were Henry Adams larger, more administrative staff might be needed, but at its current size, Bernadine, Lily, and the town's mayor, Trent, were enough to keep the ship on an even keel.

At precisely eight o'clock, Lily stuck her head in Bernadine's door. "Morning, Bernadine."

"Morning, Lil. How are you?"

"I'd be better if I wasn't living in a house full of men."

Lily and Trent had been married in November. After the honeymoon they'd combined households. Trent promised to build her a private room where she could escape all the testosterone emanating from him and their two sons, Devon and Amari, but so far the weather and his duties had kept him from starting the construction.

"You know you love your men."

"I do, but what I don't love is going to the bathroom in the middle of the night and almost falling in because a certain mayor forgot to put the seat down—again. Told him he'd be building me my own bathroom, too."

Bernadine knew Lily was just fussing. The former Henry Adams high school track and field queen loved her husband and sons as much as she loved breathing. "So what's on your plate today?"

"Typing up the agenda for tonight's town meeting and then putting on my hard hat and boots so I can walk the construction sites. I'll see what else shows up as the day goes along. How about you?"

"Sheila and I will be meeting about the groundbreaking festivities for the new church and her plans for this year's August First festivities. At eleven I'm scheduled to talk to Franklin's mayor about something or other, and Katie's flying in Jim Edison. His firm's handling this mess with Leo."

Leo Brown was Bernadine's ex-husband, and the snake in her Henry Adams paradise. He and his oil company bosses were attempting to make a land grab, claiming eminent domain in order to run a pipeline from Canada to Mexico. Problem was, the land was legally owned by local farmers, who were none too pleased with the company's intimidation tactics. According to the reports she'd been getting from her people, it appeared as if the oil snakes and their lawyers were having a hard time prevailing in court, but she wanted to talk to Jim Edison, the high-powered legal eagle she'd hired to protect the farmers' interests, and get his thoughts on where the case stood.

"What time's he due in?"

"Around two this afternoon. I'd like for you and His Honor to sit in."

"Not a problem. I'll let Trent know."

"Thanks. Anything else we need to do before we start the day?" Bernadine asked.

"No. I think we're good."

Lily made her exit, and Bernadine powered up her laptop to check her e-mail before Sheila arrived. The first message was from construction supervisor Warren Kelly. He wanted to add two more bodies to the cleanup crews, and she sent him back a message giving her approval.

After buying Henry Adams off eBay, Bernadine had made it a point to hire as many local people as she could in an effort to help the area's flat-line economy. It had proven to be a wise choice. Under Kelly's direction, the contractors worked hard, and the pride they took in their craft was evident in everything they built, from the houses in the subdivision where she lived to the new recreation center to the town's awesome, jaw-dropping school. Her dream of revitalizing Henry Adams would never have borne fruit had it not been for her dedicated workers, and she counted them as one of her many blessings.

At a bit past nine o'clock, Sheila Payne knocked on her opened door.

"Hey, Sheila. Come on in."

Bernadine loved the confidence Sheila appeared to have gained since being named head of social affairs. The woman who'd acted afraid of her own shadow when the Paynes first came to town was no more.

They spent a few moments discussing her thoughts on how she wanted Saturday's groundbreaking to go, and once that subject was done, they moved on to the August First celebration.

"Tamar wants a July Fourth celebration this year instead of August First. She's decided we need to alternate."

Bernadine might own Henry Adams, but Tamar ruled like Good Queen Bess ruling England. "Did she say whether she wants a parade, cookout?"

"Cookout, yes, and Henry Adams Idol, too."

"Like the television show?"

"Apparently."

"I may regret saying this, but that sounds like a great idea."

"But I don't know anything about hosting something like that. I do dinners and receptions—things with tablecloths and china."

Sheila looked so distraught, Bernadine had to suppress a smile. "Roni will be back in a few weeks—have her be one of the judges. Mal and Clay play instruments, and you know Siz over at the diner has a band. Have them help you out."

"I'm supposed to be in charge of social affairs, Bernadine, and holiday celebrations falls under that."

"I know, Sheila, but do you really want to take on Tamar?"

"No."

"Me either, so guess it'll be Henry Adams Idol for the Fourth of July."

Sheila didn't look happy.

"Think of it as something unique to add to your résumé."

Sheila cut her a look.

Bernadine shrugged. "I'm sorry, but that's all I have."

Sheila sighed audibly. "Okay. My hissy fit's over. Henry Adams Idol it will be. I'll do my best to make it shine, but if it turns out to be a debacle, I'm washing my hands like Pilate right now."

"Duly noted."

Sheila stood. "I'll make the announcement at the town meeting this evening."

"Sounds good."

Starting toward the door, she said, "Let the madness begin."

"It's going to be fine. Oh, and before you go—has Preston opened that e-mail yet?"

"No—I think he's moving toward it, though. I'll keep you posted."

"Thanks."

Sheila departed, leaving Bernadine to ponder what the e-mail from Preston's biological grandmother might say. It also brought back to mind Dr. Winthrop's parting warning about Lenore Crenshaw. Although Bernadine had kept her promise and not contacted Winthrop again, she didn't feel good about it. In her mind, Preston had a right to at least know his mother's name.

Because there was no solution to that problem for now,

Bernadine's mind switched gears to Tamar's Fourth of July event. Henry Adams Idol. Bernadine still liked the idea, but as always, she harbored concerns over what might happen before, during, or after the competition. In Henry Adams, events like the one Tamar was proposing had a tendency to get out of hand. She only had to look back at the chaos caused by the innocent-sounding pet parade idea Amari'd come up with the last time they celebrated August First. Add to that the memorable visit of the Oklahoma Julys during Lily and Trent's wedding last fall, and it was a wonder she wasn't already packing up to leave town, but both functions had turned out fine in the end, and this one would too.

She turned back to her desktop but froze when she heard, "Morning, Bernie."

Leo.

She eyed him coolly. "What do you want?"

He was dressed as impeccably as always, in a dark green summer-weight silk suit.

"Just stopped in to say good-bye. Your lawyers have been kicking my company's ass so thoroughly, we've decided to cut our losses and not throw any more money down the toilet. You win, Bernadine. We're pulling up stakes, and you can rest easy, knowing you've saved your hick farmers from the evil empire."

"Good. Are you saying good-bye to Marie, too?"

When he first came to town two years ago, he'd wanted them to reconcile, but when Bernadine told him to kick rocks, he began seeing Marie Jefferson.

"Ah, the little schoolmarm. Another item to cross off the balance sheet."

He'd dropped Marie when she refused to sell him her land. Bernadine wondered if she could beat him to death with something on her desk—maybe the stapler—and plead temporary insanity. "Why would you treat her that way?"

"How's that old seventies tune go? If you can't be with the one you love, love the one you're with."

He was truly disgusting.

"Still love you, Bernie—probably always will. Going to salve my broken heart with a little honey I met last week in Santa Barbara. Wish me luck?"

"Get out," she snarled softly.

"I'm going, but just a word of advice. Not everybody's happy with your court victory. Some of those farmers were counting on that money we were going to give them, so I'd watch my back if I were you. Ciao, beautiful. I'll see you around."

He winked and made his exit, leaving behind the lingering scent of his expensive cologne.

Bernadine fumed, then gave his parting salvo some thought. Until that moment, it hadn't occurred to her that providing the lawyers for the farmers' suit might result in enemies, but thinking on it now, she admitted that Leo could be right. The rising economy was slowly making its way across the nation, but few farmers were feeling any relief. The escalating cost of fuel and equipment, coupled with the backbreaking debts many agricultural families continued to carry, probably made the money Leo's company promised seem like a godsend. Now, thanks to the lawsuit, her lawyers, and the state agencies that threw in on their side because of the oil company's abysmal environmental record, it was gone.

However she'd not heard anything from Bing or his friends about anyone being mad at her, so she put the thoughts aside and chalked it up to Leo just being himself and trying to stir her up.

Bernadine's next visitor was Austin Wiggins, the new mayor of Franklin. The old mayor had resigned after a prank played on him and his wife by some of the Oklahoma Julys during their visit last Thanksgiving, which resulted in him breaking his arm and divorcing his wife of twenty-five years.

Wiggins wasn't someone she liked. She assumed the feeling was mutual, but he pretended otherwise. Since meeting her over the winter, he'd made a point of pestering her to let him in on whatever she had planned for Henry Adams's future. He was an elected official, he reasoned, born and raised in the county, and knew much more about what the two communities needed to make the region viable again than she.

He entered wearing his plastic smile and a black suit shiny from too many trips to the dry cleaner. The too-short jacket matched the flood-length pants, but nothing in nature, living or dead, matched the jet-black toupee on his head. He saw himself as suave and handsome; everyone else saw him for the pudgy, bad-toupee-wearing know-nothing that he was in reality.

"Ms. Brown," he called cheerily. "How are you, hon?"

She hated being called "hon," and had politely pointed this out on more than a few occasions. He'd either chosen to ignore it, or was suffering from amnesia. Her bet was on the former. "What can I do for you?"

Because she hadn't offered him a chair, he stood, seemingly caught between taking a seat anyway and waiting for her to make the offer. She didn't move.

"Um." He finally sat, and the plastic smile returned. "I was checking out all the construction going on. You folks are busy as bees over here."

"We're pleased with the progress."

"I hear you're going to be opening a health clinic soon."

"Yes."

"The two docs in Franklin have been talking about building a clinic for years."

"I hope they do well with theirs."

"Economically, there's no reason to have two such facilities in the area."

"Have you told them that?"

His lips thinned, letting her know that wasn't the response he'd been after. Why he thought she'd abandon a clinic scheduled to open next week to allow two doctors in Franklin to continue to *talk* about building one was beyond her. Then again, she was dealing with a man wearing an imitation black squirrel on his head.

"Mayor Wiggins, I have a very tight schedule today. Is there anything else?"

"Yes. We have the opportunity to have a Big Box built in Franklin."

"Congratulations. How soon will you break ground?"

"Soon as we can get good-faith funds from all the nearby communities."

She studied him silently for a moment. "Good-faith funds?"

"Yes. If we help subsidize the store's building costs, the parent company promises to bring jobs and low prices."

"And if we don't?"

"They move elsewhere."

She wanted to wave bye-bye, but decided that would be rude. "And how much are they asking?"

"From Franklin and Henry Adams, two-point-six million."

"Is that all?"

"I knew that wouldn't be a problem for you," he declared, grinning widely.

"I was being sarcastic."

"Oh."

Inwardly, she shook her head. "Henry Adams will have to pass on Big Box's wonderful offer, Mayor Wiggins. We have other priorities at the moment."

"But this is Big Box, hon. They're one of the biggest corporations in the good old U.S. of A."

"I'm aware of that, but we have other priorities, *hon*."

He turned cranberry red.

"Is there anything else?" She wanted him gone.

"Why are you turning down this opportunity?"

"We plan to build our own supermarket right here in town." It was a lie, but it came to her that a grocery was needed, so she decided, Why not? Local residents were having to drive hither, thither, and yon to stock their refrigerators and pantries. Better to spend that money at home.

"But you can't," he protested.

"Sure I can. It's one of those other priorities I just mentioned. Hope to have it up and running before the fall."

"But if the Big Box gets built, they aren't going to want competition."

"Not my problem."

"You won't be able to match their prices," he countered, with distress in his voice and face. "They'll crush you."

"Maybe, but this is the good old U.S. of A., and if I want to try something, I'm allowed."

He hadn't like the idea of a Henry Adams health clinic, and by the look on his pumpkin-round face, he disliked the grocer idea even less. Too bad.

He got to his feet and tried one last time. "Ms. Brown, I'd appreciate it if you'd give the Big Box proposal more thought.

Maybe talk it over with Mayor July. I'm sure he'll be able to see the benefits of throwing in on this."

"Even if I don't?"

"Mayor July was born here. You weren't."

"Get out of my office."

He puffed up as if planning to confront her, but she wasn't having any, especially not from a little jerk with a squirrel on his head.

"And to save you the trouble of thinking I may change my mind. My answer on Big Box is no, now and forever."

She swung her chair around to face her laptop. The slamming of her office door signaled his exit.

Lily entered a few seconds later. She had on her construction boots and carried a yellow hard hat in her hand. "On my way to walk the sites with Trent and Mr. Kelly. What did Mayor Piggly Wiggly want?"

"Two-point-six million dollars."

"For what?"

Bernadine explained.

Lily shook her head. "Big Box's nothing but a dollar store with groceries."

"Which is why I declined his offer. Thought maybe we'd build our own store instead."

"You know, that's not a bad idea."

"Think you can pull together a feasibility plan and get it to me in a few days?"

"To have a place to shop in town—oh, yes, ma'am. Folks around here will build a statue in your honor if we can make this happen."

"I'm telling you now, I know absolutely nothing about starting a grocery store."

"You didn't know anything about building a town, either, and look how that turned out."

They shared a smile, and Bernadine asked, "Have I told you lately what a blessing you are in my life?"

"No, but the feeling's mutual. I'll talk to Kelly and Trent and see what we can come up with."

"Didn't Gary Clark sell cars at one time?"

"Yes. Why?"

"I think I'll appoint him the manager."

"Yet another great Bernadine Brown idea. He's really struggling economically, and a job will help a lot. Let me know what he says."

"Will do."

"Okay, let me get going before Trent calls, wanting to know where I am."

She exited, crowing, "A grocery store! Hallelujah!"

Pleased, Bernadine returned to her computer and Googled "How to open a grocery store." To her delight, a number of links popped up right away.

An hour later, armed with a rudimentary knowledge of the subject, she pushed her chair back from the desk and called Gary Clark.

CHAPTER
4

Bernadine didn't tell Gary what she wanted, only that she needed to speak with him about something. He sounded a bit taken aback by her request—they'd never spoken on the phone before—but he arrived at her office a short time later.

"Have a seat, please, Gary."

"Why do I feel like I've been called to the principal's office?"

She liked his sense of humor. "Sorry I was so vague over the phone, but I wanted to speak with you in person. There's a job opening in town."

He went still.

"I've decided we need a grocery store, and I think you should manage it."

He appeared a bit stunned. "I don't know anything about groceries. I sold cars."

"Think you can learn?"

"Well, yeah, sure, but—"

She waited.

"Are you serious?"

"No, Gary. I really want Zoey and Devon to run the store. I'm just practicing my spiel on you. Of course I'm serious."

He dropped his head, and when he raised it again, he whispered emotionally, "Thank you."

"You're welcome."

"You've no idea how much this means. Worrying about finding a job and how I'm going to provide for my girls in the meantime has been keeping me awake at night."

"Now you can sleep."

He was silent for a moment, and then met her eyes. "Now I can sleep. Thank you, again."

"No problem. First order of business is for you to start the learning process. I found out the basics of starting a store online, so begin there if you like, and if you run across any classes or seminars or conferences you think you need to attend, bring me a list."

"When's the store scheduled to open?"

"Soon as it can be built, so you'll need to get up to speed quickly."

"Okay. We'll probably make a few mistakes at first, but as long as we don't make the same mistakes, we should be okay."

"I agree. So, get on out of here and get busy. I want to make an announcement about the store at the town meeting tonight."

He stood and told her in a sincere voice, "You've no idea how much I've been praying."

"You were heard."

"Thanks, Ms. Brown."

"Bernadine."

"Bernadine," he echoed, and departed.

Before she could blink, the opening bars of "Smooth Operator" by Sade sang on her phone. Smiling because she hadn't talked to the person the ringtone was assigned to yet that day, she picked up. "Hey, Mal."

"Hey, sweet thing. How goes the turning of the world?"

She grinned. "Hasn't fallen off its axis yet. How are you?"

Next she knew, he was walking into her office, still holding his phone against his cheek and ear.

"Doing pretty good, as you can see."

Loving him for always making her days fun, she ended the call. "You are so special."

The mustache lifted with amusement. "Always have been. Came to take you on a lunch picnic."

"I've a meeting this afternoon."

"Then we'll have to eat fast."

Bernadine absolutely adored Mal July, and the idea of running away with him was way too tempting, but she needed to go over the reports on the farmers' lawsuit before the legal eagle flew in at two.

Mal must've read her mind. "I know you have a ton of stuff to do, but sometimes you need to stop and smell the roses on the way to world domination—especially on a Monday—and the weather's perfect."

"Is that from the Tao of Malachi?"

"Matter of fact, it is."

"Are we picnicking in your truck again?"

Because it had been too dark and cold to sit on the grass the first time he took her on a picnic, they'd had it inside his classic Ford pickup. Now they used the cab for that purpose on a regular basis.

"No," he answered. "Real picnic this time. Basket, blanket, and everything."

"I'm not dressed for sitting on the ground."

"Did I mention the blanket?"

She dropped her head to hide her amusement. Looking back up at him now, all the good times they'd had together, be it kite flying or just sitting on her deck enjoying the sunset, rose up and made her realize what a true blessing he'd become. After having her heart smashed to pieces by Leo, she'd had no intentions of opening herself to anyone again, but Mal changed that, along with her life. "Okay. I give. Let me send Lily a text letting her know where I am."

And once that was done, she stepped out into the sunshine with the only man capable of making her leave her desk and not care about the day's to-do list still resting on top.

He drove them to the bank of the creek that ran on the edge of Tamar's land and parked. Her ears were instantly filled with the silence unique to the plains, and the busy morning melted away as if by magic.

"Thank you for kidnapping me. I didn't realize how full the morning's been until now."

"Let's get out, and you can tell me all about it."

He spread the blanket on the grass, and they sat and ate salads and she told him about her morning, beginning with Leo.

She asked him seriously, "Are some farmers going to be upset about not getting the oil money?"

"People being people, probably. Some of them are on their last legs, and Leo's money would've helped. Doesn't mean you did the wrong thing by heading him off at the pass, though. Claiming eminent domain and basically stealing land would've made a lot more people mad. And what if there'd been some kind of environmental catastrophe? Didn't Trent say at the last meeting that Leo and his boys are known for not cleaning up after themselves?"

"Yes."

"Another reason to run them out of the county. And you can't please everybody all the time, anyway—that's life."

"I'm starting to feel bad, though."

"Understandable—you got the whole world in your hands." She grinned.

"But sometimes not even you can make the world a fair place, so I wouldn't worry about it."

Bernadine knew she would, however, and he probably knew that, too, so the discussion moved on to Henry Adams Idol.

"What kind of prizes?" he asked.

She shrugged. "Planning's just beginning."

"Maybe Clay and I will dust off our old Temptation moves. Bet I can talk Trent and Gary into signing on. Or we can be Tammi and Marvin?" he said excitedly.

Bernadine choked on the water she was sipping.

"No?" he asked.

Wiping her mouth with a napkin, she shook her head and croaked, "No."

"But I can sing," he said, coming to his own defense.

"I can't."

"What do you mean, you can't? Aren't you from Detroit? Everybody from Motown can sing."

She found that amusing. "Says who?"

"Every person I've ever met from Detroit."

"They lied then, because I can't sing a note."

He looked skeptical.

"Have you ever heard me sing anything in the three years we've been together, besides the hymns at church service?"

When he didn't respond, she said, "I rest my case."

"Okay," he grumbled mockingly. "Guess we can't be Tammi and Marvin."

She shook her head. "You're a mess."

"But I'm your mess." And he leaned over and kissed her softly.

When the world stopped spinning, she whispered, "Yes, you are."

Preston had a list of reasons why he enjoyed life in Henry Adams, and at the top was school. Back in Milwaukee, he'd been dissed and bullied for being smart. Kids laughed at him, flung taunts his way, and accused him of trying to act White. That reasoning made him wonder what it meant to be Black, but he hadn't had the nerve to ask because he didn't want to be answered with more kicks and poundings. The routine daily thumpings had been enough.

In Kansas, however, his big brain was celebrated. His peers and the adults always offered encouragement and thought his dream of being an astrophysicist like his idol, Dr. Neil de Grasse Tyson, both attainable and special.

Another reason Preston enjoyed school in Henry Adams was being allowed to eat lunch outside. He never got to do that in Milwaukee. Because of the winter weather, he and the other students had only been allowed to eat outside occasionally, but now that spring had finally shown up, they were using picnic tables for lunch again on a regular basis.

There were nine students enrolled at the Marie Jefferson

Academy. Preston's best friend Amari was at another table, teaching his little brother Devon how to play chess. His other bestie was Leah Clark. She loved physics just as much, and he sort of had a crush on her. At the moment she was across the yard with Crystal and Eli and the two new girls from Franklin: Megan Tripp and Samantha Dickens, nicknamed Crue and Ella by Amari. They didn't like the Henry Adams kids, and the feeling was mutual.

Two students were absent: Leah's younger sister Tiffany Adele, home with a cold, and Zoey Garland. Zoey and her dad were in Paris, touring Europe with her famous Grammy-winning mom, Roni Moore, in support of her new platinum CD. Reverend Paula had been invited on the trip, too. The Rev, Zoey, and Dr. Reg were due back later in the week, but Ms. Roni would be staying overseas and heading for Australia next.

Preston looked up at the cardinal singing from the school's roof. Another bonus of being in Henry Adams was the fresh air. He hadn't had an asthma attack in over a year. Dr. Reg said it was likely due to relocating to the plains. Many inner city kids had asthma because of all the junk in the air from car exhaust, cockroach feces, and cigarette smoke, all of which had been present in most of Preston's foster homes. Kansas's clean air, in tandem with all the bike riding with Amari, hadn't only helped his lungs; he'd shed fifteen pounds and grown three inches taller since being away from Milwaukee. Instead of the overweight unhappy kid he used to face in the mirror each morning, he now smiled at his reflection.

He saw Leah walking his way. His heart began to beat so hard and loudly, he was scared she'd hear it. When she sat down across from him, he forced himself to act calm. "What's going on over there?"

"Dumb and Dumber said Crystal was lying about going to Spain with Ms. Bernadine last year. They don't believe Ms. Bernadine has a jet either."

Crystal had given a report on Spanish architecture that morning. "So what did Crys tell them?"

"That she doesn't talk to plants."

Preston laughed.

"Which of course made them madder. Samantha's not so bad. I mean, she's uber smart, but it's like she doesn't want to show it because Megan really is a plant. That dandelion growing over there is smarter than she is. Think I might try and turn Samantha away from the dark side and bring her into the light with us."

"Good luck."

She quieted for a minute, then said, "My parents' divorce is final today."

Preston didn't know how to respond. Leah loved her mom, but her mom hadn't wanted custody of Leah or her sister Tiffany and was now living somewhere on the East Coast.

She added, "Maybe now Tiff will finally believe Mom and Daddy aren't getting back together. Reason number seventeen I'm never getting married. Too much drama."

On numerous occasions, Leah had recited the reasons why she wasn't going to marry, the main one being that once she got her Ph.D. and went to work for NASA, she wouldn't have time.

"Have you opened the e-mail yet?" she asked him pointedly.

"No." He thought she had the prettiest brown eyes, even with the glasses.

"You really ought to, you know."

"I know. Tonight."

"Text me if you want to talk after."

"I will."

She left the table, and he was so focused on her, he almost didn't see Mr. James signaling that lunch was over. Preston quickly disposed of his trash and hurried to join the other kids going back inside.

After school, Preston saw the note on the kitchen table addressed to him and read that the colonel was in the basement lifting weights. Walking to the top of the steps, he called down. "I'm home."

"Okay. Be done in just a bit."

He remembered Mrs. Payne saying something that morning about meeting with Tamar this afternoon, but he'd been in the middle of a text to Amari and admittedly hadn't been paying her much attention, so he had no idea when she'd be home. After dumping his backpack on a chair, he washed his hands, grabbed a snack and something to drink, picked up the backpack again, and went up to his room.

Now he was ready. Having fortified himself with his snack, he sat down with his laptop. After it booted up, he clicked on the e-mail that had been haunting him since its arrival. When it opened, he read, "Dear Preston. My name is Lenore Crenshaw. I am your biological maternal grandmother. I'd like to meet you. Unless I hear otherwise, I will be in Henry Adams on . . ."

His jaw dropped. Over the pounding of his heart, he took a quick look at the calendar. Horror gripped him. Oh, he'd really messed up. Quickly clicking the message closed, he ran to find Mrs. Payne, only to remember she hadn't come home yet.

The only other person in the house was the colonel. Pres-

ton found him still in the basement, lying on his back, lifting weights. In spite of their on-again, off-again relationship,
Preston always found the sight impressive. As a budding
physicist, he appreciated the rhythm and symmetry of the bar
going up and down and the almost effortless way the colonel
controlled it. Of course it wasn't effortless. Sweat beaded the
colonel's face, and the strain in his arms, face, and neck testi-
fied how heavy the bar really was.

When the colonel glanced over and saw Preston standing
in the doorway, he didn't stop pumping, but asked, "What can
I do for you?"

"Don't mean to bother you, but do you know when Mrs.
Payne's coming home?"

The colonel set the bar on the bench above and sat up.
He picked up the blue towel lying beside him and wiped his
face. "I'm probably the last person you should be asking that
question."

Preston didn't reply to that. He had enough of his own
problems without playing marriage counselor.

In the long silence that followed, the colonel stood and ran
the towel up and down his damp arms, all the while assessing Preston, who fought not to squirm under the former drill
sergeant's steady gaze.

"So, since I don't have a clue when she'll be home, is there
something you need, something wrong?"

"Yes and no."

"Trick question, huh?"

Preston couldn't help it; he smiled. The colonel did the
same. Preston enjoyed being with the colonel when they connected. He just wished it would last longer than a few minutes. "How long have you been lifting weights?"

Preston waited while he picked up a bottle of water and unscrewed the top.

"Since around your age." After taking a long drink, he lowered the bottle. "Wanted to get big enough to stop my father from beating on my mother."

It was another one of the things that connected them; they'd talked about this before. Preston had been beaten a lot in foster care too, but watching somebody bigger and stronger beat up your mom had to have been bad. "My grandmother's coming tomorrow."

He appeared surprised. "Does Mrs. Payne know?"

"No. I didn't even know until just now. I was too scared to open her e-mail when it first came, so I finally did, and she'll be here tomorrow." He looked the colonel in the eye. "I know you think me finding my birth family is a dumb idea, so I'll wait until Mrs. Payne comes home and talk to her about it." He turned to go.

"Son."

Preston stopped but didn't turn around. "Yeah."

"It's hard for a man like me to say I'm sorry, but I need to."

A wary Preston turned back.

"I enlisted in the marines when I was seventeen. I've been a warrior all my life. Feelings are not our thing, because on the battlefield feelings can get you killed. Can you understand that?"

"Intellectually, yes."

A small smile curved the colonel's lips. "A little over a year ago, we made a pledge to each other, do you remember?"

Semper Fi. "Yes, sir, I do."

"I haven't honored the spirit of that pledge."

Preston drew in a deep breath to keep himself steady. That

day had meant so much to him, but when it became clear that the pledge had been nothing more than words, he'd put his heart back under lock and key.

"And so, you know, I have been talking to Reverend Paula," the colonel confessed, which surprised Preston. "I've also been yelled at all winter by the other dads. Everybody wants me to get myself together. Hard to do when you think you already are. Gets even harder when you finally realize you aren't. So. My apologies, Preston. I didn't want you hurt by whatever you found out on this search, and I thought maybe you weren't happy here."

"But I am. Really. I tried to tell you that."

"I know. I was hearing but not listening. All I thought I heard was a kid not wanting to be the son of a hard-ass. We've been doing this father-and-son thing in fits and starts, and I keep messing it up because I don't know what the hell I'm doing. I envy what Trent has with Amari. Looking back, it's what I wanted with my own father, and what I'd like to have with you, but I'm not real sure how to start over, or if you even want to, after all this."

Preston envied Amari's bond with his dad, too, and deep down inside he wanted the same kind of relationship with the colonel, but all this back-and-forth had made him gun-shy. As he'd told Amari the other day, he was tired of getting his feelings hurt, and so far, that was all he'd ever gotten from Barrett Montgomery Payne. "Do you really want us to be like Amari and his dad?"

"I do."

"And you aren't going to change your mind?"

"No."

"But you said that before. Why should I believe you now?"

"Because if I don't man up, I'm going to lose you, and probably Mrs. Payne, too. I don't want that."

Preston didn't know what to say.

"All winter I watched you and Sheila become closer and closer while I stayed on the outside looking in. I kept telling myself it didn't matter, but truthfully, it did, so I'm asking for another chance."

"So, suppose I say yes. How do we start?"

"Going back to playing chess in the evenings might be a place to begin. I miss that."

Preston didn't want to admit it, but he did, too. They'd played only a few times over the winter. Looking into the colonel's eyes, he thought he saw honesty, but what did a fourteen-year-old kid know about adults and their feelings, except that a ton of them had lied to him in the past? "Okay, I'd like that, but do you mind if I hold back a little at first?"

"Don't trust me?"

"Not really."

He nodded solemnly. "That's honest, and what I deserve, I suppose. No, I don't mind."

"Then let's try it."

As if they were unsure what to do next, their gazes held.

"Thanks, Preston."

"You're welcome."

"Since we don't know if Sheila's coming home before the town meeting, how about I give her a call, and you and I go get something to eat at the Dog."

"Sounds good, and I have to stay for the meeting."

"Why?"

"Civics class."

"Ah. More of Mr. James's topical teaching."

"Yeah."

"Okay. Let me grab a quick shower, and we'll go."

Preston waited out on the deck. Surrounded by the silence, he thought back on the do-over they'd agreed to. Would it work this time, or pop like a balloon stuck with a pin? He got the sense that the colonel meant well, but when life makes you a skeptic, it's hard to believe.

CHAPTER
5

Rocky added the last platter of wings to the evening's buffet and hoped there'd be enough food. Usually, the monthly town meetings weren't well attended, but for this one people were arriving in droves. According to Mal, the hotshot lawyer Bernadine had hired to take on Leo Brown's oil company was on the agenda, and apparently everyone wanted to hear what he had to say.

She went back into the kitchen to grab more plates and found Siz preparing to leave for the evening. Sporting spiky turquoise-and-black-streaked hair, he asked, "You sure you don't want me to stay and help with cleanup?"

"No. I'm good. You go on home. I'll see you tomorrow."

While Siz made his exit, she walked back over to the kitchen's double doors and peeked out to gauge the size of the crowd. People were still streaming in. At this rate, by the time Trent called the meeting to order, there'd be no place to sit. Again she hoped she had enough food.

Many of the faces were familiar, others not. She spotted

Mal over by the door, talking with Bernadine and a brown-skinned, middle-aged man wearing a gray polo and khakis. She guessed he was the lawyer.

Through the knots of people standing and talking, she saw Devon seated with Tamar, Marie, and Genevieve, and on the far side of the room, a laughing Amari in a booth with Eli, Crystal, Preston, Leah, and Tiffany Adele. She wondered why the kids had come. But then all questions faded when she spied Jack talking with Barrett Payne and Gary Clark.

The dark-haired schoolteacher with his distinctive good looks and Boston accent had gotten under her skin and refused to be ignored, no matter how hard she tried. Fighting off the urge to fake a reason to approach him, she remembered she was supposed to be ignoring him and retrieving more plates instead, so she picked up a small stack and carried them out to the buffet table.

Jack saw Rocky exit the kitchen. Watching her walk over to the buffet table and set down the plates she carried, he wanted to politely excuse himself from his conversation with Barrett and Gary and weave through the crush to her side. He wasn't bothered by the fact that she probably didn't know he was in the room; just the sight of her talking with Sheila Payne drove home his growing attraction. On the phone last night his mother, Janet, had gently quizzed him about dating again. Expressing his interest in the manager of a diner had resulted in a long silence on the other end. He'd smiled, however; although he loved her dearly, he never missed an opportunity to throw her off her conservative patrician stride.

And now, that same manager was looking him dead in the face. He greeted her with an almost imperceptible nod, only to watch her turn abruptly and stride through the kitchen doors. Amused, he directed his attention back to Gary and Barrett.

Once most of the attendees had helped themselves to the buffet's tasty offerings and were either enjoying them from booths and tables or doing their best with a hand-held plate as they stood against the walls, along with the others who'd arrived too late to score a seat, Rocky brought out a chair for herself from the kitchen. As soon as she sat, Trent gaveled the meeting to order. She looked over at Jack and, before he could sense it, looked away.

The first item on the agenda was Trent's construction report. Now that Main Street was paved, the sidewalks put in, and the solar streetlights installed, the next project would be Reverend Paula's church.

"It'll be built on the land between the Power Plant and the rec center," he informed them, and proceeded to give details about the ribbon-cutting ceremony scheduled for Saturday morning. He also expressed his hope that the house of worship would be ready for occupation before the end of the summer.

While he was talking, Rocky noticed Mayor Wiggins slipping into the meeting, followed by three men in business suits, and wondered what they were doing there. She watched them search vainly for a place to sit, in the end resigning themselves to standing with the other people ringing the room. For as long as she'd been alive, Franklin's citizens had looked down on Henry Adams. Now, because of Bernadine's refurbishing projects, they wanted in on everything Henry Adams was doing, and the hypocritical attitude was met with much derision. She had a good view of Bernadine and Lily seated in one of the front booths; from the way their eyes followed the late arrivals, they too seemed to be wondering why Wiggins had come.

No one challenged their right to attend however—it was a public meeting—so Rocky ignored the men for the moment and refocused her attention on Trent, who was now introducing the lawyer James Edison.

Applause greeted Edison when he stood, and it increased when he waved before taking his seat again. Looking around, she noted that not everyone considered Edison a hero for making Leo's company back down and pull up stakes. There was distinct dissatisfaction on the faces of some and an icy glare in the eyes of others, like Big Al Stillwell. It was no secret that the Stillwells were drowning in debt, and she could only imagine how devastated they'd been upon learning they'd be unable to lease their land. Al was a well-known hothead, and as Trent announced that there'd be a Q and A with Edison after the meeting, she hoped Al would keep his cool if he stayed.

Next on the agenda were the reports.

Tamar stood. "The movies at the rec this weekend are *The Princess and the Frog*, followed by *All About Eve*. Also, Sheila and I have decided to have a July Fourth celebration this year instead of August First. Main event will be a cookout and Henry Adams Idol."

Gasps greeted the announcement, followed by wild applause that rolled around the room. Rocky saw pure excitement everywhere. Amari and Preston slapped hands, and Crystal and Eli stared at each other with wide-eyed glee.

Rocky was ecstatic. She had no idea if anyone in the area had any talent, but decided it would certainly be fun to see.

Sheila Payne stood. We'll post details about prizes and all that at the rec, soon."

Amari stood and asked, "Can we rap?"

"No!" loud voices replied in unison. Laughter followed.

"Haters!" he called back, grinning, and sat down again.

The room continued to buzz for a few more moments until Trent gaveled the meeting back to order.

"Anybody have anything else they want to talk about? If not, I'll close the meeting."

Up went Mayor Wiggins's hand.

Trent paused, and Rocky watched him eye the mayor of Franklin critically before saying, "Go ahead, Mayor Wiggins."

But instead of speaking from where he stood, Wiggins and his bad toupee, followed by the three suits, walked up to the podium. Trent appeared caught off guard, but stepped aside and let them have center stage.

"First off," Wiggins began, "let me say how pleased I am by all the great things being done here in Henry Adams. I really like the Idol idea, and if we in Franklin can help, please don't be afraid to ask."

That was met with dead silence.

As it lengthened, he cleared his throat. "As I mentioned to Ms. Brown in our meeting this morning, there's a plan afoot to make this region even better. These gentlemen are lawyers from one of the largest and most profitable corporations in America—Big Box—and they've graciously taken time out of their busy day to come and share with us what I think will be a golden opportunity for not only Franklin but Henry Adams as well."

Rocky saw her own skepticism mirrored on faces around the room.

One of the lawyers, introduced as Kevin Epps, stepped up and began a spiel on Big Box's history. After about three or

four minutes of this, people began to get restless, so Trent interrupted. "Excuse me. We're all familiar with your stores, so
how about you get to why you're here."

Mal's voice rose from the back. "Yes, please get to the point."

Epps appeared flummoxed but gathered himself. "Okay. To
cut to the chase, we'd like to build one of our award-winning
establishments nearby."

Trent added, "And?"

"Um, well . . ." He looked over at Wiggins as if for help.

Wiggins put on his best politician smile. "As I told Ms.
Brown this morning, opportunities such as this don't come
around very often—"

Bernadine interrupted him. "Mayor Wiggins, what did I
say to you when we met this morning?"

He stilled and slowly turned her way. "You said many
things."

"Yes, I did—chief being that Henry Adams wouldn't be
contributing one-point-three million dollars to help you build
this store."

Startled buzzing filled the air. Rocky blinked. *One-point-
three million dollars?*

Epps, apparently trying to be helpful, corrected her. "The
figure is two-point-six million."

Eyes popped all over the room, and the buzzing grew.

Bernadine assessed the now visibly squirming Piggly
Wiggly before saying succinctly, "Mayor Wiggins gave me the
impression that Henry Adams would be putting up half of the
two-point-six, and Franklin the other."

"No, ma'am. Mayor Wiggins assured us that Henry Adams
would be footing the entire bill." He shot the mayor a hard
look.

Piggly Wiggly squirmed some more, then finally tried to wave off the debate and the skillet heating up beneath him. "What's important here is whether the people of Henry Adams—*those born and raised here*—want to have a say in this decision."

Bernadine's irritation at the dig was plain.

Bing yelled, "Are you crazy, man?"

Laughter rang out.

The lawyers didn't appear amused.

"What's the two-point-six for?" Bing wanted to know.

Rocky did, too.

"Good-faith money in lieu of tax breaks," the lawyer explained. "Currently up on our Web site is an application form for construction workers seeking employment. We know the economy here's been hit hard, so we'd like to hire as many local tradespeople as possible."

Tamar called out in a puzzled voice, "So let me get this straight. You and Wiggins want us to come up with two-point-six million so you can build your store. Do we get a share of the profits?"

Epps smiled as if interacting with a small child. "No, ma'am."

"That's what I thought." Tamar turned her hawk-eyed glare on Wiggins. "For the record, what exactly did Ms. Brown tell you when you proposed this to her this morning?"

Bernadine answered for him. "No!"

Applause greeted that, along with yells of approval.

Epps shouted, "All you farmers, think about this. We pay a competitive price for your crops."

Bing shouted back. "Then do away with the two-point-six, and we'll consider selling to you."

Epps replied tightly, "Oh, you'll deal with us anyway, or watch your crops rot in the silos. We have influence with the distributors. You don't."

The room went silent.

Bernadine stared and stood up. "Is that a threat?"

"No, but let's just say that if they don't sell to our designated suppliers, we can make it very difficult for them to sell anywhere else."

"And you're sure of that?"

He boasted, "As sure as I work for Big Box. Our company is very influential, in case you don't know."

She shook her head and said to the assemblage, "We'll be building a grocery store here in Henry Adams, and if our store can't take your crops, my good friend Celeste Reems, the owner and CEO of Reems Foods, will."

Rocky dealt with food distributors, too, and knew Reems Foods was the largest food processor in the nation.

Upon hearing Bernadine invoke the Reems name, Epps and the two lawyers froze.

Bernadine asked silkily, "Something wrong, gentlemen?"

They didn't reply.

"Celeste and I have been good friends for a long time," she continued. "We're sorority sisters of a sort, and if I'm not mistaken, she owns a big fat chunk of your elite level stock."

Their eyes widened, and Rocky grinned, as did many of the other people in the room.

Then, in a pleasant voice, Bernadine quoted Beyoncé: "You must not know 'bout me."

Chuckling could be heard on the heels of that, but it wasn't coming from the still frozen Big Box legal beagles.

When Bernadine added in a steely voice, "I suggest you do

your homework before you visit us again, gentlemen," Rocky wanted to cheer.

A smiling Trent stepped in front of the stricken-looking lawyers and brought his gavel down hard. "This meeting is adjourned!"

Applause and more hoots of approval raised the roof.

Wiggins and his team made a hasty retreat, and a satisfied Rocky went to the kitchen to bring out fresh coffee.

She'd just pulled two full carafes away from the industrial-size coffeemaker when Jack walked in, immediately rendering her speechless.

"Mal's playing host, so I thought I'd come see if you needed assistance."

She forced her heart and breathing to start again. *Why is he so fine!* "Um, no. I—yes, here, take these out and set them on the buffet table." Putting some distance between herself and him was the only way she'd be able to pull herself together.

"Okay. Be right back."

When he made his exit, Rocky drew in a calming breath and prayed for strength.

Out in the dining room, some of the farmers came up to Bernadine to ask if she really planned to build a grocery store, and how they might get on the list to provide produce. Others asked if she could get them in touch with Reems Foods. She answered yes to both questions, and upon telling them that Gary would be managing the place, promised further info on the store later. Feeling pretty proud of herself, she walked over to the smiling Mal.

He gave her a big kiss on the cheek. "Love your style, girl. I thought the Big Box guy was going to choke."

"I hate it when people threaten me and mine. If that squirrel-wearing Wiggins ever shows his ugly little self in my town again, I'll be calling those FUFA nuts to investigate that toupee."

Mal chuckled.

While the farmers gathered for the meeting with Edison, she went to the buffet table for coffee and a bit more to eat. Lily, Crystal, and the kids had gone home, along with nearly everyone else. Across the room, Sheila was talking with a few people wanting more info on the Idol competition. In spite of her misgivings, Bernadine still thought the idea was great, and the excitement greeting the announcement showed that a bunch of other people did too.

Seeing Tamar and her crew heading for the exit, she gave them a wave and sat to enjoy her food and coffee.

"Ms. Brown."

She looked up into the unfamiliar face of a man as tall and as wide as a Back East oak. "Um, yes."

"Name's Albert Stillwell. Just wanted to get a good look at the woman who cost me my livelihood."

She froze.

"We owned our land for over a hundred years. Now we got nothing—you happy?"

"Oh, course not. It wasn't my intention to—"

"You and that big-city lawyer with your big-city ideas could care less that folks around here could've used that oil money."

"That's not true."

He slammed his fist on the tabletop, and both she and the dishes jumped with fright. "Yesterday the county took my hogs for back taxes—you going to pay that? You going to pay my daughter's tuition, or the rest of the bills choking me to death?"

His angry shouting made people look up, and brought Mal to her aid. "Al, you should probably leave." Mal took his arm.

He pulled away. "Get off me. She needs to know what her meddling's done."

Mal grabbed him. "You're leaving."

The resulting tussle knocked over a table. Cups and silverware crashed to the floor. Men hurried over to assist Mal in forcing Stillwell toward the exit.

He raged back at her, "I'll get you, you bitch! See if I don't! See if I don't!"

The horror on Bernadine's face mirrored that of everyone else in the room.

Riley had skipped the town meeting for a host of reasons: he didn't want to be around his self-righteous ex-wife, Genevieve; Bernadine Brown was still running the town into the ground; but mainly because he was feeling so blue. As he did every morning, he'd ridden out to the county pens to check on Cletus. Mentally Cletus seemed fine, he always came when Riley called, but physically he'd lost weight. When the county first locked him up, Riley made it a point to tell the vet in charge, a lady doc named Marnie Keegan, that Cletus was more accustomed to human food, but she shrugged him off and fed Cletus what she fed the rest of the animals. Riley even volunteered to pay for some of Cletus's favorite snacks—Doritos, Quarter Pounders, and Popsicles—but had been turned down flat. He got the impression that the county people weren't happy that he checked on Cletus every day, but he was the hog's only advocate and wanted to make sure they knew that Cletus wasn't just a run-of-the-mill, everyday hog. He was family.

Eustasia's fancy antique wall clock told him it was time for one of his cable news shows, so he picked up the remote and turned on the TV. The anchor man began reciting the day's top stories. Riley'd always wanted Cletus to be a television star, but the dream fell apart the night Cletus sat on Morton Prell and crushed the old fart to death. The anchorman continued to drone on about nothing Riley wanted to see, so he decided to change the channel, maybe watch Animal Planet, Cletus's favorite. However, as the anchor segued into a story about the animal rights organization Folks United for Animals, aka FUFA, he paused. FUFA had brought suit against a county in Illinois for spaying stray cats, and the court proceedings had been held earlier in the day. According to the reporter, FUFA's lawyers argued that the county's program violated the strays' reproductive and civil rights, and demanded the county stop the procedures immediately. The reporter turned the mic to the FUFA president, a skinny, bespectacled young woman who angrily denounced the judge's decision to summarily dismiss her organization's case after less than thirty minutes of testimony. While she continued to fuss, Riley sensed a plan forming. When her name appeared on the screen, he quickly wrote it down. Heather Quinn. If he could get in touch with her and explain Cletus's story, he might be able to get FUFA to take the case, and maybe even provide a lawyer. The dark cloud that had been looming over him since Cletus's incarceration suddenly gave way to sunshine. Turning off the TV, he picked up the phone and dialed the library. If anybody knew how to find the phone number for FUFA, the lady librarians would.

CHAPTER
6

It was dark by the time the farmers' meeting with Edison ended, so Mal trailed Bernadine home in his truck to make sure she arrived safely. The incident with Al Stillwell was on everyone's mind.

After pulling into her driveway, she got out to thank him, only to have him say first, "Make sure you call Sheriff Dalton."

"I will."

The lights from his dashboard illuminated the taut set of his jaw. He was still upset. "He had no business threatening you like that."

"Because of the lawsuit, he may lose his place. I understand why he's so mad."

"He was already underwater," he countered. "Trying to put it on you is bullshit. Especially if it makes you start doubting you did the right thing. Thought we talked about this."

"We did, but that was talk, Stillwell is reality. And I don't want you going out to his place and confronting him."

He didn't reply.

"Mal?"

"Trent went instead."

Bernadine sighed her irritation.

"Just us taking care of our own—don't worry about it. They went to school together. Al's always had a temper, but this was extreme even for him."

"Is he married?"

"Divorced. Mother lives with him and his daughter, Alfreda. Freda's finishing up her first year at KU."

"What about his father?"

"Died when Al was a teenager. He's been the man on the place since. Raises hogs and corn."

Bernadine's lips thinned. She continued to feel bad. "Thanks for seeing me home."

He said seriously, "Anything happen to you, not sure what I'd do."

The sincerity in his voice and manner made her heart swell with the love she had for him. "Give me a kiss."

He obliged and then drew back, saying, "You get some rest. If anything jumps off tonight, call me."

"I will. Promise."

"And make sure you lock that garage door after yourself."

"Check."

Concern remained in his manner and voice. "Night, baby girl."

"Night."

She got into her truck and drove into the garage. Only after the door began to lower behind her did he back out of the drive.

Weary, she cut the engine and sat in the darkness. The confrontation with Stillwell had left her shaken. She'd never had such fury directed her way before, and it was scary. She hated to admit it, but Leo had been right. There was at least one person so angry over the outcome of the lawsuit he'd threatened her. Mal, Trent, and Edison wanted her to call Sheriff Dalton there and then to report the incident, but all she'd wanted was for it to go away, at least for the present. She needed time to think things through. She felt awful. In her mind, she could still hear the pain in Stillwell's voice. Mal had tried to explain earlier that she couldn't make life fair, but that didn't lessen the guilt churning inside.

She wasn't planning on pressing charges; not of fear but out of not wanting to add more weight to the heavy burden Stillwell was already shouldering. He'd had his livestock foreclosed on, no way to pay his child's tuition, and he'd looked upon the oil money as his saving grace. Were she in his shoes, she'd've lashed out at the closest target around too—which in this case happened to be herself. She understood that, and hoped that once Stillwell returned home and had the opportunity to view the situation in a calmer frame of mind, he'd see the rightness of the stance taken against the oil company by a majority of his neighbors. His anger aside, she'd even offer to foot his tax bill and help with tuition if that would allow him and his family to breathe and not lose their land. Exhaling a big sigh, she left the truck and went in the house.

Crystal was seated at the kitchen table, drawing. Colored pencils and opened books were spread out around her. The smile on the teen's face when she saw Bernadine sent the blues packing. "Hey, Mom."

Bernadine had officially adopted Crystal during the Christmas holidays, and it was one of the best presents she'd ever received. "Hey, Crys. I thought you'd be chilling. What are you working on?"

"Mississippi River assignment."

Bernadine set her bag on the table. "Knowledge is power."

"I guess, but some of this is kind of interesting. Did you know that one time, way back in the day, the Mississippi flowed backward?"

"No, I didn't."

"Says so right here," Crystal said, indicating one of the books. "Mr. James thinks we should learn about the river because of all the flooding on the news. He calls it topical teaching. I call it a lot of work. He gave us each an assignment, and mine is to find out how the river has changed in the past hundred years because of the increase in population."

"Sounds deep. How was your day otherwise?"

"Okay. School was okay, too. Eli asked me out on a date last weekend."

Bernadine paused. Crystal finally looked up from the drawing she was making of the Mississippi.

"Since this is the first I'm hearing of this, I assume you told him no?"

"I did. Told him we were friends."

"How'd he take it?"

"Okay, I guess. He said some dumb stuff after I turned him down, but he was the same old Eli this morning at school."

Bernadine got the impression that she might need to delve just a bit further into this, so she went to the fridge and withdrew a bottle of water before asking nonchalantly, "What kind of dumb stuff?"

"Just some dumb stuff about me wanting to date Diego July."

Bernadine was swallowing, and then she was choking. "Diego?" she asked after her throat finally cleared. "Why he'd bring up Diego?"

"Eli thinks I like him."

"Do you?"

Crys shrugged while drawing. "He's kinda cute."

Bernadine didn't want to make a big deal out of this, but Diego I-steal-cars-and-been-to-jail-a-hundred-times July? Not while she was living. "He is cute. Most of the July guys are."

"I know. Eli said, Why would I want to date somebody dumber than me? I guess Diego never finished high school." Crys looked up. "But I don't think that makes a difference. You're way smarter than the OG, and you're good as a couple. Right?"

It took Bernadine a moment to find her voice. "I think it's different when you're adults. We have life experience to keep us balanced."

"Oh." Crys appeared to think on that for a moment before going back to her drawing.

Bernadine asked casually, "You haven't heard from Diego since he and the family were here at Thanksgiving, have you?"

"Tried to e-mail him a couple of times just to say hi, but it bounced back. It must be an old one."

Bernadine regularly monitored Crystal's e-mail and social media accounts. The other parents kept a sharp eye on their kids' online activities as well. Since she hadn't seen anything come in from Diego either, all she could think was, Thank you, Holy Ghost!

"So, how'd the rest of the meeting go?" Crys asked.

"Okay." She didn't want to tell Crystal about Stillwell because she didn't want her to worry or to think she needed to do something to keep her mom safe. She'd tell her eventually, however. "How are you and the Witches of Franklin getting along? Are they still working your nerves?"

"Only when I pay them any attention. Today they tried to tell me I made up going to Spain with you. I refused to participate in stupid discussions."

"Good for you. Keep taking the high road."

"Be easier to just kick their butts, but I'm trying the high road for now."

Bernadine bent and placed a kiss on her cheek. "I love you, Crystal. I'm heading up to my room. How close are you to being finished?"

"Almost done. I'll lock up down here before I come up for bed. You just go relax."

"Okay."

Upstairs in her bedroom, Bernadine took off her work clothes, put on sweats, and after stretching out on the bed, tried not to think about Stillwell. Picking up the remote, she clicked on the flat-screen. There were other things on her mind competing for attention too, like deciding what temperature the oil needed to be when she fried squirrel-head Wiggly and the Big Box lawyers, because she doubted she'd seen the last of them. Then there was the arrival of Preston's maternal grandmother, apparently tomorrow, according to the text she'd received from Brain earlier. Bernadine had only talked with Lenore Crenshaw on the phone a couple of times, and frankly hadn't liked the superior tone of the voice on the other end. According to the background check Lily had done on the Crenshaws, they hailed from Massachusetts. Old money. Free Black ancestors fought for the colonies during the war. Lenore Crenshaw was one of the first fully documented African American women admitted into the hallowed ranks of the Daughters of the American Revolution.

She thought back on the short visit she'd had with Preston's birth mom, Margaret Winthrop, and the painful story the NASA scientist had shared. That Lenore had mentally pummeled her daughter into giving Preston up for adoption while being happy about his father's death said volumes about who Lenore Crenshaw was as a person. For Lawrence Mays to have earned a scholarship to MIT, he must've been brilliant, but Lenore had chosen to ignore that in order to berate him for where he'd come from. Had he lived, life might have been different. Preston would have blossomed as the son of incredibly intelligent parents, and sadness wouldn't be still pouring out of his birth mother's soul. To say Bernadine wasn't looking forward to the arrival of Lenore Crenshaw was an understatement, and for some unnamed reason, she had a deep sense of foreboding, as if something bad loomed on the horizon. Hoping it was nothing more than spillover from Stillwell's anger, she picked up her phone and put in the promised call to Sheriff Will Dalton.

Rocky finished the prep for tomorrow's breakfast and looked around at the now-sparkling kitchen. The floor had been swept and mopped, counters wiped down. The only items still on her to-do list included checking on the state of the dining room and assembling the one hundred napkin and silverware packs common to every eatery. Placing the large tub of clean silverware on a cart, she added a bundled stack of napkins and pushed her way out to the dining room.

And the first thing she saw, of course, was Jack. He was

bent over, wiping down one of the tables. His back was to her, so it gave her a moment to view him at her leisure.

His dark hair was touched with gray and worn a bit longer than was deemed trendy, but she'd never paid any attention to such things. As a teen, he'd probably been as gangly and thin as his son, Eli, was now, but age had added weight to his frame, making him no less tall, but fit, like a swimmer. The small gold hoop in his ear added a rakishness to his already good looks, and Rocky knew she could stare at him for the rest of her life. After the farmers' meeting ended, he'd asked if she wanted his help with the cleanup, and because his presence had her so off her game, she'd said yes. A few other people stuck around to lend a hand taking down the buffet table and putting the chairs back in their normal configuration, but they'd gone home a while ago. Now the two of them were the only ones in the building.

Jazz great Sonny Criss was playing on the jukebox. The sweet, velvety sound of his horn against the diner's silence gave the air a hushed, intimate feel. She pushed the cart farther into the dining room. He glanced her way and slowly straightened.

"I have a couple more tables to do, and I'll be done. What's in the tub?"

"Silverware I need to wrap in napkins, but I can do it alone. You don't have to stay any longer."

"How many do you have to make?"

"One hundred."

"Wouldn't four hands be faster than two?"

"It's almost ten o'clock," she said, fighting the parts of herself that wanted him to stay.

"And?"

She sighed around a smile. He was persistent, if nothing else. "Okay. Finish the tables and then come sit over here, and I'll show you how to do this."

He joined her a few minutes later, and she demonstrated how the wraps were made. His first few attempts were crude, but he improved steadily.

"How's this?" he asked, holding up one of his better attempts for her inspection.

"Perfect."

Their gazes held—longer than was necessary. Rocky ducked her head and resumed working. They didn't talk much, but words didn't seem necessary. With only the silence and the hushed jazz between them, she took a few peeks at him and found him peeking back. She decided the time had come to make a decision; if she didn't, she was going to lose her mind. "Are you busy Saturday morning?"

He stopped and searched her eyes as if trying to discern the reason for the question. "Um, not that I know of. Why?"

"I'm driving down to Hays to pick up a bike. Thought you'd like to ride along."

He appeared so shocked she almost smiled.

"Is this like a date?"

"No, Jack. It isn't. Do you want to go or not?" She loved his accent.

"Yeah, sure. What time?"

"Leaving here at six."

"In the morning?"

She waited.

"Okay. Where should I meet you?"

"I'll pick you up at your place. Just be ready."

"Sure."

Now he was the one who looked rattled. For her, that made them even.

He was right, four hands were faster than two, and when they were done, she set their handiwork at the hostess station and prepared to call it a night. "Thanks again, Jack."

"You're welcome, Rochelle."

"Do me a favor."

"Anything."

"Cut the Rochelle stuff, okay?"

He dropped his head but came up with a smile. "Got it."

Rocky knew she should be heading to the exit, but he was so easy on the eyes, she lost herself in his for a moment.

"You ready?" he asked quietly.

She sensed there was more to the question than its simplistic wording. "Yeah, I think so."

"Then I'll walk you to your truck."

Out in the dark, the new solar lights illuminated the two lone vehicles in the parking lot: her big black Dodge Ram and his squat Swedish import.

She asked him, "When are you going to get something that's made in America?"

His laugh was soft as the night. "Are you hating on my vehicle?"

"How many miles do you have on that thing?"

"About a hundred and twenty grand."

She shook her head. "Out here, you need a truck, professor."

"So I keep hearing."

Rocky hit the clicker in her hand and the lights on her truck flashed in conjunction with the doors unlocking. "You have a good night."

"You, too."

She nodded and climbed up and in. Closing the door, she started the engine. In her rearview mirror, she saw him walking to his car. A moment later he was pulling out. He headed east toward the subdivision. She made the left onto Jefferson and drove north.

When Jack arrived home, Eli was on the couch, watching a poker tournament. Jack was still reeling from Rocky's invitation, and it must've shown on his face.

"You okay?" Eli asked, sounding concerned.

"Rocky wants me to ride with her Saturday to pick up a bike."

"Wow. Really? What kind of bike?"

"Not sure."

"Is this like a date?"

"She said no."

"Sounds like a date to me."

He looked into Eli's eyes, eyes he'd inherited from his mother. "If it does turn out to be a date and something comes out of it, will it bother you—Mom's passing and all?"

"I'm not sure. Can I say that?"

"Sure. I always want to know how you feel. And you should also know that no matter what the future brings, Eva will always be in my heart. The love she and I shared isn't something I can just turn off."

In the silence that followed, Eli seemed to think about his words, then said finally, "Good to know. Can I ask you something else, some advice?"

Inwardly, Jack was bowled over by the surprising request. Eli wanting advice from his dad? "Sure, shoot."

"It's kinda complicated."

"How about I sit down and see if we can uncomplicate it?"

"Okay."

Wondering who this Eli was, and what had happened to his real son, Jack took a seat in the old olive green recliner. "So what's up?"

"I like this girl, but she just wants to be friends. How do I change her mind?"

"You can't make her like you, but you can show her who you are by being a good friend, and maybe over time, her feelings about you may change."

"So there's no magic line I can run, or anything like that?"

"Not that I'm aware of. The OG may have a couple, though."

Eli smiled, and the sight of it filled Jack's heart with all the love he felt for his mercurial child.

"You know I'm talking about Crystal, right?"

"I kind of figured that, yeah."

"Dad, since the first day she got in my face, she's all I can think about. I want to be with her, do what she does, go where she goes. I don't even care if she yells at me, just so she talks to me. I've been telling Eddie back home about her, and he says it sounds like I'm whipped."

"We're men, Eli. We all wind up whipped at some point in our lives. Your mother had me whipped from the moment I met her. Thought she was the most beautiful thing God ever made. Hadn't been for her, I probably would've never finished undergrad."

"Why not?"

"Too busy drinking and fighting."

Eli stared. "What!"

Jack found the reaction priceless. "I wasn't always your father."

Eli was bug-eyed. "Fights? You?"

"Had a biker for a roommate my freshman and sophomore years. Guy by the name of Smith "Smitty" Black. Parents were bikers, too. He was the first person in his family to finish high school and attend college."

"Did Gram and Gramps ever meet him and his parents?"

"Very first day I moved into the dorm. I thought they were going to have a heart attack." The memory of the shock on his parents' upper-crust faces as they took in the tattooed, leather-wearing Black family evoked a smile. "Smitty and I had some good times."

"So when were these fights?"

"Seemed like every weekend during freshman year. Frat boys took exception to Smitty's presence in the area bars, and he took exception to their exception, and the next thing we knew we were knocking heads and tearing up the place."

Jack thought if Eli's eyes grew any larger, they'd pop out of his face and roll around on the carpet. "One weekend, during homecoming sophomore year, a bunch of his biker relatives and their biker friends came up for the festivities. Preppies and bikers don't mix. The cops hauled everybody off to jail that night for over ten thousand dollars' worth of damage done to the pancake house."

Eli's mouth dropped.

"Even worse, I had to call Gramps to get me out of jail. Having to call your parents for something like that isn't fun, as you well know."

"Yeah," Eli answered sheepishly. A few days before Jack took the teaching position in Henry Adams, Eli had been arrested for car theft.

Eli was studying Jack as if he'd never seen him before. "So what ever happened to Smitty? Did he graduate with you?"

"No. After the big fight at the pancake house, he transferred. Said he was tired of being hassled by the dean about his behavior."

"What's he doing now?"

"Like me, he got himself together and is now a pediatric orthopedic surgeon in Houston."

"You're kidding?"

"Nope. Still has the tattoos, too."

Eli fell back against the sofa. "Wow."

Jack could see him still processing what he'd revealed.

"No offense, Dad, but I thought you were like the nerdiest of nerds."

"I was, but when you hang with a biker, it sort of changes you. Meeting your mother put me back on the right track."

"That was some story. How come you never told me any of this before?"

"Your mom always told me, nothing happens until it's supposed to. Guess now was the time. Makes you look at your old man differently, doesn't it?"

"Oh, yeah."

"Good." He eyed his son, and said sincerely, "Eli, eventually Crystal may turn out to be the girl for you, but right now, she's not feeling it, so don't press her, okay?"

"I won't. Besides, she's all hung up on Diego July."

It was Jack's turn to stare. "Diego, of the Oklahoma Julys?"

"Yeah. Dumb, huh?"

"I can't say it's dumb, but it is surprising."

"He never even finished high school."

"Then when you graduate, you'll have one up on him."

"But will she appreciate it, is the question."

Jack shrugged. "You're going to find out that women are the most complicated and complex beings on earth."

"Figuring that out now." He got to his feet. "I need to get to bed. Don't want the teacher yelling at me for sleeping in class."

Jack gave him a smile.

"Thanks for the advice, Dad, and for the story."

"You're welcome. I enjoyed this."

"Me, too."

After Eli went up to bed, Jack stepped outside onto the deck. The night sky was clear and dotted with stars. Even though he could hear the soft sounds of the nocturnal insects, the silence was so pervasive, it was as if the entire world was asleep. He thought back on the evening. First Rocky and then Eli. Eva came to mind too, and he wondered what she thought of the new life he and Eli were trying to build, and what she thought of Miss Rocky Don't-Call-Me-Rochelle Dancer. A shooting star blazed across the sky. He closed his eyes and made a wish upon it for peace and happiness for his son. At the end he added a prayer, thanking God for Eva's presence in his life, for the blessings of the past and present, and for those yet to come.

He stayed outside a short while longer, then quietly reentered the house.

Remote in hand, Rocky was lying in bed. She flipped through the channels, looking for something that might distract her, but there was nothing. Her workday usually started at 5:00 A.M., so she clicked off both the TV and the lamp on her nightstand, plunging her bedroom into darkness.

On her drive home, the part of herself that usually ruled her psyche declared the invite she'd given Jack a stupid idea. What could she, a half-wild woman from the plains of Kansas, possibly have in common with a college professor? She considered herself well read and fairly intelligent, but she had no idea what a man like him talked about off duty. Suppose his conversation was so deep she had no idea what he was talking about, and wound up looking country and dumb?

Usually she paid attention to this side of herself, because she'd relied on it for so long. When you have a mother with mental illness and the kids laugh because she comes to school to bring your lunch with her hair looking like a fright wig, wearing a muddy nightgown, and barefoot, you have to be tough, physically and mentally. You learn to stare down the teasing and the hurtful remarks about her being picked up by the county sheriff because she somehow got out of the house again and was found wandering through the streets of Franklin in that same dirty gown. How do you explain to a bunch of kids that your mom refused to wear anything else, and would get violent if your dad tried to get her to change clothes? Or that Crazy Debbie, as she was derisively called, had a mental illness, and wasn't responsible for the way she acted, and that outside of institutionalizing her, the doctors said they couldn't help?

When you're eight years old, you don't explain it, because you don't know how, and it wouldn't matter if you could. So instead you get into fights and get kicked out of school, and you're angry all the time. And when your mother finally ends her pain by taking her own life, you go to Tamar and cry so no one else will see your tears.

Growing up had been a bitch, and the cautious, take-no-prisoners side of herself was the part she'd always relied upon because it was all she had. Her father, who would have given his soul and everything he owned to have his Deborah back the way she used to be, was never the same after her death. The man who'd given Rocky horseback rides, taught her to pitch a softball and break down an engine, seemed to shrink right before her eyes, as if the life were slowly leaking out of him like air from a balloon.

So she'd gone through those years, and the ones after, with her chin stuck out and fists balled up; not an attitude conducive to lasting relationships of the heart. Looking back, had she listened to her inner voice and not tried to change her spots by accepting Bob Lee's marriage proposal, she could have saved herself from having the memory of him posing in her underwire permanently seared into her brain.

That inner voice asked, *Why are you trying to change your spots again and open up your life and feelings to Jack James?* The only answer Rocky could come up with was that, from the moment they met, something in his eyes had offered solace, and she felt drawn to the calm she sensed there.

Maybe she was crazy, but the other inner voice, the one that represented her softer side, asked, What if she wasn't? What if Jack was the person she'd been needing, to finally find the peace and happiness she'd always craved? Last fall, Reverend Paula told her that life was too short to be unhappy, and no guts, no glory. Well, Rocky had plenty of guts, and now it was time for some glory.

With that, she banished both inner voices for the time being, made herself comfortable beneath the bedding, and drifted off to sleep.

CHAPTER
7

The next morning, Jack watched his students file into the classroom and thought how wonderful it was to teach in Henry Adams. Unlike some teachers in the nation, he had the support of the parents and the community, along with a very nice compensation package. But more importantly, his students were a joy. They were typical kids, filled with the angst, silliness, and hormonal surges of their national peers, and sometimes they made him want to pull out his hair, but he cared about each and every one of them. "All right, everybody, let's get the day started. Leah, start us on the Pledge of Allegiance, please."

She stood, and after the others followed and faced the flag on the stand near his desk, she began, "I pledge allegiance to the flag of the United States of America . . ."

The rest of the students picked up the verse, and when the recitation wound down to the words "and liberty and justice for all," the room faded into silence. A second later, Leah looked Jack's way, and he gave her a nod. She began to sing in her teenage soprano: *"Lift every voice and sing, till earth and heaven ring. Ring with the harmony of Liberty."*

Jack and the others added their voices: *"Let our rejoicing rise high as the listening skies. Let it resound loud as the rolling sea . . ."*

Jack had never heard of the Negro National Anthem, "Lift Every Voice and Sing," before coming to Henry Adams. On his first day as the teacher, the kids recited the pledge, and after it was over he began to introduce himself, but Zoey scooted over to the old piano, hit the opening notes, and Devon began singing, all of which took Jack by surprise. Although there were only four voices that day—Amari, Crystal, Devon, and Preston—they sang with a fierceness and a beauty that blew him away. Only after they were done singing did he ask about the song, and was informed that it had been written first as a poem in 1900 by the great African-American educator and writer James Weldon Johnson to commemorate a Lincoln's Birthday address by Booker T. Washington. Johnson's brother, John Rosamund Johnson, set the poem to music in 1905. Only Devon had known the anthem before coming to Henry Adams, but during their first school year, Marie Jefferson made the rest of her new students learn the words and the history behind it. Now Jack and Eli knew the words by heart, too, and that the song had been a way for African Americans to showcase inner pride and subtly voice their protest during a time when lynchings were rampant, and segregation and Jim Crow were the law of the land.

As the song drew to a close, Jack nodded a greeting to Bing, who'd come in during the end of the first verse and added his bass line to the melody. The two new girls from Franklin, Megan and Samantha, sang while rolling their eyes and making faces, as if the anthem were a joke of some sort.

Jack made a mental note to speak to them before the end of the day; he was tired of their disrespect.

"All right, everybody. Let's give Mr. Bing a hand for coming in today."

Bing beamed under the welcoming applause. He was decked out in a nice black suit and had his World War II vet beret perched stylishly on his gray head. The eighty-two-year-old retired farmer was known for his sharp mind and withering wit. Jack liked him a lot.

The purpose of Bing's visit was to share his experiences as a member of the Black Army Corps of Engineers during the building of the Alaska-Canadian, aka AlCan, Highway.

When all the kids were settled, he began, "There were three Black regiments: the Ninety-Third, Ninety-Fifth, and Ninety-Seventh. We also had a battalion—the 388th."

At his signal, Amari, the designated tech of the week, put a large map of Alaska and northwest Canada on the screen at the front of the room. Bing pointed out the beginning of the highway in Dawson Creek, Canada, and its end point at Delta Junction, near Fairbanks, Alaska. "When we started, there was nothing but snow, forest, and glaciers, but when the highway was completed, it was over sixteen hundred miles long."

Devon said, "That's a long way."

"Yes, it is, and it wasn't easy to build." He told them about winter nights when temperatures sometimes dropped to sixty degrees below zero, and zoomed to ninety degrees in the summertime. "It was so cold the oil would freeze in the trucks, and we had to put lit torches beneath some of the equipment so it would start in the morning."

Leah asked, "How did you keep warm?"

"As best we could. You have to understand that we'd

trained in the south, and figured we were going to be sent to Europe to help fight the Germans, but we ended up in Alaska instead, and we weren't dressed for the weather. Some of our guys had never even seen snow before, and none of us had been anyplace that cold."

"But the army gave you warm gear, right?" Preston asked.

Bing looked over at Jack, who responded by saying, "You don't need my permission to tell him the truth, Mr. Shepard. It's history. They need to know the realities back then, and frankly, so do I."

Bing nodded in agreement, and told the kids just how rough it had been in the segregated U.S. Army, where they were given inferior clothing, housing, and equipment, and commanding officers who made it well known that the Black soldiers weren't wanted. "While the officers and other troops stayed in Quonset huts, we had to make do in canvas tents. In the wintertime, they were like trying to stay warm inside a sheet."

The army routinely sent them broken-down equipment, and when the Black soldiers did get quality machines, they usually wound up being reassigned to the White engineers also working on the AlCan.

"Some of our guys had to cut through glaciers with hand tools when their heavy equipment got reassigned. We weren't allowed to go into the air force bases, where it was warm, couldn't go to the movies at the bases that other troops got to enjoy on days off, and we were forbidden to go into the local towns, even though we were building them roads."

"That stinks," Crystal said.

"Yes, it did, but you know what?"

"What?"

"We got the job done, and we did it well. Only time there

was any real trouble was when a group of our guys refused to ride cross-country in the back of an open truck."

"Sorta like Rosa Parks?" Amari asked.

"No. They knew they'd risk frostbite or paralysis sitting for such a long ride in below-freezing weather."

"What happened to them?"

"They were court-martialed."

"Wow, that stinks, too."

"Yep. But as I said, we got it done, and we took pride in the roads and bridges we built. In fact, when the Ninety-Fifth was at Sikanni Chief River, we bet our paychecks that we could build that bridge in record time."

"Did you do it?" Eli asked.

"Yep. Took us eighty-four hours, half the time it normally took."

Amari crowed, "Now that's what I'm talking about."

Bing grinned. "And when all hundred and thirty-three bridges were finished, along with the roads and the eight hundred culverts that held the pipelines, we'd proven to the army that yes, Black soldiers could handle heavy equipment and perform under extreme conditions, and that our engineers were just as able-bodied and smart as the other side of the army."

He spent a few more minutes telling them about the Ninety-Fifth's transfer to Europe after leaving Alaska, and when his talk was done, the kids applauded. Jack did, too. He'd learned a lot. "Any questions?"

From the hands that shot up, they had a ton, so Jack sat back to enjoy the rest of the morning.

At lunchtime, Preston sat at the picnic table he and Amari claimed as their own and ate the burger Siz brought over from the Dog. The Dog usually provided lunch for the students—yet another bonus of living in Henry Adams.

Like everyone else in town, they were excited about the Henry Adams Idol competition.

Preston asked, "Are you going to enter?'

"Not sure. After being dissed on the rap idea, I've been trying to come up with something else. I can't sing, so that's out. What about you?'

"Unless I can do a talk on the periodic table, I'll be in the audience."

Amari laughed. "My parents were talking this morning about entering as somebody called Peaches and Herb, whoever they are."

"No clue."

"Me either." Amari asked around a bite of his fries, "Do you know what time your grandmother's coming?"

"No, but I figured if she was here, Ms. Bernadine or Ms. Lily would've brought her over by now. Maybe she changed her mind."

On one hand Preston kind of hoped she had, but on the other, he hoped she hadn't. He was pretty mixed up. "The colonel says I should play it by ear, and that he and Mrs. Payne have my back."

Amari paused in mid bite. "You two talking again?"

"Sorta, I guess. He gave me this long speech yesterday about wanting to start over as father and son, and that the issues we've been having are mostly his fault because he doesn't know how to be a dad."

"At least he's honest. What did you say?"

"That I was okay with trying again, but didn't trust him."

"That was honest, too."

"That's what he said."

Leah sat down with her bag from the Dog and pulled out a takeout container holding her usual salad.

Preston asked, "Tiff still sick?"

"No, she's faking. Just doesn't want to come to school. She's missing Mom. Dad told her she's coming tomorrow whether she wants to or not."

Preston knew that Amari wasn't missing Tiffany Adele one bit and waited for him to say something sarcastic, but Amari remained silent.

Leah asked, "So when's your grandmother coming?"

"I don't know."

"I think she's going to be real nice."

"How do you know?"

"Woman's intuition."

Preston saw Amari roll his eyes, but he hoped Leah was right.

She wasn't.

Right after lunch, while they were working on their Mississippi River reports, a short, gray-haired woman wearing an expensive red suit, fur stole, and gold jewelry swept into the classroom. A guy in a chauffeur uniform trailed in her wake. Before anyone could react to the surprising entrance, she looked from Amari to Preston and asked, "Which one of you boys is Preston?"

No one moved.

Mr. James asked, "Um, who are you?"

"Lenore Crenshaw. Preston's grandmother. Where is he?"

"Does Ms. Brown know you're here?"

"Who?"

"Ms. Bernadine Brown?"

"Oh, her. Yes. I spoke with her when I got off the plane. She said my grandson was at the school. I am in the right place, aren't I?"

Preston saw Crystal take out her phone and go out into the hallway.

Mr. James asked, "Did she give you permission to come here without her?"

Preston glanced over at Amari, and the look on his face confirmed that Preston wasn't the only person studying the newcomer warily.

"She said to stop by her office, but I didn't think that necessary. After all, I am his grandmother."

Preston stood. "Who gave up all legal claims when I was sent to foster care. How are you, Mrs. Crenshaw?"

She stopped, turned, and after a silent moment of regard, replied, "I should have known. You look just like him."

"Who?"

"The man who fathered you."

"Do you know where he is?"

"Dead. Which made everything easier, if you don't mind my saying. A boy from the projects was not my idea of the man my daughter should have been with, and definitely not one she should have a child by."

Preston felt like he'd been punched in the stomach.

Mr. James stepped in front of her. "I'm going to have to ask you to leave."

She looked him up and down. "You obviously don't know who you're talking to."

A strong voice rang out, "And you obviously don't know where you are."

They all turned, and there stood Colonel Barrett Montgomery Payne, dressed in full uniform, eyes blazing. "Are you always so disrespectful of the dead? How dare you say something like that to my son?"

She had the sense to step back.

Preston was still reeling, but he wanted to cheer. Like the colonel, he wanted to know, What kind of person said hateful stuff like that to a kid? Especially when she claimed to be his grandmother! Did she expect him to feel the same way about his dad? It made Preston wonder if his birth mother knew about this visit, and if so, why she hadn't come along. He was now more confused than ever, and although he was trying not to let it show, hurt too.

Beside him, Amari asked quietly, "The colonel showed up right on time, but what's he doing here?"

"He said something this morning about meeting Mr. Bing here so they could ride out for a vets' event together. He must have gotten his times mixed up."

"Well, if this lady has any sense, she'll book before Ms. Bernadine gets here."

Too late; Bernadine came striding in a moment later. She took a look at Preston, then at the angry faces of the colonel and Mr. James, before settling cool eyes on the woman in the fur with the chauffeur.

"I thought we agreed on the phone that you'd come to my office when you arrived?"

"You must be Ms. Brown."

Ms. Bernadine didn't respond; she just looked mad.

His grandmother gave her a snooty up-and-down glance. "I didn't realize it was mandatory, nor did I expect such a rude introduction to this tacky little place. What exactly is your function here?"

Ms. Bernadine leaned in. "I own this tacky little place."

"Are you the mayor or something?"

"No. I'm the ow-ner."

"Well, I'm here to retrieve my grandson."

Preston stared, wide-eyed.

Ms. Bernadine appeared just as surprised. "Retrieve, as in how?"

"I'm taking him back east. I was about to explain that when I was verbally accosted by this so-called colonel."

Preston wondered if this woman was crazy. He prayed that whatever she had wasn't genetic.

"Do you want to talk to her, Preston?" Ms. Bernadine asked.

"No, ma'am." If he never saw Lenore Crenshaw again, life would be good.

"Barrett, do you wish to speak with her in my office?"

"Yes, I would. Sheila's at Tamar's. I'll give her a call and have her meet us there."

The tension in the air was thick.

Amari leaned over and whispered, "This is better than TV."

"Shut up!" Preston whispered out of the side of his mouth.

"Ms. Crenshaw, you can come to my office, or you and your chauffeur can leave my tacky little town. Your choice."

"I will not be bullied."

"Nor will I, so what'll it be? I can have you escorted off the property if you prefer."

Preston's and Amari's eyes widened again.

"You're threatening me with the police?"

"Nope. County sheriff. We can also slap you with a restraining order if you want. I'm sure Judge Davis won't be hard to find."

It was apparent to Preston and everyone else in the class-room that Lenore Crenshaw was unaccustomed to having someone get in her face who wouldn't back down. She viewed Ms. Bernadine as if she'd never seen anything like her before, and he was pretty sure she hadn't; the owner of their tacky little town was one of a kind.

"All right, fine," Mrs. Crenshaw finally huffed out. "Your office it is. Come, Phillip."

She swept out, and Phillip the chauffeur, who'd remained as emotionless as a statue the entire time, followed as ordered.

After their departure, Ms. Bernadine told Preston reassur-ingly, "Don't worry. Even if she had the right to take you any-where, I'd tie her up in court so long, you'd be forty years old before the final ruling came down."

He gave her a smile.

The colonel asked him, "Are you okay? Do you want to go home?"

"No, I'm good." Preston wanted to tell him how great it was that he'd shown up when he had, but didn't want to get all emotional in front of his classmates.

"We'll get this straight and talk about it when you get home then."

Watching Payne and Ms. Bernadine exit the classroom, Preston felt better, but he didn't want to see Lenore Crenshaw ever again.

He glanced over at Crystal. "Thanks for calling in the big guns."

"No problem."

From the front of the room, Mr. James said, "Okay, every-body, let's get back to our reports."

CHAPTER
8

By the time Bernadine entered her office, she was so out-done, she was sputtering. She'd specifically told the Cren-shaw woman not to approach Preston without her, but she'd done so anyway. Then again, she was probably unaccustomed to having anyone tell her what to do. Judging from the atti-tude she'd displayed at the school, it was no wonder Dr. Win-throp had changed her name. "Have a seat, Ms. Crenshaw, Barrett."

Both chose a chair and complied. The hard set of Barrett's face showed he was still steaming, and from the phone video Crystal had sent Bernadine of what transpired at the school before she arrived, he had every reason to be. Crenshaw, on the other hand, just looked haughty.

Bernadine was about to begin the interrogation when Sheila Payne rushed into the office. "Got here as quickly as I could."

Bernadine did the introductions. Lenore Crenshaw gave Sheila a dismissive glance and turned away. Sheila's jaw tightened at the obvious slight, but she took a seat next to her husband and sat silently.

The rude behavior only increased Bernadine's ire. "Now, why are you here again?"

"To fly Preston back to Boston so he can take his rightful place in my family."

Sheila pointed out icily, "Legally, you forfeited all rights when he was put up for adoption."

"I understand that, but when I explain to the courts that it was a mistake, I'm certain it can be straightened out."

"A mistake?" the colonel echoed skeptically. "Are you saying your family wanted to keep him?"

"Oh, of course not. No one wants their only child impregnated by a boy from the projects, no matter how smart he's supposed to be."

Bernadine bit down hard on her tongue. She wanted to curse the woman up one wall and down the other, but that might delay her departure, and Bernadine wanted her gone—as did her blood pressure. "So where was the mistake supposedly made?"

Her chin rose. "I didn't realize the impact the adoption would have on my relationship with my daughter. She hasn't spoken to me since the day the nurses took him away fourteen years ago."

Bernadine went still. Dr. Winthrop hadn't mentioned that. She looked at the Paynes. They appeared equally taken aback.

"Margaret didn't even attend her father's funeral," she added bitterly

According to the report, Martin Crenshaw had passed away two years ago.

"Did your husband agree to the adoption?" Sheila asked.

"Oh, yes. He didn't find the Mays boy acceptable son-in-law material either. Martin was one of the first African-American jurists in this country. We're both descendants of free Black men who fought in the Revolutionary War. There was no way we could have welcomed a boy with his roots into our bloodline. We'd always encouraged her to set her sights on an Ivy Leaguer, or a Morehouse man—as long as his people weren't descendants of slaves."

Bernadine blinked. She'd heard there were people in the race like the Crenshaws, but never wanted to believe it was true.

Barrett said emotionlessly, "You and your husband must have been quite a pair."

The sarcasm went right over Mrs. Crenshaw's head. "Yes, we were. And when Margaret began showing serious interest in this Mays character, my husband and I presented a united front."

With a mother like this, Bernadine was surprised Margaret hadn't volunteered to go on a deep space, no return mission.

"Let me be frank, Mrs. Crenshaw. Even with your husband's connections, no court in the land is going to void the adoption papers that your family signed, nor will they force Preston to live with you if he chooses not to. He's fourteen, not four."

"I'd still like to speak with him."

"He's chosen not to speak to you, remember?" Barrett reminded her.

"I demand that you bring him to this office now! Did you not hear me say I need him to get my daughter back?"

Bernadine kept her voice even. "Shouting at us like we're servants is not going to change the situation. I suggest you fly back to Boston, Ms. Crenshaw. There's nothing for you here."

"I want to speak to someone in authority!"

Bernadine hit the button on the speaker. "Lil, you there?"

"Yes."

"Can you call Sheriff Dalton for me. Tell him I need assistance in escorting someone off the property."

"Right away."

Lorene puffed up. "You wouldn't dare!"

Bernadine sat back in her navy blue leather chair and folded her arms.

Although Lenore Crenshaw might've been arrogant and full of herself, apparently she wasn't stupid. She obviously sensed that Bernadine and the Paynes weren't playing. She stood. "This is not over."

Sheila countered evenly. "Yes, it is. Bother our son again, and we'll have you arrested."

Face filled with fury, Crenshaw turned to Bernadine, who responded with a smile that didn't reach her eyes. "Have a safe flight."

She snapped at the chauffeur, "We're leaving, Phillip."

And they did.

Bernadine hit the button on the speaker and had Lily cancel the call in to the sheriff.

"Sheila and I will be following through on the restraining order," Barrett said.

"Good, because if you don't, I will."

Bernadine knew he'd had issues with the birth search, so she was a bit concerned about how he might handle discussing this meeting with Preston.

Apparently, Sheila had misgivings, too. "You aren't going to tell Preston I told you so, are you, Barrett?"

He shook his head. "I saw his face when she said those

awful things about his father. I'm not going to pour salt on the wound."

"Good," she said softly.

Bernadine was pleased, but she had one more question for him. "Why are you all dressed up?"

"I was supposed to meet Bing at the school and ride with him to a meeting about the Memorial Day parade some of the vets want to organize, but I must have written down the wrong time. He was already gone when I got there."

Sheila said, "I think you were supposed to show up at the school when you did."

He nodded. "You could be right, but let's not make it any deeper than it is. All that matters is that I was around when Preston needed someone." He then spoke thoughtfully. "You have to wonder why that woman thinks having him back will help her reconcile with her daughter after such a long time."

Bernadine wondered, too. "Maybe it's her age. Sometimes when we see the grave looming, we want to make amends. She doesn't have any other children, and with her husband gone, she might be looking back over her life and regretting some of the things she's done. Who really knows?"

"Maybe she should try talking to her daughter instead of throwing her weight around," Sheila pointed out tightly.

"I'm with you on that. I was surprised to hear about the estrangement, though. When I met Dr. Winthrop last winter, she admitted that she and her mother weren't close, but to not speak for fourteen years? That's a lot of anger and bitterness."

"And the doctor hasn't called you or e-mailed you since?"

"Nope. Nothing. As I told you and Sheila, she doesn't want further contact, but I'm hoping she changes her mind. If she were to meet Preston, she'd be so proud."

"I agree. He's a great kid," Barrett voiced.

Bernadine added, "And Winthrop didn't seem anything like her mother either, which is a good thing."

"Yes, it is," Sheila said, nodding.

Pleased with how the situation had turned out, Bernadine told Barrett, "Thanks for your help at the school."

"I didn't do anything but scare her off my son, but you're welcome."

He got to his feet. "I should find Bing and apologize for missing the meeting. Feels good wearing the uniform again."

"And you wear it well, Barrett," Sheila added.

He snapped off a salute, gave them a smile, and left them alone.

In the silence left behind, Sheila said, "He was the handsomest man I'd ever seen when my cousin Gayle introduced him to me."

"He's still real easy on the eyes, Sheila."

She chuckled in reply. "That he is, and I'm glad he was there for Preston today. I've never wanted to strike another person, but I wanted to pound Mrs. Crenshaw."

"I wanted her in a cage match, myself. Let's hope she takes our advice and stays away. Were you and Tamar working on the Idol project?"

"Yes. We already have ten contestants, and we haven't even put the word out yet. I texted Roni and received a reply this morning. She's pretty excited about being one of the judges."

"Good. Anything you need my help with?"

"Not at the moment. Genevieve and Marie have volunteered to be on the steering committee, so if we need more hands, I'll let you know."

"Okay."

Sheila stood. "Thanks again for taking on the Dragon Grandmother, and for bringing Preston into our lives."

"He's a special young man."

"And a blessing. Too bad his biological mother will never know him."

"Yes, it is."

Sheila departed, and Lily's voice came over the intercom. "So, what happened?"

Bernadine gave her a quick rundown.

When she finished, Lily said, "Wow. Glad I missed all that. Hope she'll stay in Boston."

Bernadine agreed. "So what's on your plate?"

"Going to ride out with Trent and Gary to look at grocery stores. He wants to check out square footage, displays, lighting, that kind of thing. Says he's also putting together a survey for residents to fill out on what brands they prefer when shopping."

"He's hitting the ground running."

"Yes, he is. I'll call when we get back."

Lily signed off, and Bernadine heard her stomach rumble a reminder that she hadn't had lunch. Grabbing her purse, she was on her way to the door when a familiar presence walked in. She sighed. "Mr. Epps. What can I do for you?"

The Big Box lawyer looked very uncomfortable. "May I speak with you for a moment, please, Ms. Brown?"

Wondering what this was about and why he seemed so meek and mousy, when last night at the meeting he'd been yelling and threatening people, she said, "I have a moment. Go ahead."

She could tell by his body language that he wanted a seat, but she didn't offer. "You were saying?"

"Um, first of all, I'd like to apologize for losing my temper last night. It was very unprofessional."

She waited.

"And my, um, district manager sends his apology as well."

"Really?" That was surprising. Had Epps been called on the carpet?

There was a sheen of perspiration on his forehead, and he mopped at it with a white handkerchief withdrawn from inside his blue suit coat. "He also hopes you won't inform Ms. Reems of the incident, and that I make it clear Big Box was unaware Mayor Wiggins lacked permission to speak on your behalf during the negotiations."

She found this all very interesting. "So, you told your manager you'd been unprofessional?"

He wiped his brow again. "No. One of the lawyers with me last evening is his son-in-law."

"Ah, and he tattled on you."

"Yes," he clipped out.

So if the son-in-law hadn't outed him, would Epps still be acting as if the residents of Henry Adams were a bunch of uneducated hicks he could just steamroll over? She had no answer.

Epps revealed, "We've informed the mayor that we won't be building in Franklin."

"And his response?"

"He's threatening to sue."

Since she hadn't been party to the negotiations, Bernadine had no way of determining whether Wiggins had a legitimate claim or not, but knowing what she did of him, she'd go with not.

"However, as a token of goodwill, the Big Box corporate

office would like to make a donation in your name of fifty thousand dollars to the charity of your choice."

She found the offer amusing. Apparently they were so scared she'd call Celeste and tattle that they were willing to bribe her, because basically that's what the donation amounted to. She'd never been offered a bribe before and didn't know whether to be sarcastically flattered or flat-out offended. "Send the money to Doctors without Borders."

"Who?"

She walked over to her desk and found one of the nonprofit organization's business cards.

While he studied it, she said, "I'll have their board notify me when they get your check."

He paused and scrutinized her for a moment, making her wonder if he was surprised she knew someone on the charity's board. She wanted to quote Beyoncé again, but didn't. "Is there anything else?"

"Just that if and when we decide to build in this area, Big Box hopes to have your support." She assumed he was waiting to hear that his bribe had purchased both that and her silence. She hoped he wasn't holding his breath.

"I'm sure Doctors without Borders will appreciate your donation. Now, I'm on my way to lunch. If there's nothing else, have a good day, Mr. Epps."

He appeared to want to say more, but apparently decided not to chance it and made his exit.

She made a move to follow him, but the sight of a young woman in the hallway carrying a large something wrapped in voluminous green paper made her stop. Would she ever get to the Dog for lunch? "May I help you?"

"I'm from Franklin Flowers. Are you Ms. Brown?"

"Yes," Bernadine replied surprised.

"These are for you."

Bernadine sent the young woman away with a nice tip, then carried the flowers over to the coffee table. Wondering who on earth would be sending her flowers, she gently unveiled the contents. Inside was a lovely cobalt blue vase holding the most beautiful and colorful arrangement of long-stemmed roses she'd ever received. "Oh, my," she whispered.

There were yellows and reds, corals and whites. Blown away, she found the little folded note attached and read: "Roses for my rose. Mal."

Tears sprang to her eyes. "Oh, my." Emotion rose with such strength, she covered her mouth as if to hold it inside. After she and Leo began drifting apart, she had spent the last twenty years of her marriage going through the motions. He made sure she had everything money and status could buy, but her heart had ached for love like the Kalahari ached for rain. And along came Malachi July—her wellspring, her source of all things fun and good—and her heart was in bloom again, just like the roses. She dabbed at the tears in the corners of her eyes. Mal made her look at herself in ways no one else had, and prompted her to take time out of turning the world to stop and smell the roses. Leaning over, she let the fragrance fill her nose and soul. When she first came to live in Henry Adams, everyone around had advised her to avoid Mal at all costs because he was made out of snake oil. She took in another long draw of the aromatic roses and smiled. Whoever thought snake oil could smell so sweet?

He was behind the counter, bopping to the music of "The Cisco Kid" by War, when she walked into the Dog, and he greeted her with a smile. "Hey, baby doll."

"Thank you for the beautiful flowers."

"You're welcome. After that ugliness last night, figured you might need some beauty."

"You are so wonderful."

"That I am. How about I treat you to lunch?"

"I'd love that."

He came out from behind the counter, offered her his arm, and escorted her into the dining room.

CHAPTER
9

Jack checked out the mutinous faces of Megan and Samantha as they sat in their seats, and felt not an iota of sympathy. He'd assigned them both a five-page research paper on the state of African Americans, politically, economically and socially, going into the twentieth century, so they'd get a sense of why "Lift Every Voice and Sing" was so important. They had a week to turn it in.

"But how come we're the only ones who have to do this?" Megan whined accusingly. BFF Samantha appeared equally put out, but let her friend do the complaining.

"Because you're the only ones being disrespectful when we sing the Negro National Anthem."

"No, we aren't."

"So that wasn't you rolling your eyes this morning?"

Megan huffed and blew out an exasperated breath. "My father's not going to like this."

"Have him call me, and we can talk about it."

She rolled her eyes and gathered up her back pack. "Come on, Samantha."

Neither said good-bye as they made their exit, but Jack wasn't bothered by it. The research paper was still due next week. He doubted Megan would complain to her dad about the assignment. She and Samantha came from comfortable middle-class homes and had parents who cared about their education—otherwise they wouldn't be forking over the money to have their daughters attend Jefferson Academy. Jack had supported the ideas of opening up the school's enrollment to students who didn't live in town, but Megan and Samantha were making him question the rightness of his stance. In truth, Megan was the problem. She was academically lazy—only turned in half of her homework assignments, and what she did turn in was partially completed and rife with spelling and grammatical errors.

Samantha, on the other hand, was a very good student. Her work was always completed and in on time. Intellectually, she could hold her own with the likes of Leah and Preston, but she wouldn't stretch herself in class, probably so she wouldn't show Megan up. He wanted Samantha to spend more time with the Henry Adams crew so she'd realize it was okay to be smart, but she'd only been at Jefferson a few months. It was probably too soon for her to think about expanding her horizons.

Speaking of expanded horizons, he was still trying to get over Rocky's invitation. What had made her descend from her goddess perch and decide to rub elbows with a lowly mortal like himself? He hadn't a clue, but he liked the idea of hanging out with her on Saturday, or any day for that matter. He wondered what kind of bike she was picking up. A dirt bike, maybe. She was definitely the type.

"Dad!"

He started at being called. It was Eli, standing less than a foot away from his desk. "What, Eli?"

"You daydreaming? Had to call you twice."

Jack pulled his thoughts back to the present. "Uh, no. Just thinking about something. Are you going home?" Eli and Crystal often stayed after school to work on the big L.A. art contest they'd entered.

"Crys has to work at the Dog until six thirty, so I thought I'd go in with her and see if Rocky needs me to do anything."

This from a boy who'd complained so much the first day in the diner's kitchen that Rocky paid him less than the other kids because of his Oscar the Grouch attitude. Now, he was volunteering his services, and that could only mean one thing: young love. He didn't say that to Eli, though. "Okay. I'll be over there for dinner in a bit. I've some work to take care of here first."

"Okay." And he was gone.

Jack liked the transformation Eli had undergone since the move to Kansas. For a while after Eva's death, Jack had loved his son but hadn't liked him a whole lot. Smiling at how great life was going, he turned his attention to the next day's lesson plans.

Twenty minutes later, he was just about finished when a knock on the opened door made him glance up. It was Trent. "Hey. What's up?"

"Can you sing?"

"Yeah, I guess so—why?" he asked, wondering where this might be leading.

"Trying to put together a male singing group for the Idol competition. You sing bass, tenor, what?"

"Tenor."

Trent seemed to mull over the response. "Ever sing in public?"

"Does three years in a boys' choir and having my own band in high school count?"

A smile spread across his face. "Oh, yeah."

"What are we singing?"

"Not sure. Just doing recruiting right now. How's your dancing?"

"Okay."

Trent looked skeptical.

"Better than okay."

He didn't appear convinced.

"I'm not Michael Jackson."

"Neither am I."

"Who else is in the group?"

"So far, you, me, and Gary. We may not need anyone else, providing we don't wind up sounding like cats caught in a fence when we start rehearsing. How about we get together in the next couple of days and figure it out?"

"Sounds good."

Trent left with a wave.

A pleased Jack went back to his work. Life in Henry Adams kept getting better and better.

Usually Preston hung out with Amari or Leah after school, but today he went straight home instead. Neither of the Paynes were there when he arrived, which suited him fine because he wanted to be alone. Lying on his bed he clicked on the TV, found the Science Channel, and muted the sound.

He was still recovering from his crazy grandmother's visit. Although he knew Ms. Bernadine and the colonel had taken care of everything, he still wondered how their meeting had turned out, and if he was going to have to see Lenore Crenshaw again. He hoped not. Once was enough to almost make him thankful he'd been given up for adoption—almost. She obviously couldn't stand his father, and although Preston had never known the man, he was angry and offended on his behalf. The only positive about her coming was getting the answer to one-half of one of the questions that had plagued him since he was old enough to figure out he was being raised in foster care—the whereabouts of his parents. Preston still didn't know their names, but he did know now that his dad was no longer living. That hurt. Holding on to the hope that he would somehow meet him had kept him going when life became unbearable—like the night he set the house on fire so the state would be forced to move him away from the foster mom who refused to buy him an inhaler. Afterward, sitting in the CPS office with the social worker, he'd thought about his dad, and fantasized on how wonderful it would be to be rescued by him. Now? He shrugged. One more disappointment in the messed-up life of Preston Mays. He wiped away the dampness in his eyes. Crying wouldn't help. It never had.

There was a soft knock on his door. He gave his eyes another quick swipe. "Come in."

It was the colonel. If he saw the tears in his eyes, he didn't mention it.

"How're you doing?"

"I'm okay."

"I'm sorry you had to endure that."

"Me, too. Is she gone?"

"Yes, and hopefully for good."

That made him feel better.

"And we'll be getting a restraining order so she doesn't bother you again."

"Thanks." He could see the colonel trying to assess how he was really feeling, but Preston wasn't in the mood to open up, at least not then. "I appreciate what you did at school today."

"Anytime. Mrs. Payne's coming home in about an hour, so how about I start dinner?"

"Will it be something we can eat?"

Humor sparkled in his eyes. "Jokes, huh?"

Preston asked quietly, "You want some help?"

The colonel nodded. "Sure. I'd like that."

"I'll be down in a minute."

"Take your time. I have to change clothes." He was still in uniform. "No kid should have to hear what Crenshaw said to you, so if you want to talk, I'm here."

Preston nodded a reply.

The concern on Payne's face remained, but he exited.

Preston had offered to help because he didn't want to be alone with the thoughts and hurt circling in his head any longer. If foster care had taught him anything, it was the futility of wallowing. Being with the colonel would give his brain something else to do, and if the truth be told, he also wanted to make sure that whatever he cooked was edible. Letting the pain resonate for the final time, he swung his feet off the bed and went downstairs.

To his surprise, he and the colonel had a good time. Preston mashed potatoes, and the colonel fried chicken. They talked about the Memorial Day parade and laughed at Crystal's rebuttal to the Witches of Franklin during lunch. After that, he washed the salad greens while the colonel sliced tomatoes.

Once everything was ready, they filled their plates and sat down. After the colonel said grace, it was time to eat.

"So," the colonel said, "other than Crystal taking on the witches, how was school?"

"Pretty good. Mr. Bing was a special guest and told us about working on the AlCan highway during World War II." Preston bit into a chicken leg and was stunned. "This is really good," he said, surprised.

"Thanks." The colonel chuckled.

"You really can cook, just like Mrs. Payne said."

"I do okay. Your potatoes aren't bad either."

"Thanks." It was a good shared moment.

"So now, tell me about Bing's talk."

In between bites of the colonel's slamming chicken, Preston told the story of Bing's Alaskan deployment. When he'd finished, the colonel appeared impressed.

"I didn't know all that. The conditions must have been terrible. Torches beneath the equipment—wow."

"Yeah. He said only one man froze to death, though."

"I'm surprised there weren't more."

"Me, too."

"Wish I'd been there to hear him."

"What was it like during Desert Storm?"

"Hot. Where Bing and his buddies froze, we roasted. The gear made it even hotter, and we also had to deal with sandstorms, sand fleas, and spiders. Some days I would have loved being stationed someplace glacial."

They heard the front door open and the tap of Mrs. Payne's high heels on the wood floors. "Evening, gentlemen. Smells good in here."

"Just me getting over myself," the colonel replied.

She walked over and gave him a kiss on the cheek. "Good to hear."

"And Preston, how are you? I'm so sorry she said those terrible things about your father."

"The colonel got her off me, though. It was awesome. He showed up like the marines."

"Did he, now?"

"Yep. You should've seen her step back. Me and Amari wanted to cheer."

"You were a hero today, Barrett."

"Just doing my job as dad."

For the first time in his life Preston experienced having a dad who had his back. It felt good. He saluted the colonel with his glass of milk. The colonel raised his glass and saluted him in return. Preston thought the colonel's eyes looked a little misty but figured that was his imagination, so he politely helped himself to another piece of the off-the-hook chicken.

Afterward, while the three of them cleaned up, he asked, "Do you know if Mays is my real name?"

He saw them both pause. Mrs. Payne met his eyes. Seeing what appeared to be guilt reflected there, he asked suspiciously, "What do you know that you haven't told me?"

He glanced between them and watched her look over to the colonel as if seeking guidance or maybe support—he wasn't sure which.

He waited. They appeared torn, and because they had yet to answer, frustration rose. "How much do you two know about me?" he asked again, trying not to shout.

The colonel took the lead. "Your name is Mays, and according to what we were told, your father's name was Lawrence.

He was from Philadelphia and lost his life in a car accident a few months before you were born. You're named for his grandfather."

Tears stung his eyes. "And my mom?"

Mrs. Payne replied quietly, "Her name is Margaret."

"So she's alive?"

"Yes," the colonel confirmed, "but she doesn't want to be contacted."

That hurt, really hurt. Now he understood how Amari must've felt last fall when he was told the same thing about his birth mother.

Mrs. Payne said, "But, Preston, apparently she hasn't spoken to her mother for fourteen years for making her give you up. I think she must have loved you very much."

He saw her tears and swiped at his own. "May I be excused?" he asked around the thick emotion clogged in his throat.

"Of course," the colonel said.

Preston hurried from the kitchen. Up in his room, he closed the door, sat on the bed, and cried uncontrollably. His mom was alive, and according to Mrs. Payne, she hadn't wanted to give him up. That mattered, but that she didn't want to be contacted added to his already broken heart.

A time zone away, on the outskirts of Boston, Lenore Crenshaw entered the formal dining room of her stately old mansion, feeling alternately angry and blue about her trip to Kansas The moment she returned to Boston, she had gotten on the phone to the former clerks and colleagues of her late husband, Marvin, explained her dilemma, and been informed that the Brown woman was correct. Not even she, a member of the

DAR and wife of one of the nation's first Black jurists, could rescind the adoption request she'd signed nearly fifteen years ago, nor was there anything to be done about the threatened restraining order, either.

So what was she supposed to do? she'd asked in a last-ditch phone call to one of Marvin's frat brothers, a member of the Supreme Court, but he didn't have an answer.

Neither did anyone else, it seemed. If she couldn't use her biological grandson as a means to soften her daughter's stance, Lenore faced the prospect of spending her remaining years estranged from her own flesh and blood.

No one had faulted her and Marvin for making the decision they had made concerning Margaret's out-of-wedlock child. It hadn't mattered that Margaret and the boy were planning to marry; that wouldn't've been allowed either. What mattered, once the father of the child was dead, was extricating Margaret from the embarrassing situation so the Crenshaw family could get back their well-heeled, scandal-free lives. Lenore couldn't have imagined showing off a baby with such questionable parentage as her grandchild—the gossip would've been intolerable—but for some reason Margaret refused to view the matter in that light.

After the baby boy was handed over to the adoption agency, Margaret left the hospital and went to live with Marvin's younger sister, Ellen, a woman Lenore refused to have in her home because of her loosey-goosey lifestyle. Lenore didn't care that Ellen was a world-renowned artist. A woman with her upbringing had no business opening her mansion to fund-raisers for Angela Davis, Bobby Seale, and the like; those hoodlums were jailed because they were supposed to be jailed. But she and Ellen always disagreed. That Margaret chose to live with Ellen over her own parents had been quite a blow, but Lenore and Marvin stuck to their guns, even though he hadn't been as stoic as she might have wished. He'd always wanted to call and work things out, but Lenore had nixed the idea, believing Margaret would eventually come to her senses and return home.

She hadn't, and now that Marvin was no longer among the living, Lenore had no one in her life outside of the backbiting women in her social clubs, her priest, and the small cadre of house servants and groundskeepers who tolerated her and her constant corrections only because she paid them well. She turned to watch the housekeeper, Mallory, setting the table for dinner. "Don't forget to set a place for Mr. Crenshaw."

"Yes, ma'am.

Marvin had passed on, but Lenore continued to act as if he hadn't because it made her feel less alone. Having Margaret in her life again would help with that as well, if she could just find a way to bring her back into the fold. During her initial phone conversation with the Brown woman, Lenore got the impression that Preston really wanted to meet Margaret. If she could somehow bring that about, Preston might be so grateful, he'd willingly talk to Margaret on her behalf.

"Dinner is served, Mrs. Crenshaw."

"Thank you, Mallory."

Lenore took her seat at the head of the elegantly set dining table. As Mallory quietly placed a salad in front of her for the first course, Lenore began to formulate a plan. She'd given the Brown woman Margaret's phone number, and even though she'd no idea what transpired afterward, she was certain something would happen if she shared Margaret's contact information with her son. Her mind made up, she decided to send Preston an e-mail first thing in the morning. After which she'd cross her fingers and hope it all worked out in her favor.

Over at the Power Plant, Bernadine slowly packed up for the ride home. Her eyes brushed the beautiful roses, and she debated whether to take them with her or not, but decided she liked having them where they were. She and Mal often met at the end of the day but he was at his weekly AA meeting, so she was going home to relax, enjoy Crystal, and try and come down from the long day that had begun with the visit from Preston's grandmother. She was tempted to put in a call to Margaret Winthrop to let her know about her mother's antics, but she didn't because of the no-contact mandate she'd agreed to.

Bernadine still thought Margaret should be alerted, but she had enough on her own plate at the moment. She'd figure out what to do about that later.

She took one last look around her office to make certain she had everything. Before she could start toward the door, the desk phone rang. Lily was already gone for the day, so she picked up.

"Good evening, Ms. Brown." The voice was deep, sinister, and electronically altered.

Ice filled her veins. "Who is this?"

"We're going to play a game. It's called Run Bernadine Out of Town, and if you don't leave, you die. Hope you're ready." The laugh that followed sounded like Satan himself, and then the line went dead.

Heart pounding, she dropped into her chair. With shaking hands, she called Sheriff Dalton, and then Mal.

CHAPTER
10

Dalton arrived fifteen minutes later, accompanied by a younger man wearing a suit she'd never met before.

"Thanks for coming so quickly," she said. Henry Adams had no police force, so it and other small towns relied on the county sheriff and his deputies for law enforcement.

"Lucky I was just up the road and not two hundred miles away. This is my son, Kyle. He's currently with the Bureau, but for some reason wants to give that up and come home and be a county sheriff like his old man."

"Pleased to meet you, Kyle."

"Same here."

Dalton said, "So tell me about this call."

Bernadine related the chilling phone call.

"Any chance you taped it?"

It came to her that it had been. "Yes, Lily has the answering machine set up to record everything that comes in on the landline." She forced her hands to stop shaking.

"Will it upset you too much to play it back for us now?"

Even though she could still hear the satanic laugh echoing in her head, she told him no. She replayed the call, running it through the speaker on her desk.

When it was over, she noticed Kyle take out his phone and step out into the hallway.

The sheriff said, "That's one of those cheap voice-alteration devices. Outside of Al Stillwell, have you had any run-ins with anybody lately?"

She managed a smile. "When do I not have run-ins?"

He nodded understandingly.

Since purchasing Henry Adams, Bernadine had crossed swords with everybody from the phone and cable companies to Leo's oil bosses. She'd never imagined someone would threaten her life, though.

Dalton said, "Then how about just this week?"

She thought back. "Let's see, we have Leo and his oil company. Preston's birth grandmother, Lenore Crenshaw." She spelled the last name for him. "Franklin mayor Wiggins, and the legal eagles from Big Box Inc."

He looked up from the pad in his hand. "Big Box? How'd you get on their bad side?"

She told him.

"Why would Wiggins want them around? They'll bankrupt every mom-and-pop business from here to the Nebraska border."

"Tell me about it."

"Anybody else I need to add to this list? Riley giving you any problems?"

"No. He's been keeping a pretty low profile." She hadn't seen him since winter began.

"You fire anybody in the last, say six months or so? Know of anybody fired on the construction crews?"

"You'd have ask Warren or Trent about the crews, but I personally haven't fired anyone."

He made a few more notes before placing the small spiral-bound book into the shirt pocket of his uniform.

Kyle stuck his head around the open door and pulled the phone from his ear. "Ms. Brown, what's the number on your landline?"

She replied, and he stepped back out of view. "I didn't know you had children, Will."

"Vicky and I have three—two boys and a girl. Kyle's in the middle."

"Do you think this could be a prank?"

"Helluva prank, if you ask me, but we'll be treating it as if it isn't. Can't have folks trying to scare you off. You leave town, my carpenter brother-in-law will be out of work, and talking about moving in with me and my wife. Not having it."

Bernadine had liked Will Dalton from the moment they were introduced. The former UK linebacker was in his forties, but he looked like he could still suit up.

Kyle reentered the office. "Called in a few favors to put a trace on the call. I'd like to record it too, if I may. Lab folks can run it through special software and hopefully come up with a real voice."

"How long will it take?"

He shrugged. "Depends. Hopefully not very."

"Thank you."

"No problem. On the way over here, Dad was telling me how great you've been for the area. Least we can do is find the

person responsible and make sure they're prosecuted." Kyle
Dalton was a younger, less broad version of his father. His hair
was sandy, as opposed to Will's corn gold, but both men had
eyes the color of a Kansas blue sky.

Mal came rushing in. "Are you all right?"

She was so glad to see him. "Yes, I am."

He and Dalton exchanged greetings, and afterward she
told Mal about the call.

"Do you think it was Al, Will?"

He shrugged. "Hope not. I talked to him yesterday and told
him Bernadine wouldn't press charges if he stayed away from
her. He assured me he would."

"Do you believe him?"

Will shrugged. "I don't know. We'll wait and see what
the lab people find out when they analyze the tape. If it's his
voice, I'll pick him up."

Mal looked her way. "Anybody wanting to hurt you will
have to go through me."

"I know."

Mal seemed to notice Kyle for the first time. "Kyle? Long
time no see. What're you doing home?"

"Hey, Mr. July. Maybe moving back permanently, but
we'll see."

"Are you still with the FBI?"

"Yes, sir."

"You helping your dad with this?"

"Unofficially, yes."

"Good." He directed his attention back to Bernadine. "How
about I follow you home?"

"Good idea," Dalton said. "Soon as we get word on that
tape, I'll be in touch. In the meantime, keep an eye on your

surroundings, Bernadine, and let someone know where you'll be at all times."

She nodded.

He and his son departed, and the first thing Mal did was ease Bernadine into his arms and hold her tight. He placed a kiss on her forehead, and his strength buoyed her own. "Thanks for coming," she said.

"Please. Where else am I supposed to be when you're in trouble?"

She could hear his heart beating. This would be the second time he'd be escorting her home, but she wasn't going to eschew the offer like some stupid woman in a movie determined to prove her toughness, only to end up dead. The phone call scared her. On the surface she felt better, knowing Mal was with her and law enforcement was on the case, but inside, beneath the fancy suit, makeup, and gold jewelry, she was a mess. The demonic laughter rang out again, taunting her as if reminding her it was still there.

Mal drew back and looked down. "You ready?"

"Yes."

"I'll be letting everybody know about the call so they can keep an eye out. Like I said before, I don't know what I'd do if something happened to you, so I want to make sure nothing does."

"And I appreciate that."

He looked so serious, she hugged him tight. He had become her world, and she didn't want anything to mess that up.

On the drive home, she decided Crystal needed to know about the call so she could be on the alert as well. Mal planned to have a short meeting at her house to inform Trent, Lily, and the rest. In truth, all she wanted to do was go home and fall out, but his idea was a good one. Those closest to her needed to know what was going on, and a meet-up would eliminate having to tell the story to each of them individually.

Once Mal had everyone rounded up and in her living room, she shared the details.

They all looked shocked.

"You okay?" Lily asked, scanning her features for clues. "Oh, my goodness, Bernadine."

Everyone expressed their outrage and peppered her with questions. An angry-looking Crystal stood with her arms crossed tightly, shaking her head.

"Why would someone do this to you?" Sheila asked heatedly.

"The better question is who?" Jack added in disgust.

She shrugged, wishing she knew.

They spent a few more minutes discussing the matter but Lily must have seen the tiredness Bernadine felt rising inside because she brought the gathering to a close.

"Okay, let's get out of here so she can get some rest. Bernadine, if you need anything call me, you hear?"

"I will."

"And Crys, you too."

"Yes, ma'am."

Bernadine walked them to the door.

Trent told her very seriously, "Whoever it is will have to run a Lakota gauntlet before they can even think about getting to you, so don't worry. Town's got your back."

Payne added, "And so do the marines."

The last part lessened the tension a bit, but their worry and anger was still evident in the hugs and kisses on the cheek they bestowed as they exited. She let their silent affection buoy her as well.

Mal stood at the door. "I can sleep on the couch if you want."

"No, babe. Crys and I should be good, but thanks—for everything."

"Call me when you get up, so I'll know you're okay."

"Will do."

He said to Crystal in parting, "Take care of my girl, Crys."

"Don't worry. I got this."

He nodded, gave Bernadine a peck on the cheek, and left the house.

Once they were gone, Bernadine opened her arms to Crystal and held her close.

"This is scary," Crystal whispered.

"Yes it is, and no sense denying it, but I'm going to be fine. Sheriff Dalton will find whoever it is."

She hugged Crys tighter, letting the love she had for her child fill her heart instead of the terror of the taunting laughter that kept echoing in her head. "Not going to let whoever it is keep me from loving you, or doing what I need to do for Henry Adams."

Crystal pulled back to meet her eyes. "You need to get a permit."

"A permit for what?"

"A gun."

"I don't need a gun, Crystal."

"Then I'll get the permit. Until this is over, somebody in this house needs to be armed and dangerous."

As always, in situations such as this, Crystal Chambers-Brown was dead serious. "In fact, I should be the one, because

I know you—if a perp comes in here, you're going to try and talk to them, and be all nicey-nice and wind up getting hurt. Me—I'll light that sucker up. Think I won't?"

"Crystal—"

"No. If something happens to you, I don't know what I'd do—maybe run off with Diego or . . ."

In response to Bernadine's shocked and then narrowed eyes, her voice trailed off. Bernadine instantly went into mama mode, and asked quietly, "Why would you run off with Diego?"

The teen queen of Henry Adams squirmed. "I was just using that as an extreme example."

"Again, why would you run off with Diego? Thought you said your e-mails bounced back?"

Looking-guilty-as-hell added itself to Crystal's squirming.

"The truth, please."

Crystal chewed on her bottom lip and viewed Bernadine as if trying to determine just how much trouble she might be in. "Um—"

Bernadine waited.

"We've been e-mailing since Thanksgiving."

Lord! "He's too old for you, Crystal."

"Only three years."

"Too old in terms of life."

"But I lived on the street."

"Yes, but not anymore. You have a different lifestyle now. Are you seriously willing to give up all you've become to ride on the back of a bike with someone who hasn't even finished high school?" Bernadine wanted to scream at her.

"I miss the old me."

"Life is meant to go forward, Crys, not backward. Aren't you happy?"

"I am, but after meeting him I feel like I'm living in a cage, and all I want to do is get my freak on."

"You only have a year of school left. Once you head to college, you can get your freak on as often as you like, as long as you keep those grades up."

Crystal crossed her arms impatiently.

"I know he's tempting. All bad boys are, but he's not for you, Crys, at least not now. You have your whole future ahead of you, don't blow it on a July who can't stay out of jail."

It was obvious that Crystal wasn't feeling the lecture, but Bernadine didn't care. She was not going to let her child get sidetracked by a stupid crush. "Do you remember what your mother said to you the last time we saw her?"

"Yeah. Listen to you."

"And?"

"I don't remember."

"Stay away from fast boys. Go to college. Do something with your life."

Silence.

Bernadine wasn't done. It hurt, knowing Crys had been lying to her all this time. "Since you know I monitor your e-mail, I assume you either have another account or you've been deleting his messages. Which is it?"

Busted. "Both."

She held out her hand. "Your phone, please."

Crystal responded with wide eyes, but the cool steel in Bernadine's manner forestalled any arguments. She gave it up.

"Now, go get your laptop."

Crystal looked stricken. "But—"

"I have never lied to you, Crys. It isn't fair for you to lie to me, or play Secret Squirrel behind my back." Bernadine was sure Crystal had no idea that Secret Squirrel referred to an old-school Saturday-morning cartoon character, but she apparently got it; looking shamed, she dropped her eyes and whispered, "Okay."

After a prompt return, she set the computer on the end table.

"Now. Do any of the other kids have duplicate accounts?"

The squirming began again. "I—I'm not sure."

That response was all Bernadine needed to hear. She'd be making a few phone calls once she was done putting Miss Chambers-Brown on punishment. "You will have no electronics for two weeks."

"That's not fair!"

"And lying to me is?"

Silence.

Bernadine knew that Crys might use the punishment as an excuse to run off with Diego—she got that part—but her only alternative as a parent was to look the other way and let the girl do whatever she wanted, and that wasn't happening. "Right about now, you probably think I'm the meanest old bitch in the world, and hooking up with Diego looks better and better, but the real world has rules, and if you can't follow the rules at home, how are you going to follow them once you begin your own life?"

More silence.

"And I will be calling Diego's grandfather to let him know what's going on."

Blazing eyes locked on Bernadine.

"I'm not going to apologize for taking my parenting duties seriously, or loving you enough to act like it."

"Anything else?" Crystal snapped.

"Yes. For that bit of attitude, you get to paint the Jefferson fence, starting in the morning, too."

Crystal visibly blanched. So far, Crys and Zoey were the only two of the original Henry Adams foster kids who'd not had to paint the Jefferson fence. Zoey now held the title alone.

Crystal had tears in her eyes. "May I be excused now?"

"Yes, you may."

She ran up the stairs to her room but had sense enough not to slam her bedroom door, and for that Bernadine was thankful.

Bernadine dropped onto the sofa and placed her head in her hands. *Lord.* This was not what she'd expected to come home to. The threatening phone call had been enough, and now Crystal's shenanigans had pushed their way onto her decidedly full plate. She wanted to strangle Diego. Had the two really talked about Crystal running away to meet him? Did they have a plan in place? She scrubbed her hands over her eyes. *Lord have mercy.* Children always thought they were smarter than their parents; she knew she had though that, growing up. Then reality would hit when your parents proved you wrong and dropped the hammer. She could now relate to how they must have felt. Having to come down on Crystal made her feel like crap. Playing the role of a heavy wasn't something she relished. Most parents wanted to be loved and liked by their kids, and she was no exception. However, unlike some parents, she didn't consider Crystal her friend; Bernadine had friends. Crystal was her child, and children needed guidance, structure, and love that was sometimes tough, so that if they were lucky, they'd grow up, get themselves together, and then be considered friends. Not now.

To her surprise, a short while later, Crystal came back

downstairs. Bernadine prayed this wasn't going to be Mother vs. Daughter, the Sequel. She waited.

"I came down to ask if you want me to cook you some dinner?"

"Sure."

"I also want to apologize for lying."

Having been a teenager, Bernadine wondered whether this confession was truly sincere or just an attempt to get back on her good side. Seeing the tear-swollen eyes, she guessed it was a bit of both. "I appreciate the apology, but you still have to do the time."

"I know."

"So what are we having?"

"I have a salmon recipe I want to try, and we can have salad."

"Sounds great. Let me go up and change clothes."

Still looking teary, Crys nodded and left for the kitchen.

When it came time for them to sit down and eat, the atmosphere at table was still strained, but the ginger salmon was fabulous, and Bernadine let Crystal know. "You're turning into quite the chef."

"Siz said he might let me work the grill this summer. Who knows, maybe after I become a world-famous artist, I'll open a restaurant, decorate it with my art, and call it Crystal's."

"I like." This moment with her adopted daughter was what she'd been needing after all the drama. The comfortable routine of a shared meal eased the stress. She was also pleased to hear Crystal's dreams. The old, tattooed, weave-wearing Crystal had arrived in Henry Adams with only one—finding her addict mother—but now her world had expanded so much that her dreams were boundless, and Bernadine felt blessed by all Crystal had and could become. She just hoped they could put this mess with Diego behind them and move on.

They ate in silence for the most part, and when the meal was done, Crys offered to clean up alone, but Bernadine declined the offer.

"I appreciate it, but if we both help, we can get it done faster. It's been a long day, and you have school in the morning."

That Crystal also had a fence to paint remained unspoken.

After the cleanup was done and the dishwasher filled, Crystal asked, "Does being on lockdown meant I can't do my art?"

"No. Doing your art is okay."

"Thank you."

"You're welcome."

Crystal stood there a moment as if she had something to say but wasn't sure how to start. Instead, she said, "I'm going back up to my room now."

She was on her way out of the kitchen when Bernadine called softly, "Crys."

She stopped and looked back.

"I just want you to have the future you've been dreaming about—not one where you're a teenager with a baby."

"I'm not stupid enough to get pregnant."

"You don't have to be stupid to get pregnant. Sometimes you just have to think you're in love."

Crystal stilled as if she'd never thought about it that way. She then nodded as if she understood.

"See you later," Bernadine told her, and watched her go. She thanked the lord for her, even on lockdown.

After a few minutes of introspective silence, Bernadine picked up her phone and called the parents of Amari, Eli,

Preston, and Leah. If her guess was right, Crystal wouldn't be the only one painting the Jefferson fence in the morning.

Later, as she lay in bed mindlessly watching TV, she thought about all the day's happenings, and about Mal. He was such a bright light in her life. Marriage to him seemed the logical conclusion, but was it? Did they really need a ceremony and a cake to declare their commitment and love? They'd been together going on three years now, but for some reason the discussion had never come up, and she wondered if it was because neither of them were ready to put the issue on the table. They'd taken a few day trips together, but nothing overnight because of Crystal and the example Bernadine felt she needed to set. She often wished, though, that they could spend more time together alone as a couple.

That admission was a big step for her. She was fiercely independent and had become even more so since purchasing and running Henry Adams. And Mal was the same way, so much so that he'd never married. She wondered if maybe matrimony had never come up because neither of them really wanted it. There was no way of getting the answer without asking him, though. For now, she'd have to set it on a back burner—too much other stuff going on. She'd deal with it when things quieted down. As if cued, the ugly voice from the phone call resurfaced in her head and laughed long and hard.

CHAPTER
11

Across the street, Preston was in his bedroom, browsing the Internet for the latest news on the Hadron Collider, when the colonel came in. Both Paynes had been up to check on him because of the tumultuous day, but this time the colonel's unreadable features sent a chill of alarm through his blood. "Am I in trouble?"

"Depends on the answer to this question. Do you have an e-mail account that you've been keeping a secret?"

Preston couldn't help it. He began shaking. His mind raced like electrons in a particle accelerator as he tried to figure out how he'd been found out, and how long Reverend Paula might preach at his upcoming funeral, because he knew he was dead.

"Waiting on an answer, son."

"Um. Is Mrs. Payne going to join us? She'd probably want to hear my answer, too."

"No. This is going to be one of those father-son conversations."

"Oh." Preston really wanted Mrs. Payne there to keep the

colonel from punishing him by making him do nine thousand pushups or something else marine-ish. Then again, if the colonel knew, she probably did, too, and was as upset as the man standing tall and straight over his chair right now.

"Amari and I just wanted to play—" Realizing he'd inadvertently given up his boy, he took in a deep breath to try and calm himself down. *Think Preston! Think!*

Too late, however. The colonel was shaking his head as if he found the response pitiful or sorry or both.

"Didn't you and Amari get in enough trouble the last time for playing overage games?"

Preston had no answer.

The colonel did. "I guess not, so this is how it's going to go. I confiscate your phone, computer, and flat-screen for two weeks. You'll come straight home after school. No movies at the rec on Friday nights. No friends over, or calls on the landline, in or out, unless there's fire or blood involved."

Preston slumped.

"And the reason I'm not yelling is because I spent my entire career yelling at recruits. You're not a recruit, you're my son. You already know how disappointed Mrs. Payne and I are."

He did, but at least the colonel hadn't added—

"And in case you're thinking there won't be a fence involved in your immediate future, you're wrong."

Preston's head dropped. *Damn!*

"I'll be taking your laptop and phone now, son."

He sighed and got up. After unplugging the laptop, he handed it over, along with his phone.

The colonel wasn't done. "I also need screen names and passwords for *every* account."

Preston got a pen and wrote them down.

The colonel glanced at the list for a moment, then stared stonily into Preston's miserable eyes. "I'll see you at oh-six hundred. Good night."

"Good night," Preston whispered.

Alone, Preston sighed heavily. He felt like he was knee-deep in hell. How was he going to survive without Internet access and his phone? More importantly, how had the colonel learned about the secret accounts? He imagined Amari was being put through the same interrogation wringer by his dad and Ms. Lily, and that they were as mad as the colonel and Mrs. Payne. Had Crystal and Eli been busted too? He wanted to wail, but instead he put on his pajamas and climbed into bed. He and the colonel were just starting to get back into a groove, and now this—and it was all his fault.

Next door, a furious Jack stared at his stone-faced son, Eli. Bernadine's call had resulted in a shouting match that left him and his son viewing each other angrily. Jack was going through the hard drive on Eli's laptop, ripping open files, cookies, and history and finding enough incriminating evidence to send Eli to a parent's version of Sing Sing. "And what is Pink Panties?"

Jack had already figured out what type of site it was, but he wanted to hear it from Eli's lips.

"A porn site," came the tight response.

Jack studied him. "Look, when I was sixteen, any chance I got to look at a naked girl, I took—I get that part—but when you get older, you realize how detrimental it is to women. They're more than tits and asses, Eli, and these sites are so full of viruses and malware, it's a wonder you don't need penicillin. And I now have the answer to why the in-house network is so screwed up."

Eli wouldn't meet Jack's eyes.

"Do you know you and Pink Panties could make me lose my job? If Ms. Marie found this crap on my computer, I'd be toast! When you get your own place and pay your own bills, you can look at all the nasty you want, but as long as you're in *this* house, you will play by my rules, or not play at all. You got it?"

No response.

Jack held on to his temper. "I need an answer, because you're about two seconds from no electronic access ever again—and aren't you the one supposedly getting a car in the fall?"

The teen stiffened and looked up.

"Figured that would get your attention. If this happens again, you'll be riding your bike until you're thirty-five."

Eli looked down at his shoes. "Okay."

"In the meantime, everything you own that communicates belongs to me for the next two weeks. Phones, iPods, laptop, television—all of it, and starting tomorrow morning you'll be painting Ms. Marie's fence along with the rest of the We're So Slick Gang."

"But that's—"

Jack cut him a look.

Eli closed his mouth.

A few minutes later, Jack had confiscated enough electronic devices to start his own store. "Good night, Eli. We'll be leaving at six A.M. Be ready to go."

Jack left Eli standing in his bedroom, Jack went outside on the deck to cool off, and saw Barrett and Trent sitting on the Paynes' deck.

Barrett called, "We decided to have a mini Dads Inc. meeting so we can all cuss these kids in one spot. Come on over."

Jack dropped his head and chuckled. Thank God for Henry Adams. He walked over and took a seat in one of the chairs.

"A little late for a beer, but grab one if you want," Trent offered. Both men were holding cans.

"I'll pass, but thanks."

Barrett asked, "So, Eli too?"

"Yeah. I was wondering why I was having so much trouble with my computer. Viruses from all the porn sites he's been viewing."

"Porn?"

"Yes."

"Gotta love 'em," Trent said. "The two knuckleheads Barrett and I live with were doing adult video games. They were busted for the same sort of thing during their first summer in town. You'd think they'd've learned, but I was young and stupid once, too, painted that damn fence so many times, might as well have had my name on it."

Jack looked up at the star-filled sky, and his wife's face shimmered across his mind's eye. He wondered if she was up there, smiling at his attempts to raise Eli. She always did have a wicked sense of humor. "So Amari and Preston just had the game sites."

Trent chuckled softly against the night. "Amari also had a fake Facebook page. Was posing as a twenty-two-year-old NASCAR driver–slash–biker. Even had a picture of my cousin Griffin on his bike as his profile picture."

Jack stared and laughed. "What?"

"My boy never does things by half. Had over a hundred so-called friends, all of them female. Last winter he swore he'd never be into girls. Now? I suppose I should be thankful the girls had clothes on."

Jack ran his hands over his eyes. "I don't think I'm going to survive this."

Barrett agreed. "Even having trained recruits all my life, this is way tougher."

"We'll survive," Trent countered. "We may be wearing straitjackets in a crazy house somewhere before it's over, but we will."

He raised his beer can high. "To fatherhood."

"Hear! Hear!" Barrett and Jack replied.

Trent added, "And may they all live long enough to have kids that drive them to drink, too."

"Amen to that," Jack cracked.

Silence settled between them for a few moments before Barrett said, "Switching gears for a minute. This thing with Bernadine really has me concerned."

"Me, too," Trent replied. "Wish I knew who it was. I can't believe someone would scare her like that. I've made some calls to put the word out, and everybody's outraged. Glad to know Sheriff Dalton's on the case, though. He'll find whoever it is if he has to turn over every rock between here and the border. In the meantime, we'll be keeping our eyes and ears open."

Jack agreed. "Do you think it was the Stillwell guy everybody's talking about?"

"I don't know. He and I had a pretty frank one-on-one after he showed his behind at the Dog. He told me he'd leave her alone. We'll see."

Trent set his now-empty beer can on the small table beside his chair and stretched. "I need to get going. See you all in the morning?"

"Bright and early," Barrett said.

"And once they get to school, I have a surprise," Jack informed them.

Trent began laughing quietly. "Should they be afraid?"

"Oh, yeah. It's going to be educational, but it's also going to teach them how lucky they are to have all the electronic bells and whistles they've been abusing."

"I like it," Barrett said.

"Whatever it is, you have my support."

"Thanks. Oh, before I go, either of you know which one of them came up with this brilliant plan to create the dual accounts? I was too mad to think about that when I was grilling Eli."

"I asked Amari, but all I could get was name, rank, and serial number."

"Guess it doesn't really matter," Barrett said. "They're busted regardless."

Jack was satisfied. He rose to his feet. "Good night, guys."

They gave him good-nights in response. When he reentered his house, he felt much better

The sun was just getting up when Crystal, Amari, Preston, and Eli were let out of their parents' trucks to begin their first morning of painting the Jefferson fence. They'd all brought their bikes along too, for the ride to school once they were done.

Trent stayed to help unload the gallons of whitewash, bags holding new brushes, tarps, and the rest of the items the painters would need, then tipped his hat and headed up the walk to visit with Marie for a minute before driving back to town.

Because Amari and Preston had done the fence before, they'd learned it was faster to work as a pair.

"Me and Amari'll take this end," Preston explained to Crys and Eli. "You two take the end way down there, and we'll meet in the middle. One person paints inside, the other, outside."

The novices nodded in agreement.

Amari pulled the new paint rollers out of a bag and grumbled, "And remember Ms. Marie expects us to clean up and stash everything in her barn before we leave."

"Dad expects us to get to school on time, too," Eli added.

Amari cursed. "What I want to know is how we got busted? Who told?"

Two denials came from Preston and Eli. Crystal said nothing.

Curious about that, Preston asked, "Crystal?"

She took one of the rollers from Amari. "Let's just paint. I don't want to be out here all day."

"Hold up," Amari declared. "Do you know how they found out? Yes or no?"

The three boys waited.

She blew out a breath. "If Ms. Bernadine hadn't gotten that stupid call, Diego's name never would've come up."

Eli made the time-out sign with his hands. "Wait. What call? Diego called you?"

"No. Somebody called and threatened her life. I told her—"

Preston shook his head, "Back up. What are you talking about? Somebody threatened Ms. Bernadine's life?"

For the next few minutes she explained about the call, and Mal escorting her home.

Preston found the story unbelievable. "What! How come they didn't let us come to this meeting? Do they know who this person is?"

"Not yet."

"That is so wrong on so many levels," Eli said angrily. "She never hurt anybody."

"I know," she said. "I'm worried about her."

Amari looked stunned. "Does this fool know how many people will kick his ass once we find out who he is?"

Preston replied, "Evidently not."

"So what are the adults going to do?"

"She said Sheriff Will and his son in the FBI are looking into it."

"Good," Amari. "We need to keep an eye out, too."

They were all silent for a moment as they digested the disturbing news. The town's benefactor meant a great deal to all of them.

Eli said, "Now, back to Diego. How's he figure into this?"

Crystal sighed. "I told Ms. Bernadine she needed to get a gun, because if anything happened to her, I didn't know what I'd do."

"And?"

"And I said, I might run off with Diego," she added in a small voice.

Eli folded his arms. "And?"

"And then she started grilling me about had I talked to him, and I lied, and she asked me if I had two accounts, because she monitors my e-mails, and it went to hell from there."

Eli threw up his hands in disbelief. "You having the hots for this loser is what got us busted?"

Amari shook his head. "Diego doesn't care about you. You're still in high school. He's probably got women in every state."

"Shut up!"

Preston sighed. "Okay, let's start painting. We're already behind."

She grabbed a brush and stomped off.

Eli asked, "Why are girls so stupid?"

Amari grumbled, "We used to be able to blame it on that bad weave squeezing her brain too tight, but now it looks like she's just stupid, period."

While the boys painted and plotted Crystal's demise, an excited Riley was driving his old white truck to the airport. FUFA president Heather Quinn was flying in at 7:00 A.M. to meet with him. During his phone call to her last weekend, she'd sounded interested in Cletus's case, but she wanted to personally check out the lay of the land before making a final decision, so Riley hoped to make a good impression.

Now, wearing his black suit with the fake red carnation in the lapel, he stood in baggage claim, holding a piece of paper with her name written on it. He searched the faces of the few entering passengers and recognized her immediately. Just like on the television, she was short, thin, and mousy-looking, with oversize glasses on her nut-brown face.

"Mr. Curry?" She extended her hand.

He pumped it in greeting and grinned. "Yep. Welcome to Kansas, Ms. Quinn. Grab your bags, and we'll go meet Cletus." It never occurred to Riley to be a gentleman and offer assistance. In his mind, he was already introducing her to Cletus and imagining her being as impressed by the hog as he was. As a result, he missed the studied glance she gave him over the thick black frames.

Minutes later, he was in the driver's seat, and she was placing her suitcase in the truck bed. When she got in on the passenger side, she sent him another look, but he was too busy telling her about how smart his hog was and all the tricks he could do. Once she had her seat belt secured, he kept up the chatter and guided them to the highway.

"So your hog killed a man?"

"But in self-defense. He didn't like Prell hitting him with a table leg, and neither did I."

"Did you explain this to the county?"

"Yes." Riley didn't know why she was asking these questions, when he'd already told her the story on the phone.

"And they still want to put him down?"

"Yes."

"That doesn't sound fair to me. Every sentient being has the right to defend itself when faced with violence."

Riley didn't know what the word *sentient* meant, but he wholeheartedly agreed with the rest of her statement. "You think FUFA can make them change their minds?"

"With the right publicity, we might."

"Cletus is pretty famous on the Internet."

"What do you mean?"

So Riley told her about Cletus's wedding to Chocolate, and the resulting video of the event that went viral.

She stared. "The hog is married?"

"Yep. Had a minister and everything. Eustasia bought Chocolate a gown all the way from Europe, and Cletus and I wore matching tuxedos. Lots of Texas bigwigs were in the audience."

"Is the video still up?"

"Far as I know."

Heather shook her head in wonder. She'd met some odd characters in her six months as president, but he had to be in the top ten. Heather had a real love of animals and had been a crusader on their behalf most of her adult life. It was her dream to make FUFA as well respected as PETA, instead of being thought of as a group of whackadoos, a label well earned considering its past actions and campaigns. One of its former presidents was currently serving time in a Canadian prison as a result of an ill-conceived operation. He and a few other members had broken into a mink farm facility and released a hundred or so of the animals out into the snowy Ontario countryside. Those that didn't freeze to death were run over by traffic on a nearby road. The Canadians hadn't been happy, and proved it by sentencing everyone involved to five years for breaking and entering, trespassing, and endangering animals. A more recent example of whackadooism was the cat sterilization debacle in Illinois. Although the case had been taken on before her watch, she was currently the president of record and thus forced to defend the organization's ridiculous stance before the media. Heather wanted a top-of-the-line animal case that would propel FUFA to legitimacy. On the face of what Curry had told her on the phone, she'd thought his hog might be the golden ticket, but now, after meeting him, she wasn't so sure. What kind of crazy people threw weddings for hogs and wore matching tuxedos?

Had Riley a lick of sense, he would've noticed she was paying more attention to the passing landscape than his tales of Cletus's accomplishments, but he kept talking—telling her about Cletus's extensive wardrobe, his love of Animal Planet, and Riley's dreams for a sitcom.

That got her attention. "You want to put him on television?"

"Wait until you meet him, you'll see. He was born for TV.

Given the right agent and director, he could be bigger than that pig on Green Acres."

Proud of himself for being the owner of such a stellar hog, he missed her sigh and the way she pinched her nose between her eyes, as if she had a headache coming on. "So are you married, Mr. Curry?"

"I'm divorced."

"Do you think your ex-wife would be willing to testify for our side anyway?"

"No. She and Cletus don't get along."

"I see."

Riley didn't offer any further explanation, so she didn't ask anything else.

They reached the pens a short time later, and he parked the truck in the gravel parking lot. They got out, and he led her onto the property. The complex consisted of a low-to-the-ground brick administrative building and a bunch of barns, behind which were the wooden pens for the animals. Riley watched the county veterinarian, a tall horse-faced woman with brown hair named Dr. Marnie Keegan, come out of the building and walk toward them with a plastered-on smile. He knew she didn't like him visiting every day, but he didn't care.

"Morning, Mr. Curry. Who's that with you?"

Heather answered for him. "Heather Quinn. President of FUFA. Pleased to meet you." She stuck out her hand.

Keegan gave Quinn a wary up and down during their shake. "Nice meeting you, too. What brings you to our neck of the woods?"

"Mr. Curry's invited me to take a look at this case. If what he told me is true, I'd think you'd consider the animal's state of mind during the death of Mr. Prell and see that he was simply trying to defend himself."

Riley stood beside Heather, looking pleased as punch.

"He sat on a man and crushed him to death, ma'am."

"I understand that, but what would you do if someone was beating you over the head with a table leg, Dr. Keegan?"

She didn't appear to like the question. "My response has no bearing on this."

"It will when our lawyer puts you on the stand."

Keegan stiffened visibly.

"I'm a vet too, and we're supposed to be advocates, especially for an animal subjected to physical abuse."

Keegan crossed her arms. "Have you met the subject?"

"No, but that's why I've come."

"Follow me, then."

She led them around to the fenced-in pen behind the barns, and as they came closer, Riley was surprised to see that Cletus had company. There looked to be a dozen or more hogs in with him. "When did these other hogs get here?"

"Late yesterday afternoon. County's auctioning them off for back taxes."

"Cletus doesn't like other hogs around him. He likes his space."

"He threw a bit of a tantrum at first, but he got over it."

The moment Cletus saw Riley, the hog began squealing as if voicing his displeasure and trotted over. A larger hog, obviously another male, blocked his path. Cletus squealed louder.

"That hog's bullying him," Riley snapped angrily. "Move him back to a pen by himself."

"They're just vying for dominance. Happens all the time, and besides, we don't have anywhere else to house him."

"Ms. Quinn, do something."

"Mr. Curry, if there isn't room, there's nothing I can do. I'm sure your hog will be fine."

He turned to Keegan. "If anything happens to him, I'm suing you."

"Noted," she responded, but didn't appear the least bit intimidated by the threat.

The big male finally let Cletus pass, and he made his way through the crowded pen to where the concerned Riley stood on the other side of the waist-high plank corral. "How you doing, boy? Those other hogs being mean to you?"

Cletus moved close enough to be petted and voiced his discontent.

"I know, big boy. I'm sorry. I want you to meet Ms. Heather. She's going to get you out of here."

Heather stepped to the fence. "Hello there, Cletus. How are you?" She reached over the wooden slats to pet him, and he snapped around and bit her hand. "Ow!"

Dr. Keegan hid her smile and said, "Hope your shots are up to date. I'll get you a Band-Aid. Be right back."

Heather stared down at the blood welling from the small break in the skin between her index finger and thumb. She eyed the hog angrily.

A dismayed Riley chastised his hog. "Cletus! Bad boy! I'm so sorry, Ms. Quinn. Must be the perfume you're wearing. It sets him off. Used to bite Genevieve all the time."

"I'm not wearing perfume."

"Oh."

"So he bites often?"

The pointed question made him hesitate. "Just if he smells perfume. Maybe it's your shampoo or your soap."

Riley saw the raw skepticism in her eyes and prayed she didn't stomp off in a huff and fly home. He blamed Dr. Keegan. If she hadn't put Cletus in with those other hogs, especially the bully, he wouldn't be all upset. That had to be the reason he'd taken a plug out of Ms. Quinn's hand. He gave Cletus a calming stroke across his broad back. "Being in with all that riffraff's got you upset, hasn't it? I'm so sorry, but we're going to get you out if it's the last thing we do, right Ms. Quinn?"

"We'll see."

Riley had hoped for a stronger affirmation, but he figured her hand was probably still hurting.

Dr. Keegan returned with some antiseptic wipes and a Band-Aid. Ms. Quinn doctored herself, and when she was done, Keegan asked, "Anything else you need, Ms. Quinn?"

"No."

"Then I'm going to get back to work. Nice meeting you. See you in court." Not bothering to hide her smirk, she strolled away.

After glaring at the hog one last time, Heather Quinn declared, "I'm ready to go to my hotel, Mr. Curry. " And without a further word, she set out determinedly for his truck.

"Sure. Okay." Riley gave Cletus a hasty good-bye and hurried off to catch up.

After dropping her at one of the motel chains on Highway 183, Riley drove home. Outside of her being bitten by Cletus, he thought this first meeting had gone well. He was a bit concerned that she hadn't spoken a word on the way to the motel, though. Not even thank you when she got out of the truck. He figured she was just tired from all the jet lag.

CHAPTER
12

The We're So Slick Gang, as Jack dubbed them, came dragging into the classroom ten minutes after school started. Paint-stained and tired, they looked a mess. "You guys are late."

They answered with grumbles and took their seats. He noticed Leah staring at them as if they were aliens. Apparently she'd been unaware of last night's parental firestorm, and he was glad to know that at least one of the teens in his class hadn't been involved. The painters were just freeing themselves of their backpacks when he announced, "Those of you who are late are getting special assignments, term papers."

Crystal's cry of, "What!" merged with Eli's "Dad!" Amari's, "No!" and Preston's, "Aw, man!"

Jack waited. When they were done griping, he continued, "The paper will be a minimum seven pages. You will not be allowed to use any electronics, so that means it'll have to be handwritten, in cursive."

Eyes widened all over the room. Even the ones who hadn't been given the assignment stared aghast.

"You can use encyclopedias or reference books here at school, in your homes, or the library over in Franklin. All of your references are to be included in your bibliography."

"Why not just take us out and shoot us," Amari groused.

"Too easy," he tossed back.

Amari slumped down in his seat.

"This assignment will serve two purposes. It will prepare you for the big papers you'll be doing once you get to the college level, and give you a lesson in the value of electronics when they are used for good. Any questions?"

None.

He wasn't finished. "And to make this even more of a challenge, I've picked your topics, so get ready to write this down."

They stared in horror.

He turned first to Crystal. "Crystal, pick a number from one to four."

She sighed resignedly. "Three."

"Eurystheus."

"What?"

He spelled it for her.

"Is this somebody's name?"

"You'll have to look it up."

He turned to Eli. "Numbers one, two, and four are left."

"Two."

"Eurybiades."

Eli's mouth dropped.

Jack spelled it for him and moved on to Amari. "You're next."

He sighed heavily. "Give me number one."

"Euripides."

"I hope that's some kind of car," he grumbled, writing down the letters as Jack gave them.

"Preston, you get number three by default. Eurydice."

Shaking his head, Preston wrote while Jack spelled.

"Now, the rest of you aren't allowed to help them in any way, unless you want a paper of your own."

The look on the faces of Tiffany, Devon, Leah, Megan, and Samantha said they had no intentions of getting anywhere near the projects, especially Megan and Samantha, who were under the gun with their own papers, but at least allowed to use their laptops.

A disgruntled Eli asked, "When's this due?"

"Two weeks. A week to do the research, and a week to write the paper."

"That's all?" Crystal cried. "But we have to paint the fence, too!"

"Not my problem. No extensions will be given."

"Man!" Preston declared.

"Any questions before we move on?"

None. They appeared to be too mad.

"Okay, let's get started on last night's math homework."

Bernadine's morning wasn't going so well either. Having tossed and turned all night because of the threat, the laughing voice, and Crystal, she was still unsettled as she got dressed for work.

She'd never dealt with anything this bizarre before, and she wasn't sure what kind of precautions she needed to take other than being careful and on alert. Would the person or persons threaten Crystal, or someone else close to her heart, next? Did she need to hire private security? She probably should've asked Will Dalton that. She and the residents of Henry Adams lived under such idyllic conditions, it was easy to lose sight of the fact that they actually lived in a world where security precautions were de rigueur. She sighed, then forcibly pushed aside the troubling thoughts, along with all the rest of the scenarios and questions clamoring for attention, and concentrated on getting herself ready to head to the Power Plant. All the drama notwithstanding, she had a town to run.

The phone played the "I'm Every Woman" ringtone, so she picked up. "Morning, Lil."

"Morning. I'm at the Dog. Reporters are camped outside the Power Plant."

"What? Why?"

"Probably to interview you about that call last night. There's a story about it on the front page of the morning paper."

She blew out a breath.

"See if anyone's out in front of your house."

Bernadine moved to the window. Making sure she stayed behind the open drape, she peeked out at the street. Sure enough, there were three vans, all bearing logos of local television outlets. "I'm not giving any interviews. Why would they want to give this nut publicity?"

Her text alert chimed. "Hold on. Mal just sent a text."

What she read made her smile. "Lil, he's on his way. I'll see you after I run the gauntlet."

She ended the call and went downstairs to wait for Mal. While there, she brought up his message again. She'd paraphrased it to Lily, but in actuality it read, "Whitney. On the way. Kevin Costner." Amused, all over again, she put the phone in her purse. Yes, he was her light.

He arrived a short while later and parked his truck in her driveway. In response, the press poured out of their vans in pursuit, but he was already on the porch and inside before they could catch up and stick their microphones in his face.

"Not happy with all this," he said after greeting her with a kiss.

"Me either."

"Have you heard from Will?"

"Not yet." Logically she knew the lab wouldn't have been able to provide any information overnight, but that hadn't kept her from hoping. "Thanks for coming."

"You could handle those jokers outside on your own, but I thought it might be fun saying, 'No comment,' over and over again. Never knew anyone besieged by the press before."

She could always count on him and his humor.

"Ready?"

She was.

"They're probably going to follow us."

"I know, and I don't want them hanging around the building all day, making me crazy."

"Then we implement Plan B."

"Why am I suddenly afraid?"

He gave her that July grin. "You're going to love it."

"All right, Hannibal," she replied, making reference to the leader of the A-Team. "But I want to get to work in one piece."

"Trust me," he said, Hannibal's usual response.

She punched him playfully in the arm. "Come on, crazy man. Let's go."

As soon as they stepped out of the door, the press pounced. Bernadine had never been besieged before either, and although there were only three reporters—two men and a woman—the scene was just like on TV. Making her way through the tangle of them and their cameras, she ignored the questions and focused on not falling down the stairs. Shoving microphones in her face, they barked out: "Ms. Brown! Do you know who the caller is?"

"Ms. Brown!"

"Ms. Brown! What time did he call?"

"Ms. Brown! Do you have a message for him?"

On the other hand, Hannibal Costner, shielding her as best he could, kept up a steady reply of, "No comment. No comment." His voice was terse, and he was glaring, but he shot her a sly wink, so she knew he was having a ball.

Because his truck was parked only a short distance away, the entire ordeal lasted maybe three minutes. Then she was in the passenger seat, drawing on her seat belt. He jumped in on the driver's side, slammed his door, and keyed the engine.

The reporters swarmed the truck like zombies, waving their mics and yelling questions at the glass on the raised windows.

Her threw the truck into reverse. "Hold on!"

He backed down the driveway on squealing tires. In the side mirror she saw people diving to get out of the way. With another squeal the truck hit the street, and the souped-up old Ford took off.

Just as they'd predicted, the reporters and crews ran to their vans and sped off behind them.

"Let's lose these jokers!" he crowed with glee.

They roared up the road that led from the subdivision to Main Street, hooked a screaming left, and blazed down Main. A knot of vans and people was clustered in front of the Power Plant, but the truck blew by so fast that she only saw them for a second. "More press?" she called.

"Probably!"

Bernadine assumed that once the group outside the Power Plant saw their brethren chasing the Ford, they'd join the chase too.

A few seconds later, Mal let her know she'd called it right. "We have a train behind us, baby girl. Let's see if those fancy vans can keep up!"

The Ford barreled past the mound of rubble that was once the old Liberian Lady saloon and onto the unpaved road that led into the countryside. The view from her mirror showed the vans in the distance bouncing up and down over the ruts and gullies. Their truck was taking a pounding too, but there was no expensive electronic equipment to worry about, and unlike the vans, it was fitted with a heavy-duty suspension.

"Where are we going?"

"To have brunch."

"What!"

"Trust me," he called out, and gave her that smile of his again.

Bernadine wanted a further explanation, but she was too busy hanging on.

He was driving like a bat out of hell, and she could only imagine the bruises forming on her behind as she was tossed up and down like a bull rider at the rodeo—thank God for seat belts!

About a mile later he took a right and headed north. Originally there'd been six vans in pursuit. Looking back, she saw one pull over, smoke pouring from beneath the hood. And then there were five.

They were coming up on Bing and Clay's farm, and she wondered if Mal was planning on swinging in there, but when he approached the split that led to their private road, he made a two-wheeled right and headed on east onto Jefferson instead.

There were now only four vans in pursuit. Mal sped past the land belonging to Genevieve Curry and the spot where her now-razed home once stood. Another half mile, and they were passing the partially painted picket fence that sat between the Jefferson homestead and the road. Seeing it made her think about Crystal and the boys, but he didn't stop there, either.

They were approaching the Jefferson road split. A right would take them south toward the Dog and back to town. The left led to Tamar's. The vans were still behind them.

He took the left, and they approached Tamar's at warp speed. Up ahead, Bernadine saw Tamar standing by the open gate that led onto the property. She was cradling a shotgun.

Mal flew through the gates, wheeled the truck around as if they really were filming an episode of *The A-Team*, and came to a stop. Tamar had already closed the gates on the fence when the press vans roared up. Bernadine took in a deep breath to calm her racing heart and got out of the truck, wondering what might happen next.

Mal came around and draped an arm around her waist. The smile on his face spread from ear to ear.

"Nice job, Hannibal."

"I love it when a plan comes together."

She threw back her head and laughed.

The press wasn't laughing, however.

"This is private property!" Tamar yelled. "Move along!"

Bernadine didn't know if it was arrogance, hearing loss, or just plain stupidity that made them ignore the July matriarch, but they left their trucks with their mics and cameras and quickly approached the fence.

Tamar rarely repeated herself, and she didn't this time, either. Instead, she purposefully primed the barrel on the pump-action shotgun, and the ominous sound froze the entire contingent in their tracks.

Bernadine saw their surprise. They looked from Tamar to the smiling Bernadine and Mal, standing by the Ford.

One of the reporters called out boldly, "Ms. Brown. Are you going to—"

The blast from the shotgun drowned out the rest of the question.

"I'll be shooting tires and windshields next! You got fifteen seconds to get off my land!"

They ran like Godzilla was on their heels, and scrambled back into their vehicles.

The road was public property, and if they wanted to sit on the shoulder in their vans until the first snow fell, they had that right, but no way were they going to get anywhere near Bernadine Brown in the foreseeable future without trespassing on July land.

She was pleased.

Tamar looked pleased too. As she passed them on her way back to the house, she said, "Bernadine, I don't ever remember us having this much fun before you moved in, but thanks. You keep this old girl young."

Mal said, "Thanks for the backup."

"Anytime."

She climbed the steps to the porch and disappeared inside. Bernadine asked, "So she knew we were coming?"

"Yep. Gave her a call on the way to your place. Come on.

Let's drive down to the creek. I figure if we stay here long enough, they'll eventually get tired and go home, but until then, I'm declaring a Bernadine Brown Mental Health Day."

"But I have to go to the office."

"Where you will spend the day being pestered on the phone and in person by stupid questions from obnoxious people."

She had to admit he was right. The press were still positioned on the side of the road. She got in the truck.

They drove down to the creek bank, where they were out of sight of the road. The weather was a bit cool and windy, but the sun was shining, and there were no microphones or cameras, just peace and quiet.

After parking, Mal walked around to the back of the truck. When she joined him, he was removing a cooler and a small hibachi grill from the bed.

"What's this for?"

"Our brunch. I swung by the rec and grabbed a pair of your sneakers out of your locker. They're in that sports bag."

She was impressed by his forethought. "You really did have a plan."

"Told you."

She took the sneaks out of the bag, put them on instead of the Choos—nothing worse than attempting to walk on spring-softened earth in five-inch heels—and followed Mal to the bank to begin the Bernadine Brown Mental Health Day.

A short while later, they had the blanket spread out and were sitting on it, sipping cold water from bottles he'd taken from the cooler. "I've never been in a high-speed chase before," she said.

He chuckled.

"You obviously learned to drive from Tamar."

Before he could offer a reply, they were interrupted by the buzz of her phone. She glanced at the caller ID. "It's Will Dalton."

She and the sheriff chatted for a few minutes before she ended the call, sighing.

"What did he say?"

"They traced the call to a phone booth at a gas station up on 183. Manager didn't remember seeing anybody suspicious around the time the call came to me, and his outside security cam's busted, so Will's people can't get a look at any images it may have caught."

"That's disappointing."

She agreed. "Secondly, Kyle's buddies at the Bureau won't be able to get to the voice print for at least another ten days. Some big-ticket case they received this morning bumped us out of line, but they promised they'd get to it soon as they're able."

"Don't worry. Dalton will figure it out," he said supportively.

"I know. I just wish we had an answer now."

"Well, let's put that aside for now and see if we can catch us something to eat."

"I know you didn't bring me out here to go fishing in this suit."

"You're so beautiful when you're angry."

She punched him again.

"No, I'm going to do the fishing. You're going to sit on the blanket and look gorgeous."

"That I can do."

Back in town at the Marie Jefferson Academy, the We're So Slick Gang didn't feel so slick by the time lunch rolled around.

Leah carried her salad over to the picnic table where they'd gathered and sat down. Taking in the gloomy faces, she asked, "What did you all do to make Mr. James so mad that he gave you that messed-up term paper assignment and made you paint the fence?"

The boys shot Crystal a dirty look, after which Preston explained, "We got busted for having those secret e-mail accounts, like that kid you told us about."

"You actually did it? Didn't I tell you the kid got caught by his parents? I wondered why my dad asked me about that last night." Leah's story about a teen in Baltimore who'd successfully pulled off the ruse for nearly a year had intrigued them all. "I can't believe y'all are that dumb."

"Me, either," Preston sadly agreed. He wasn't looking forward to more painting after school.

"I can," Tiff chimed in, and was roundly ignored.

Amari cracked, "If it hadn't been for Ms. I'm Hot for Diego—"

"Shut up, Amari," Crystal snarled.

And he did, which surprised Preston. Then again, Amari probably sensed that Crystal was about two seconds from kicking major butt from having people in her face all morning, and although he'd grown a lot taller over the winter, Crystal could probably still whip him like he was Devon's size.

Leah raised an eyebrow. "Diego? Diego July?"

Crystal concentrated on the straw in her soda and didn't reply.

"You know he's probably just playing you, right?"

"Exactly," Eli said, throwing up his hands. "Finally a girl with some sense. Will you marry me, Leah, please?"

She answered with a roll of her eyes. "I'm not marrying you. Artists starve, and so do their wives. Even if I do get married, and I'm not, it would be to somebody like Preston. He's smart, and physicists make big bank."

Preston coughed so hard he thought he might need his inhaler. When he turned his widened eyes to Leah, she smiled and gave him a cute little wink that set him wheezing. Amari pounded on his back.

"You okay, man?"

Still in the throes of the coughing fit, he pulled out his inhaler, gave himself a few puffs, and got some relief. "I think I choked on a piece of carrot."

When he glanced Leah's way, she was eating and acting as if nothing had happened.

"Let's change the subject," he said around the tangle in his throat. "So who do you think made that messed-up call to Ms. Bernadine?"

Leah shook her head. "My dad talked about that this morning, too. He said if we see anything suspicious, to let somebody know."

Amari said, "What's really messed up is that it could be anybody. Lots of folks are mad at her for trying to do the right thing. The Big Box lawyers, Mr. Brown, that wack oil company, and everybody in Franklin, seems like."

Devon had been sitting quietly but asked with concern, "Is somebody really going to kill her?"

Preston shook his head. "I don't think anybody's going to allow that, Devon."

"Especially not us," Amari pledged. "Messing with her will get somebody jacked—they better ask somebody."

Ms. Brown meant so much to everybody, Preston couldn't imagine what would happen if somebody did hurt her. Like the rest of the people in Henry Adams, he was worried.

Devon said, "I want to be in Henry Adams Idol."

Amari shrugged. "Okay. Go for it."

"I need help."

"What kind of help?"

"I want you and Preston and Eli to be my Flames."

A confused Preston met the eyes of the equally confused-looking Amari. "Are you talking about real flames, as in fire?"

"No. I want to be James Brown. His backup singers were called the Flames."

Leah asked, "James Brown, that old dead guy?"

Crystal got up from the table. "I'll see you all later. I'm not in this."

"Why do you want to be him?" Preston asked, wondering if they should all maybe follow Crystal.

"Because he's cool, and he was my grandma's favorite soul singer."

They were staring at him as if he were from Mars.

Devon explained, "All you have to sing is 'Please, please don't go.' I do the rest. Somebody has to put the cape on me, though."

Eli asked skeptically. "Cape?"

"Like Batman?" Amari asked.

"No!" Devon said in a frustrated voice. "Don't y'all know anything?"

Amari cracked, "I know I'm not being a Flame."

Tiff snapped. "Stop being so mean. He's your little brother. You're supposed to be helping him."

"And you're supposed to be keeping your nose out of my business."

"Cretin!"

"Brat!"

"Both of you cut it out!" Leah yelled.

Preston was pretty sure Amari didn't know what the word *cretin* meant, but if it came out of Tiff's mouth, he knew it wasn't a compliment.

While Amari and Tiff engaged in a battle of mean mugging, Eli asked Devon, "Is there a YouTube of this guy we can look at?"

"Yeah, probably. He's in the Rock and Roll Hall of Fame."

"But we can't access any electronics, remember?" Preston pointed out. He couldn't dance or sing, and he had no interest in flamcs or capcs.

"But Idol isn't until July," Eli countered. "We get our stuff back in two weeks. That's plenty of time."

"My grandma said Michael Jackson copied the moonwalk from James Brown."

"I didn't know that," Leah responded, looking impressed.

When no one pledged to commit, Devon pleaded, "Please, be my Flames. I'll never ask for anything again for the rest of my life. I promise."

"Yeah, right," Amari responded, sounding unimpressed. "Let me think about it."

Devon grinned. "Okay. Thanks." He left the table and went back to the school building.

Preston asked, "Are you really going to think about it?"

"If I don't, he'll just whine to Mom, and she'll *suggest* I do it anyway. I think I hate having a little brother."

"But's he's so cute," Leah cooed.

"Uh-huh."

Preston knew that if Miss Lily made Amari be a Flame,

Amari would convince him to throw in. Preston thought he hated Amari having a little brother, too.

Leah said, "I think it's nice that you're going to do this."

"Yeah, yeah."

When Preston and the others saw Mr. James waving their way, they gathered up their stuff and left the picnic table to return to class. On the way, Preston glanced hesitantly over at Leah, but she was talking to her sister and didn't seem to notice him. She wasn't hot like Megan Fox or Beyoncé, but she was nice, liked sports, and was super smart. In his book that made her a babe. He kept hearing her say she wanted to marry someone like him. He knew she'd been generalizing, but that she'd actually thought of him in those terms was thrilling for a fourteen-year-old kid who wanted to pursue physics as a way of life and who'd never had a girlfriend.

At three o'clock that afternoon, Bernadine and Mal were seated side by side on the blanket. They'd grilled and eaten the fish he caught, flown their kites, and enjoyed each other's company and the day. A call to Tamar confirmed that the press was no longer out on the road, and another call to Lily revealed that there weren't any reporters hanging around the Power Plant or the Dog either. Apparently they'd grown tired of waiting and left town to besiege other prey. Bernadine was pleased. "I've had a great time, Mal."

"Good. We need to do this more often."

She studied him silently, seeing everything she'd hoped to see in the hypothetical man of her dreams. "Are we heading for marriage?"

He shrugged. "Are we?"

"I asked myself the question the other day, and to be truthful, I don't know if that's what I want. I know I want you in my life forever, lord willing, but we've both been single for so long—I don't know. Maybe I'm not explaining myself well."

He seemed to be concentrating on something off in the distance only he could see.

"I haven't hurt your feelings, have I?"

He gently covered her hand with his. "No, darlin', you haven't. Just thinking over what you said. Appreciate the honesty, by the way."

He remained quiet for a little while longer, then said, "I want whatever you want."

"Mal, you need to be honest, too."

"I am, and in a way, I'm kind of relieved, to tell you the truth. I love you like I love breathing, baby girl, but I don't think either of us is ready to have somebody underfoot twenty-four/seven, three-sixty-five for the next twenty or thirty years. You know we Julys live a long time. After Crystal goes away to school and you and I get a chance to really hang out, maybe we'll change our minds about this. For now, though, I want what you want. We can let the future take care of itself."

She slipped her fingers into his and leaned her head against his shoulder. I love you."

"You'd better."

That short talk and the loving kiss that followed sealed their hearts and commitment to each other.

CHAPTER
13

Mal dropped Bernadine at her house so she could retrieve her truck and then followed her over to the Power Plant parking lot. Only after he watched her go inside did he pull off and drive away.

Just as Lily said, there were no reporters either outside or in, so Bernadine entered her office, glad to be free of them. She gave herself a few quiet minutes to sit and think about how blessed she was to have Mal in her life, then prepared to start turning the world.

Apparently, Gary Clark had stopped in earlier; she found a note from him on her desk. Attached to the note was a sample of the grocery survey he would be handing out to everyone at the Friday-night movies. She was scanning through it when the landline rang. The memory of last night sprang to life, and she tensed and waited for it to go to voice mail. To her relief the caller was Greer Parker from CNN. Surprised to hear from him, she picked up before he could finish his message. "Hello, Mr. Parker. How've you been?"

They chatted for a moment while she prayed he wasn't calling about the threat she'd received. "So what can I do for you?" she asked, hoping her voice was light.

"All the news outlets were given a call a little while ago from Heather Quinn."

"Why's that name familiar?'

"Quinn's the president of Folks United for Animals."

"Those silly animal rights people?" She was confused. "What's this have to do with me?"

"She's in Henry Adams."

"Really? Why?"

And what he shared made her almost fall off her chair. "FUFA's representing Cletus!"

"Yes, ma'am."

"Lord have mercy," she whispered.

"I'm wondering if you have a place that my camera crew and I can lease for our stay?"

"Stay?"

"Yep. We're coming in to cover the hearing."

"Oh, my goodness." All manner of insane scenarios began filling her head, rendering her speechless for a moment.

"Ms. Brown? You still there?"

"I'm sorry, yes." She told him about the empty trailer on Tamar's land. Parker had been very instrumental in her purchase of Henry Adams and the subsequent search for foster parents for her kids. Offering him and his people a place to stay was the least she could do to reward him for his many kindnesses—but FUFA and Riley, together, Holy Ghost help us!

She and Parker finished pulling together the arrangements for his arrival, and with a thank-you, she hung up. Immediately afterward she dialed Lily, who was out at the church construction site. And when she came on the line, Bernadine said, "Girl, you are not going to believe this."

For the rest of the afternoon, she fielded calls from the press, both local and national, about the upcoming hearing. So many came through that she finally sent them all to voice mail, so she could get some work done. She'd play them back in the morning, but the entire time, all she could think about was the circus that would be coming to town, with Riley as the ringleader.

After school Jack drove down to Fort Hays University to meet with the chair of the physics department. The graduate student who'd worked with Preston and Leah last year had left the university over the winter to begin work on her doctorate at one of the big schools on the East Coast. The meeting would be to talk about replacing her. It was important to Jack and Marie that Preston and Leah continue to be challenged and get the best support they could as they prepared for college.

The meeting went well, he spoke with a couple of potential candidates, and two hours later, he was on Highway 183 again, heading north for home. There was virtually no traffic, a fact that always amazed him, as did the miles and miles of open land that stretched to the horizon on either side of the highway. After driving for decades in southern California, it had taken him a while to get used to the emptiness of the Kansas countryside, but he'd adjusted and now enjoyed the relatively stress-free travel.

It began to rain as he approached the small town of Plainville, and then pour buckets. Turning on his wipers, he decreased his speed as a precautionary measure and concentrated on driving safely so he would make it home in one piece.

He came up behind a battered, slow-moving pickup piled high with baled hay. The unsecured load was wobbling back and forth as if threatening to spill out onto the two-lane road, so Jack inched his car out a bit to the left and peered through his wipers to check for oncoming traffic, hoping to pass. In that half second, the truck lost its load, and huge bales of hay were bouncing around on the road in front of him. Panicked, he steered sharply to the left to avoid running into them. The car spun on the rain-slick pavement like an ice skater in the Olympics, then barreled off the road and tumbled down the embankment into the wire fencing strung along the adjacent field. The air bag deployed, and that was the last thing he remembered before the world faded to black.

Jack hated hospitals. They all reminded him of the eternity he'd spent sitting in them while Eva was fighting for her life. Radiation. Chemo. Experimental protocols. She'd been fearless. He'd been terrified.

And now here he sat in the ER of the Hays hospital with a broken left wrist and stitches in his forehead, waiting to be released. The trucker who'd come upon the accident scene had called 911 and stayed with him until an ambulance arrived. Jack had regained consciousness, but the pickup that caused the crash apparently never stopped.

An hour later, Jack and his cast, sling, stitches, and vial of prescription pain meds were given the okay to go home. He'd put in a call to Eli earlier, and after assuring his son he was okay, asked that Eli call Trent or someone to come and pick him up. So far, no one had shown.

He supposed he could call a cab, but the reality of what it would cost for a ride home from Hays made the frugal Bostonian he'd grown up as cringe. There were no other options, so he pulled out his phone and, balancing it precariously in his injured hand, hit the app for directory assistance.

While he was waiting for it to come up, Rocky walked in. He was so surprised he fumbled the phone and dropped it. Further fumbling to retrieve it and cursing himself for looking like such an idiot, he asked with wonder, "Somebody you know in the hospital?"

"Yes. You. Eli said you needed a ride."

"Eli?"

"Tall kid. Looks a lot like his father."

Jack dropped his head in amused chagrin. When he raised it again, she was smiling.

"Ready to go?"

He nodded.

For the first few miles, they drove through the pitch-black night in a silence gently broken by the jazz playing through the speakers. He was still amazed by her presence. "Why'd you come?"

"Eli said you needed an assist. Friends look out for friends."

"Is that what we are, you and I, friends?"

"I think it's a good place to start." She looked over at him, riding shotgun. "No?"

"Yes. Definitely." Because of the darkness in the cab, it was difficult to assess her reaction to his reply, but he sensed she was pleased. "I think my car's totaled."

"You needed a new one anyway."

He chuckled softly. No sympathy there. "The deputy who took the accident report said he'd call in the morning and let me know where it's towed."

Silence settled in again, and he turned to view the darkness out his window. "What was it like, growing up out here as a kid?"

She didn't respond, and just before he thought she hadn't because he'd unwittingly offended her in some way, she said quietly, "Hard. Very hard, but we'll talk about that sometime. Right now, let's just enjoy the drive, the company, and listen to some jazz."

Her enigmatic answer notwithstanding, Jack thought that a grand idea.

An hour later, she pulled into his driveway. Even though it was nearly midnight, he didn't want the ride to end. They hadn't spoken much, but as on the evening they'd spent together at the Dog, conversation hadn't seemed necessary. It was as if the vibe and being together were all that mattered, and he'd enjoyed both immensely.

However, his desire to remain in her company notwithstanding, they both had responsibilities to meet in the morning, so he reluctantly opened the door and got out. "Thanks again, Rock."

"Get some rest, Professor, and take care of that wrist. If you or Eli need anything, give me a call."

The offer sent him soaring. "We still on for Saturday morning?"

"Yes. Now go in, before Lily comes out on the porch and starts yelling at me about my engine waking up the neighborhood."

The truck did have a powerful bass rumble. "Night, Rocky."

She nodded in parting.

He stood in the circle of her headlights as she backed down the driveway and drove away.

When he went inside, the sight of Eli passed out on the

couch brought on a smile. *Must've tried to stay up and wait for his old man.*

Jack leaned down and jostled him gently. "Eli. Wake up, son."

A few more shakes, and the lids raised drunkenly.

"Go on to bed. Thanks for waiting up."

"You okay?" he slurred.

He showed him the sling and cast.

Eli sat up and rubbed his eyes. "Rock bring you home?"

"Yeah. Thanks for looking out."

"You're welcome. Going to bed." Stumbling like a zombie, he left the room.

A very contented Jack checked the doors, doused the lights, and followed his son up the stairs. After downing another pain med, he fell into bed.

Seated on the bed in her small, sad little motel room, Heather Quinn couldn't believe she'd taken on the Cletus case. The hog was mean, its owner insane, but the legal issues seemed solid. She'd taken a look at the Cletus and Chocolate wedding video. By all rights the ceremony was as laughable as it was appalling, but a viral YouTube video was priceless for PR purposes, and at this point she needed anything she could get her hands on to get this campaign under way. The home office in Dayton confirmed that e-mails had gone out to all the major media outlets, both online and off. Their interest and coverage would be crucial. Her personal distaste for Cletus aside, the hog had been defending itself when it crushed that man to death, and it was her plan to get America to agree that no animal, no matter its temperament, should have to pay for that with its life. The hearing was scheduled for Monday morning.

She just hoped Curry had been truthful about the details of the event. This being a referee-type hearing and not a human court case, she wasn't sure if the FUFA lawyers could ask to see what kind of evidence the county had that might prove Riley wrong, so she'd have to keep her fingers crossed on that one. She glanced down at the bandage on her hand, shook her head with irritation, and picked up her phone to try and round up some volunteers to start picketing the courthouse in the morning. She also needed to rent a car so she could speak with some of the locals. She'd planned on Curry being her main means of transportation during her stay, but not anymore. Having met him, she wanted to spend as little time with Riley as possible. The same held true for his pig.

Bernadine had breakfast with Mal the following morning.

"How you doing?" he asked as he slid into the booth.

She shrugged. "So-so, I guess. I didn't sleep well."

"After a high-speed chase and all that fresh air yesterday, I'd've thought you'd've slept like a baby."

She offered him a tiny smile while slowly stirring her coffee. "Bad dreams. All I can remember is being chased by somebody wearing one of the stupid V masks. You know, from the movie. Sounds silly now, but I woke up in the middle of the night, terrified."

"I'm sorry."

She waved him off. "It's okay. I'll be fine once I get to the office."

He didn't look as if he believed her, but she was thankful he didn't say anything more, because she didn't want to talk about it.

She saw Jack come in with his arm in a sling. "What happened to him?"

"Totaled his car."

He told her what Rocky had shared that morning when she came in for work.

"Shouldn't he be home in bed?"

Mal shook his head with apparent amusement. "He's okay."

Bernadine wasn't sure, and made a mental note to talk to Jack later to see if he needed help scoring a new vehicle.

Their food arrived, and as they ate, the place began to fill. She saw Bing and Clay, Lily and Trent, and Warren Kelly and some of the construction workers. Many of the other diners were familiar, and over the course of the meal a few of the farmers who'd been plaintiffs in the case against Leo's oil company came over to thank her again for her help with the lawsuit, and to denounce whoever was behind the threatening call she'd received.

Bing stopped by, too. "Don't worry, Bernadine. Whoever it is will be caught. Just hope it's by Will Dalton and not one of us, because there might not be enough left to prosecute."

"You got that right." Mal toasted him with a raised glass of orange juice.

"Thanks, Bing, but I don't want to have to scrape together bail money for you."

"Everybody knows you got it, so we'll be looking to be bailed out right quick."

"Okay," she replied, chuckling.

The visits from the farmers brought to mind the troubled Al Stillwell, and she turned serious. "I want to go visit the Stillwells, Mal."

"Why?"

"I'd like to pay his daughter's tuition, if that will help the family."

"It'll help, but he won't take your money."

"Reason being?"

"Pride, and that he blames you for the oil company backing out."

"Okay, but will you ride with me anyway, so I can try and talk to him?"

"He's not going to talk to you, baby girl, believe me." He eyed her for a moment. "You still feeling guilty?"

"Yes."

"You shouldn't. Even without your lawyers, the thinking folks around here would've fought Leo. Remember that HBO special?"

She did. *Gasland.* Trent had showed the documentary to the community during a movie night last winter. The cautionary tale about the peripheral dangers of pipelines and drilling on farms and in small towns had been an eye-opener. One woman's home was so filled with gas seeping from the pipelines on her land, her house would spontaneously flame up, as if an invisible hand had flicked a Bic. The documentary shed light on cancer clusters and livestock born with deformities, not to mention contaminated water tables, toxic air, and sick kids. When the program ended, the local farmers who'd been straddling the fence about Leo's pipeline got off the fence and signed their names to the petitions and lawsuit.

"Nobody wanted a Gasland here, Bernadine. Free money from Leo's company was great, but not at the expense of the health of our families and land."

"He's going to lose his farm, Mal."

"And that's sad, but you shouldn't blame yourself. Some of

the farmers who signed the lawsuit will be losing their places as well, if times don't get better. Are you planning on paying everybody's bills?"

"If I could."

"You don't have enough money to save the entire world, Bernadine."

He was right, of course, but she didn't like hearing it, any more than feeling responsible for putting the final nails in Stillwell's casket.

"Sometimes there's collateral damage," he said quietly. "No matter how good our intentions are."

She looked away with a sigh of resignation. In truth, she felt terrible, and yes, on some levels responsible.

Mal said, "And besides, Al's mad at everybody who opposed the pipeline, not just you."

"But maybe if I talk to him."

He chuckled softly. "Did you not hear what I just said?"

"I did, but you know I'm an eternal optimist, so let's ride out to the Stillwell place. Maybe he'll let me give him a loan or something."

Mal shook his head. "Okay, but remember, I tried to warn you."

"What if I talk to his mother?"

"Odessa? The lady who pulled a gun on Marie and threatened to kill her for keeping Al after school in the eighth grade—and went to jail for shooting a bill collector? Oh, yeah, she'll hear you out."

"Shot a bill collector?"

"That may sound comical, but Odessa Stillwell is not to be played with. She's mean and dangerous, but if you're determined to do this, we'll go."

"Thank you."

When they arrived at the Stillwell place, Bernadine looked out at the weed-choked field that should have held crops, and over at the empty pens that had probably held livestock until they were taken away. The house had been white at one time, but the paint was peeling now, and worn. The home looked tired, as if crumbling under the weight of the pain and suffering of the people inside.

Mal parked the truck, and they got out. Halfway up the walk, an older woman wearing dirty jeans and an aged T-shirt stepped out of the torn screen door and sighted them with the raised shotgun she held steadily in her hands. Bernadine froze.

"What do you want, July? You come to gloat?"

"No, Dess."

"Bank's giving us thirty days to pack up and get out. Hope you and the rest of them do-gooders are happy."

His lips tightened. He looked down at Bernadine.

"Who's that with you?" she asked nastily.

"I'm, um, Bernadine Brown." Odessa Stillwell was nearly as tall as her son.

"What the hell you want! I should shoot you where you stand."

"I—wanted to offer to pay your granddaughter's tuition, or offer you a loan—"

"Why! Trying to pay off your guilt?" The laugh was an ugly one. "It ain't going to be that easy, so get the hell off my land, and don't ever bring your ass out here again! Same thing for you, July. I see you, I shoot you."

On the walk back to the truck, Bernadine prayed her shaking legs wouldn't give out before she got inside. Her pounding heart didn't calm until they were driving on the road back to town.

All Mal said was, "See what I mean?"

She did. "I expected her to be older. Not sure why." The woman looking down the gun hadn't been the kind, elderly farm matron she'd envisioned.

"She's only in her mid-sixties. Went to school with us."

She started to ask if she had other family in the area, but went still at the sight of the traffic jam ahead. She and Mal were on the one-lane road that flowed past the county's agricultural complex. Usually there was nobody out this way, but today traffic was backed up coming and going because of all the television trucks and cars blocking the way. There was a whole slew of people of all ages, races, and sizes chanting and marching with signs, while nicely dressed men and women stuck microphones in their faces, or stood along the shoulder of the road, speaking into cameras. Locals in vehicles trapped on either side of the mayhem were honking their horns furiously.

"This must be Riley and FUFA," Mal said without amusement.

She wondered how he'd come to that conclusion, but as they crawled ahead, she saw uniformed police up ahead escorting sign-carrying protesters out of the road. It irritated her, knowing law enforcement had been taken away from their real duties—like trying to find the nut who'd called her—and she'd bet her BlackBerry that Sheriff Dalton was irritated too.

College kids were knocking on the windows of the slow-moving vehicles and holding up canisters. "Wonder what they're collecting for?" she asked.

"Who knows? If it's for Cletus, they may as well fill 'em up with rocks. Not much hog support around here."

Sure enough, when one of the kids came up to the window and held up the canister in her hand, Bernadine read: "Cletus Defense Fund." She shook her head no.

Mal's truck was by then close enough to the center of the madness for her to get a good look at what was going on. There had to be at least fifty cheering and chanting people holding signs and marching clockwise in the center of the road. Signs that read: "Free Cletus!" "Honk If You Love Hogs!" and "Hogs Have Rights TOO!" were raised next to others bearing color photos of Cletus decked out in his wedding tuxedo and Ray-Bans. FUFA had a reputation for being a bunch of kooks, and this display of crazy people, some of whom were wearing full-face pig masks, didn't dispel the notion. Traffic was inching by on the shoulder to keep from hitting the protesters, the police, and the camera people.

Mal groused, "Riley needs his butt kicked for this."

"Where did all these people come from, is my question."

Mal didn't answer; he was too busy cursing and swinging the wheel to avoid a woman who darted out in front of them on her way to the demonstration. She was wearing fat pink pig ears, and there was a large curly tail attached to the seat of her jeans. In her arms rode a black potbellied pig with a pink bow tied around its neck.

"Good lord," Bernadine voiced.

"Ditto."

All the hoopla certainly took her mind off Odessa Stillwell and her rifle-toting threats, if nothing else.

CHAPTER 14

Heather Quinn worried about what was going on with the demonstration out on the road and how long it might be before the police came and closed it down because they didn't have a permit. But her client didn't seem concerned in the least. Riley Curry was standing next to the pens, showing off his pride and joy to the assembled media. Of course, he'd had to point his hog out to them because the big city reporters couldn't tell one hog from another, but the camera crews and photographers must've taken a thousand shots of Cletus, if not more.

Earlier that morning, when she and Riley first arrived on the scene, he'd taken a suitcase out of his truck and said he wanted to wow the reporters by decking the hog out in camouflage gear, complete with beret and aviators, but Dr. Keegan vetoed the nonsense. Heather was so relieved and grateful, she could've hugged the county vet.

As it were, the reporters and photographers were going gaga over Cletus even unclothed, so Curry seemed to have put away his pique and contented himself with basking in the attention of his version of a press conference.

"Mr. Curry? What's the first thing you and Cletus plan to do if he's set free?"

He grinned like a polished politician. "*When* he's set free," he countered. "We're going to sit in front of the TV and watch Animal Planet. It's his favorite channel. Then we're going to see about taking him to Hollywood."

He pointed at a reporter standing to his right. "Yes?"

"Do you think Cletus and Chocolate will ever reconcile?"

"We'll have to see, won't we?" He turned to a female reporter who'd raised her hand. "Yes? You over there in the blue."

"Is it true your wife, Genevieve Curry, left you because Cletus made her life unbearable?"

He kept up his smile. "Only because she kept wearing a perfume Cletus didn't care for."

Heather growled inwardly. Perfume had not been the issue. Her bandaged hand bore the testament to how nasty that pampered hog was, and the more she was around Riley, the more she sympathized with Genevieve. Riley Curry was as pompous as he was delusional, and she found it surprising that the lady had stayed married to him for as long as she had. Heather didn't understand why Riley kept putting the animal in clothes, either. The practice only made him look crazier, but then again, she'd never been a big proponent of anthropomorphism. To her, animals were just that, nothing more, but nothing less, either.

He was in the middle of answering a ridiculous question as to which Hollywood actress Cletus would be best paired with when a big man in a police uniform walked up and announced, "Name's Will Dalton, and I'm the local sheriff.

You're trespassing on county property, and you got five minutes to get yourselves packed up and out of here."

His no-nonsense manner negated any discussion, and the cameras crews took a few quick parting shots before scrambling after the reporters to their vans.

"Who's in charge of the yahoos tying up the road?" he asked, turning on Riley.

While Curry stood wide-eyed and silent, she walked up and stuck out her hand. "Heather Quinn, president of Folks United for Animals."

Dalton shook. "You make a habit of trespassing?"

"Trespassing?"

"Don't play dumb with me, miss. We both know you don't have a permit, and when you don't, it's called trespassing."

"I didn't think rural areas like this one required permits to strike a blow against injustice."

"This may look like Green Acres, but it's still America, so don't give me that bull about you not knowing. The way I figure it, you were looking for some free publicity, called the rally, and figured that all you'd get this time around was a warning. Guess what, you're right. However, any more demonstrations will need a permit, or I throw you and Riley in jail."

That he'd nailed her thinking right on the head momentarily caught her off guard.

As if having read her mind, he warned, "Don't judge the smarts of folks around here by your client, ma'am."

"Good to know."

He gave her an assessing look. "Okay, get going and take Mr. Curry with you."

"Yes, sir. Thank you."

He didn't appear to buy her meek surrender at all. He folded his arms and waited and watched as she shouldered her laptop and picked up the box containing the press releases and flyers she and the volunteers had been passing out.

Curry complained, "Can I at least say good-bye to Cletus?"

"From what Doc Keegan said, you and Cletus have been holding court all morning, so get going, Riley. Now."

Heather saw him pout his displeasure, but he got going and so did she.

After the walk to the car, she dumped the box in the trunk of her rental car.

"Where you headed to now?" Curry asked.

"To Henry Adams to pass out flyers. I'm hoping the residents will come out and support us at the hearing."

"Don't waste your time. They're all on Genevieve's side. They don't like me or Cletus, and the feeling's mutual."

She paused. "You don't have one supporter in the entire town?"

He didn't respond.

"What about over in Franklin?"

"Might be a few there."

She knew he and his wife didn't get along, but the entire populace? "Okay. I'll check that out after I speak with the people in Henry Adams."

"You want me to go with you?"

"No!" she shouted, then upon hearing herself, drew in a calming breath and smiled falsely. "I mean, might be best if I went alone."

"Suit yourself, but don't say I didn't warn you."

"I won't. I'll call you when I get back to my motel room."

He got in his truck and drove away.

She ran her fingers through her hair and tried to convince herself everything would be okay. When she glanced up, Sheriff Dalton was standing next to his patrol car, watching her.

"Ms. Quinn. Have you seen the tape of what Mrs. Curry's home looked like the night Cletus sat on Prell?"

"No."

"You might want to get a copy before you go to court on Monday."

He got into his car, but he didn't pull off until she drove past. Curry hadn't mentioned anything about a tape, and it made her wonder why Dalton's tip sounded so ominous.

In the parking lot behind the Power Center, Bernadine stepped down out of Mal's truck and heard him groan. "Now what?" she asked him.

"The little guy walking toward us in the too-big suit is a process server."

"As long as he's not an assassin, I'm good."

When the man reached them, he asked, "You Ms. Bernadine Brown?"

"Yes."

He handed her a sealed envelope. "You've been served. Have a good day. Take care, July."

Opening the summons, she asked Mal, "How do you know him?"

"He served me and the rest of Dads Inc. when Riley sued Genevieve for assault."

Bernadine read the contents. Once she finished, she was so angry, she balled it up and shoved it into her tote.

"What's it about? If I'm not being too nosy."

"Mayor Piggly Wiggly and his minions on the City Council want to sue me for breach of contract."

"What contract?"

"Exactly. I may have to hire an assassin just to make His Craziness go away."

"Is this tied to Big Box?"

"I don't really know, but I'm going to assume it is."

"When's the hearing?"

"Monday afternoon."

"Same day as Cletus's hearing."

Bernadine sighed deeply. The world had gone insane. "Great. Let's hope Judge Davis is so mad after dealing with Riley, she sentences old Squirrel Head to a firing squad."

He laughed. "Let's hope."

Inside her office, she dropped her tote into the bottom desk drawer and plopped down into her chair. First Mrs. Stillwell, then the fools from FUFA, and now a court summons. Neither she nor the town had contracted with the city of Franklin for anything, let alone something that called for a court appearance, but just to make sure she wasn't mistaken, she hit up the intercom and asked Lily.

Lily entered the office, saying, "I don't even have to look it up. We haven't signed any contracts with them, because Wiggins can't be trusted."

"Just wanted to make sure I was right."

"You are, and if he brings anything to court that says otherwise, I'll eat—"

"Excuse me," called a soft female voice from the doorway.

They turned, and there stood a young woman whose small brown face was dominated by a pair of thick black-framed glasses. She was wearing a cheap gray skirt and matching jacket over a worn white blouse, all of it looking like hand-me-downs.

"May I help you?" Bernadine asked.

"My name is Heather Quinn. I'm looking for Ms. Brown."

The familiar name made Bernadine wish for the power of invisibility, but since that wasn't possible, she sighed inwardly and confessed, "I'm Bernadine. What can I do for you?"

"I'm the president of FUFA, and as you've probably heard, we're representing Mr. Curry at his hearing against the county on Monday, and I—"

Lily chose that moment to make her escape. "I think I hear my phone ringing. Bernadine, let me know when you're ready for lunch. Oh, and I'll get in touch with Jim Edison about the summons."

Bernadine cut her BFF a look that Lily promptly ignored because she was too busy leaving. "Please have a seat, Ms. Quinn."

"Thank you. You have a very nice office."

"Thanks. What brings you here?"

"Do you believe an animal should be euthanized for defending itself against an assault?"

Bernadine assumed Quinn was referring to Cletus, and to be truthful, she hadn't dealt with Prell's death from that perspective. "No."

"Would you be willing to say that on the stand at the hearing?"

"I doubt my testimony will make much of a difference."

"Why not?"

"Because once Genevieve Curry gets up and tells her story, it'll all be over but the shouting. Cletus may have been protecting himself against Prell, but that hog has no business being in a household or trotted through town like a pet poodle. He's mean, and he bites."

Quinn held up her bandaged hand. "I know."

"Then you understand."

"I do, but is that grounds for death?"

Bernadine studied her silently. She hadn't been expecting hard questions from such a nondescript little woman. "You're serious about this issue, aren't you?"

"I am, and to be perfectly honest, I don't care for Mr. Curry or his animal, but that doesn't mean the county gets to put the hog down just because. I understand that a human life was lost, but would Mr. Prell be still alive if he hadn't picked up that chair leg? From where I sit, the answer is probably yes."

Bernadine mulled that over. "Interesting. You're a very impressive young woman, Ms. Quinn. What in the world are you doing working for FUFA?"

She shrugged. "I have a thing for animal advocacy, and FUFA could be a genuine platform if it's turned into an organization that's respected."

"Is that your plan?"

"It is. I'd always envisioned myself working for one of the big names, like Greenpeace or the World Wildlife Federation."

"They do great work."

"Yes, but because of their size, they don't have time for small cases like Mr. Curry's. I want FUFA to be there for people like him, and maybe in a few years, once we're seen as legit, the public will be more inclined to support us financially."

"A worthy goal."

"I think so."

Bernadine had been prepared to dislike Heather Quinn.

Instead she found herself wanting the young woman to suc-
ceed. "I wish you well."

"Thank you. Would it be okay if I passed out some flyers
detailing our efforts on Mr. Curry's behalf?"

"I suppose, but be prepared for a backlash. He's not well
liked, and whatever you do, don't give one to Genevieve
Curry. It could be ugly."

"I've not met her. Pretty angry?"

"Extremely, and with good reason. I assume you've seen
the tape of what Cletus did to her home?"

"No."

"I suggest you get a copy so you'll know what you're up
against."

"Sheriff Dalton said the same thing."

"He knows what he's talking about. He was one of the first
responders the night Prell died."

"Okay. I'll let our lawyer know." She stood and pushed the
ugly glasses back up her nose. "Thank you very much for your
time. It's been nice meeting you."

"Same here. Good luck on Monday."

"Thanks." She exited as quietly as she'd arrived, leaving
Bernadine with some food for thought. However, before she
could further contemplate the idea of Cletus being the true
victim in the Prell death, her phone sounded with a text message from Dr. Reg Garland, letting her know that he, Zoey,
and Reverend Paula were at the airport in Hays and waiting on their luggage. Bernadine's driver Nathan was already
there, waiting to bring them home.

She set the phone aside. She couldn't wait to hear what Miss
Z had to say about their trip. Reg and his superstar wife, Roni,
had been experiencing a few bumps in their marriage due to

Roni resuming her singing career. Bernadine hoped that their time together in Europe had helped get their love affair back on track. She was also looking forward to the return of the town's new spiritual leader, Reverend Paula Grant. With all the drama Bernadine had faced over the past few days, Paula's soul-settling advice and ready smile had been sorely missed.

Lily buzzed her. "Hey."

"What's up?"

"I played back all the messages the media left last night, and that wacko is on here, threatening you again."

Bernadine's heart stopped.

"You don't want to hear it. I've already called the sheriff."

Acknowledging her fear, but determined not to let it paralyze her, Bernadine got up and walked to Lily's office. "Let me hear it."

"You know you don't have to do this."

"Lily, play the tape."

The distorted voice came through the speakers with all the evilness she remembered. "Evening, Ms. Brown. How's it feel being scared to death? Good, I hope. You and I are going to get together real soon, and I can't wait." The bone-chilling laugh ended the transmission, and she forced herself not to rub her hands over the frigid tremors running up her arms.

"Sick bastard," Lily snapped angrily and stopped the recording.

Lord. "Dalton on his way?"

"Yes."

Bernadine took in a deep, bracing breath. Her life was suddenly brimming over with worries and drama, issues and threats, and it wasn't even Friday.

CHAPTER
15

After school, had Preston been privy to Bernadine's thoughts, he would've heartily concurred. It had been a super long week in his world, too, and he still had Friday to go. By his estimation, they'd be done painting the Jefferson fence by tomorrow afternoon, but that was tomorrow. For now, they were still painting, and as he dipped his brush in the pan for what seemed like the millionth time, he swore to never do anything to put himself in this stupid position again. "I am never painting this fence again!" he yelled out in irritation.

On the other side of the fence, Amari painted and grumbled, "Me either. This sucks."

"My hands look like they belong to a ghost. Probably be months before all this stuff washes off."

"When I grow up and get my own crib, I'm not having any white walls. I'm hating on white paint right now."

"Me, too."

"Not hating on Leah though, I'll bet."

Preston paused. "What's that supposed to mean?"

"Quit playing dumb. I heard what she said about you at lunch yesterday. You coughed so hard, I thought your eyes were going to pop off your face."

"Ignoring you, Amari," Preston replied and moved to the next picket on his side.

"Too late for that, my man. I'm your BFF."

Preston had to grin on that one. He was right. They were best friends, and it felt good knowing he had one.

Amari stroked the slat on his side. "You like her, and now it looks like she likes you back."

"Maybe. Let's not get it twisted."

"I understand. This girl thing is complicated. My dad says it only gets worse when you get older."

"You talk to him about stuff like this?"

"Sure. I can talk to him about anything, at least so far."

"Must be nice."

This wasn't the first time Preston had envied Amari's relationship with Trent. From the very first day Preston came to town, he'd thought Trent July was special. He and Amari had both expressed the hope that Trent July would be their foster dad, but because each foster parent could only take one child, Amari and Trent's love for cars made them an easy match, and Preston went with the Paynes.

Amari was checking him out with the thoughtful look he always wore when family was concerned. "I've been telling you for years that you and the colonel are going to be okay. You'll see."

Preston believed it, but then again he didn't believe it, if that made any sense.

Amari added, "You and Leah too."

They smiled at each other through the fence.

"So what happened with Devon and this Flame thing? Did Miss Lily make you help?"

"Of course, so as soon as we get off this wack lockdown, she said she'd find us a video to watch. My dad said this Brown guy was the shizzle back in the day and that Devon was right about Michael Jackson copying his moves. He said every kid in America knew Brown's dance moves when he and Mom and the OG were growing up."

"The OG, too?"

"Yeah. I guess Brown would be just a little older than the OG if he was still alive."

"So we have to be Flames?" Preston asked disconsolately.

"Yeah, but at least we don't have to put lye in our hair."

Preston stopped in mid stroke. "Lye?"

"You know, I think something is really wrong with Devon. He asked Mom if he could get a process."

"What's that?"

"From the way Dad explained it, it was something guys did to their hair back then to make it real straight."

"Sort of like a perm?"

Amari stopped and seemed to think on that. "Yeah. I guess so. Mom and Dad tried to explain it to me, but I didn't get it. They talked about lye and heat and curlers."

"Curlers? Devon wanted us to wear curlers!"

"Told you. Something real wrong with him, Brain. Real wrong."

An appalled Preston agreed. He was liking this whole Flame business less and less.

When the two hours were up for the day, they gathered their gear, stashed it in Ms. Marie's garage, and washed up.

Done, they grabbed their backpacks, hopped on their bikes, and pedaled toward home.

To Preston's surprise, Mrs. Payne was seated at the kitchen table. "Hey, Mrs. Payne."

"Hey back. You look tired. How's the fence detail going?"

"We should be done by tomorrow, hopefully. Do you think you can drive me and Amari over to the Franklin library Saturday morning so we can work on our papers?"

"I can't because of the groundbreaking, but I'm sure Barrett can. So have you found out who Euripides is?"

"Yeah. He's a Greek playwright."

"Very good. I know you all are grumbling because of the assignment, but I love the way Mr. James thinks."

"We don't. What smells so good?"

"Tomato sauce. We're having spaghetti."

Her spaghetti was one of his favorites. "Where's the colonel?"

"Helping Bing with the planning for the parade. He should be here shortly. Something you want to speak to him about?"

"Maybe, but it can wait." He wanted to have a father-son talk, or at least that was his plan, even if he wasn't sure it was a good one.

"Okay. Go get your shower, and when you come back, we'll eat."

The spaghetti was off the hook. Because he was starving, he ate two big platefuls along with a salad and some garlic bread. And as he sat back, content and full, he once again noted how much better life was now than the one he'd had in foster care.

The colonel arrived home a short while later, and the discussion at the table ranged from the parade to the FUFA demonstrators to a news story Mrs. Payne had seen earlier about a young woman in Australia discovering the where-abouts of the universe's missing matter.

Preston's eyes popped. "Really?" Scientists had been trying to find the location for ages. "And she's an intern, not a real physicist yet?" he asked. That was so awesome that a young person had been able to do something the big guys hadn't.

"She's a twenty-two-year-old undergrad student at the University of Melbourne, studying aerospace engineering and science," Mrs. Payne said, apparently enjoying his reaction.

"That is so awesome."

The colonel said, "Explain this missing matter thing, Preston."

Preston was so excited all he wanted to do was run upstairs to his computer and read everything he could find about the discovery, but then he remembered he was on punishment. He couldn't even call Leah to ask if she'd heard about it. *Man!* Swallowing his disappointment, he launched into a kiddie version of why the news was so important. "Science knows there's a bunch of matter left over from the beginning of the universe, but nobody's been able to find it."

"So is this the dark matter I sometimes hear you and Leah talking about?"

"No," he said. "This is the regular kind. Mrs. Payne, did the news say how she did it?"

"Something to do with X-rays, I believe."

"Wow. I wonder where she found it?"

"Galaxy filaments?" she responded, sounding unsure.

"Man, I sure wish I could use my computer—hint, hint."

The colonel lifted his glass of water. "Hint acknowledged and ignored."

Preston looked down at his plate, but rather than feel sorry for himself, he smiled. That Mrs. Payne had taken the time to listen to the news story and tell him about it meant a lot; that said she cared. "Thanks for knowing I like this kind of stuff."

She nodded. "That's a good parent's job, right, Barrett?"

"Right."

It was Preston's day to do dishes, so after the meal Mrs. Payne went to her office to work on details for the groundbreaking, and he loaded the dishwasher while the colonel put away the leftovers. They talked about the day, his term paper, and that Ms. Brown had received another nasty call. "I hope they catch this person soon."

"So do I."

Preston closed the dishwasher door and started it up. "Can we go out on the deck and talk for a minute?"

"Sure."

They stepped outside. The colonel took a seat at the glass-topped table, but Preston remained standing, leaning back against the wooden rail.

"What did you want to talk about?"

"Girls."

The colonel appeared slightly amused. "And what about them?"

"How do you figure out what they mean when they say stuff?"

"Honestly? I have no idea, but give me an example."

He told the colonel about what Leah had said at lunch yesterday.

"How'd it make you feel?"

"After I finished sucking on my inhaler, I felt really good."

"So you like her?"

"I do. She's so smart. She's fun, and she knows how to stand up for herself."

"And catches a pretty mean pass."

Preston agreed. During the football game last Thanksgiving between Henry Adams and the team made up of the Oklahoma Julys, Henry Adams had taken a butt kicking and lost badly, but Leah had scored twice on two long touchdown passes from Trent. "I think I want to ask her to be my girlfriend, but I never had one before, so I'm not sure how to do it." Preston thought that over for a moment. "And what if she says, 'No, get away from me, fool'?"

"That's always on the table when you deal with women, but no guts, no glory. You know?"

Preston supposed he was right. "How did you know Mrs. Payne was the one?"

"Couldn't eat or sleep without thinking about her. Always wanted to know what she was doing, or where she was. Heart would speed up whenever she looked at me."

"That's sorta how I feel about Leah."

"Then do something for me?"

"I'll try."

"Whoever winds up being the one for you, don't take her feelings for granted and treat her like I did Mrs. Payne."

Preston nodded. "Are you two okay? You aren't going to get a divorce or anything, are you?"

"No."

"Good. Because if you did, I'd probably have to move to another foster home, and I kinda like it here."

"And I like having you here."

Preston wanted that to be the truth so badly.

As if he'd read his mind, the colonel added, "I really do. As for Leah? I say, go for it."

"Okay. I'll let you know what happens."

"I'd like that, too."

Preston felt some of the stress lessen inside. "This wasn't so bad."

"You mean the two of us talking?"

"Yeah."

"I think it went pretty well. We won't ever be Trent and Amari, but we can be Barrett and Preston, and who knows, I may even learn enough about physics to hold a decent conversation with you about it someday soon, so tell me more about this missing matter."

Bernadine got a late-night call from Kyle Dalton. Her tormentor had made this latest call from a pay phone at a campground up near Riverton, a small town north of Henry Adams.

"Place has no security cams, and it's located right off the highway, so still no way of knowing who our perp is."

More disappointment.

"I'll ride up there in the morning and take a look around. No word as of yet on the tape."

Frustration made her sigh. "Okay, Kyle. Thanks."

"Sorry I don't have better news, but you're welcome. Oh, and I'm no longer attached to the Bureau. All my paperwork's cleared, so I'm officially a county deputy, but I'm based in Ellis. Nepotism laws won't let me work under Dad."

"Congratulations."

"I start next week, so I'll be backing off your case. Dad'll be updating you from now on."

"Good to know, but keep in touch."

"Will do, and sorry again for calling so late, but I figured you wanted to hear what we found out about the call."

"I did, no apology needed. Keep me posted."

"Of course. Good night, Ms. Brown, and try not to worry. Law enforcement will find whoever the caller is. I promise."

"Thanks. Good night."

After the call ended, she lay there in the dark and hoped he was right.

CHAPTER
16

By Friday morning, Rocky had had it up to her eyebrows with all the visitors in town; the sooner they all disappeared, the sooner she could stop fuming. At the top of her list of the things working her last nerve were the FUFAs. After being given permission to pass out their leaflets in support of Cletus yesterday, they'd descended on the Dog like a biblical plague and proceeded to give her and the staff fits with their demands to know where her meat was processed, why there was no vegetarian menu, and why they couldn't take over some of the booths in the back to have a strategy meeting. Many of them were rude to the servers, tipped like pennies were dollars, and were constantly sending dishes back to the kitchen because "this doesn't taste right." She wanted to smack them all—especially the ones wearing the pig masks

And then there was the media. They were no less demanding and seemed to think nothing of filling the aisles with their equipment, tripods, and cameras, making it nearly impossible for the servers to do their jobs without tripping over something.

She'd had to threaten a bunch of reporters with the police to get them to leave last night so she could close up, and when she, Mal, and Siz arrived at six in the morning, people were lined up at the door like the Dog was giving away free liquor.

The local customers weren't any happier. They had to wait an hour or more to be seated, and when they did get a chance to sit, they were finding their favorite booths occupied by strangers.

Because of the sheer volume of guests, she was doing everything from greeting to cooking to busing tables. In truth, they were the same duties she handled every day, but not at such a frenetic pace. As it stood, she and the staff had been going nonstop since all this nonsense began, and she was ready for it to stop.

When she looked outside to see how many people were still waiting to get in, the only thing that kept her from snapping was the sight of Jack, standing near the end of the line. He gave her that crooked smile he and Eli worked so well, and for some reason all the drama melted away. To reward him for being her calm in the midst of the storm, she walked over, took him by the hand, and led him toward the entrance.

"Hey!" one of the FUFAs complained. "Why's he cutting the line?"

She ignored him.

Once they were inside, she pulled him into the office. He gazed down at her with a look that was part bemusement and part she wasn't sure, but it rendered her so tongue-tied, she forgot what she was going to say. It came to her then that she was still holding his hand, so she quickly dropped it and forced herself away from his mesmerizing eyes. "Um, give Siz your order. You can eat in here so you won't be late for school."

"Thanks, Rock."

"You're welcome."

She faced him, and although she'd given him his marching orders, neither of them moved. It was as if they were content to stare at each other. "Go eat, Professor."

"Sit with me tonight at the movies."

The softly spoken request almost knocked her over. She tried not to let it show. "We'll talk. Go."

"Going."

A second later he exited. Heart pounding, she headed back to the morning madness. She felt better.

As Preston and the rest of the gang biked from Ms. Marie's to school, he was feeling pretty good, too. They were done painting for the morning, and there was only a little bit left to do. By the end of the day the fence would be finished, and he and the crew could hang up their brushes and stop walking around looking like relatives of Casper the Friendly Ghost. Usually on Friday evenings, he and Amari would hang out at the movies, then head home to play video games until dawn, but being on punishment had put the stomp on that. Not only would there be no movies, video games, or sleeping in, they were going to have to get up in the morning and ride to Franklin and probably spend the entire day at the library. That meant they'd also miss the church groundbreaking; not that that sounded like a barrel of fun, but it beat being stuck in the library trying to find out why Euripides wrote a wack play about some guy in love with his mom.

In spite of the prospect of a boring weekend, he was feeling okay because of the decision he'd come to last night. He was going to ask Leah to be his girl. It was a big step for a kid like him and on the inside he was scared to death that she'd laugh or ask if he'd lost his mind, or both, but talking with the colonel after dinner had helped clear his thinking. Amari was riding beside him, but Preston hadn't shared his plan. Amari sometimes gave wise advice, but he also gave stupid advice, and if it was the latter, Preston didn't want to be thrown off course. He'd talk to his best friend after he talked to Leah and got her response.

The other students were already working when Preston and the painters made their entrance. Mr. James gave them a nod of greeting, and after they took their seats, he asked, "Does anyone know what the Eta Aquarids are?"

Leah's hand shot up.

Amari leaned over to Preston and said under his breath, "If she wasn't like a cousin, I'd really be hating on her, Brain. The girl knows everything."

Mr. James called on her. "Leah?"

"A meteor shower."

"Do you know when they occur?"

"First week of May?" she asked, sounding a little unsure.

"Correct. Very good," he said. "This year, the date's May 5. The display usually peaks around four a.m. We're on break that week, so anyone who wants to join me to check it out will get extra credit for their science grade."

The kids looked around at each other with glee. Preston couldn't remember ever getting up so early, for something like this, but he was game. He knew about meteor showers and had seen them online, but never in person.

Samantha asked, "Do we need like binoculars or telescopes?"

"No. Just your eyes. Everybody should bring blankets and wear warm clothes. Maybe something to sit on in the grass too. If it's really chilly, I'll see if Rocky can't get us some hot chocolate to drink."

Preston liked Mr. James's topical teaching. Of course, Preston could've done without the topical term paper assignment, but in reality, he and the other painters had brought that on themselves.

Mr. James went on to talk about how many meteors they might see per hour and that the Eta Aquarid meteors originally began as dust particles from Halley's Comet. Preston looked over at Leah, and she beamed back her excitement. For two kids who loved astrophysics, this opportunity was totally awesome.

At lunch they were all still talking about it. Crystal failed to understand the giddiness. "Four in the morning? The only thing I want to see at that time is my bed. You all have fun. I'll skip the extra credit."

Eli said, "Oh, come on, Crys. It'll be fun."

"Nope. Not doing it."

Preston looked over at Leah, sitting across from him, and saw her shake her head at Crystal's stance. Preston imagined himself and Leah watching shooting stars together in the middle of a field in the dark, and it gave him goose bumps. He glanced Amari's way. Amari didn't say anything, but on his face was a knowing smile, as if he knew just what Preston was thinking. Preston figured that was impossible, but with Amari anything was possible, so Preston went back to eating his lunch.

For the rest of the school day, Preston discreetly watched Leah, noting the way she pushed her glasses back up her nose with her index finger, the way she leaned over to help the dreaded Tiffany Adele with an algebra problem, and the way she smiled back at him when their eyes met. He thought she was the most perfect girl in the universe. Now he just had to figure out how, when, and where to pop the question.

The opportunity presented itself after school. He and Amari got their bikes to ride out to Ms. Marie's, but before they rode off, he said to Amari, "Go on, I'll catch up. I need to ask Leah something."

To his relief, Amari didn't ask a thousand questions. He just rode off, but he did call back, "Good luck, Brain!"

Preston grinned and decided having a best friend was great. Leah finally came out of the building, but she was walking with her sister, which presented its own set of problems. He had to separate the two, so rather than angst over it, he called out, "Hey Leah, can I talk to you for a minute?"

To his delight, she made Tiff wait on the steps while she walked over.

"Hey, Brain. What's up?"

He took in a deep breath. "Um. I was just wondering—"

She waited, but when he didn't say anything else, she asked, "Wondering what?"

He prayed she wouldn't turn him down. "I was wondering if you—I mean, if we—" The words he wanted to use wouldn't come out, so he said in a rush, "Um, if you were going to the library in the morning?"

She studied him for a minute. "I'm not on punishment. Why would I be at the library?"

"Um. I—I forgot. Never mind."

She stared at him oddly. "Are you okay?"

Over by the school steps, Tiff yelled, "Hurry up, Leah! I'm ready to go!"

"Will you chill out!" Leah called back.

He knew the opportunity had slipped away, and he wanted to punch himself. He felt like Charlie Brown talking to the Little Red-Haired Girl. "Look, I have to catch up with Amari. Maybe I'll see you sometime this weekend."

The puzzled look remained on her face. "Sure. Okay."

She hurried off to join her sister, and a miserable Preston hopped on his bike and pedaled away. *Stupid! Stupid! Stupid!* the voice inside yelled, and he had to agree.

By the time he got home, he was feeling so blue, not even the joy of having finished up the paint job on the Jefferson fence lifted his mood. His big plan of asking Leah to be his girl had fizzled like a wet sparkler on the Fourth of July, and because he'd handled it so badly, she probably thought he was a doofus. He hung his bike up on the hooks on the wall of the garage and was about to enter the kitchen when he heard the Paynes talking. One of the things Preston had learned in foster care was the necessity of eavesdropping on adults. If they were planning to move you to another home, or intent upon some other kind of stupidity—such as leaving you home alone for three days to fend for yourself so they could fly to Cali for a wedding, like one foster mom did to him when he was eight years old—it was best to know in advance and be prepared. Eavesdropping was one of his survival skills, and Preston prided himself on being good at it. Which is why when he heard Mrs. Payne say his name, he stopped just outside the door that led into the kitchen to listen.

"I talked to the court about it today, and they said the adoption process is fairly simple," Mrs. Payne said.

Preston's heart began pounding. Were they talking about making him official?

The colonel replied, "But are we ready, is the question."

His joy plummeted. Mrs. Payne must've made a face in response, because the colonel said softly, "That's not what I meant. I meant are we as husband and wife ready? Is our marriage sound enough? The last thing I want is for him to be in a home where his parents are simply tolerating each other."

"You do care about him, don't you?"

"More than I ever thought I would. Any man would be proud to call him son. He's smart, sensitive, and up-front. Calls me out occasionally, too, and I like that about him."

"He's the child I always wished and prayed for, Barrett, and we're going to be okay."

Preston felt tears wetting his cheeks, and he wiped them away, but soon they were flowing like the Mississippi, and next he knew he was sitting on the floor, sobbing his heart out. Finally, finally he had people who loved him, and cared about him, and wanted him to be in their lives, not just temporarily, or because the state was paying them to feed and house him. If what he'd heard was true, and he had no reason to doubt otherwise, he had a family. A real freaking family! And then he cried some more.

He had no idea how long he'd been sitting there, but when he looked up, the colonel was standing over him.

"Hey, what's wrong? I didn't know you were out here."

Preston quickly tried to pull himself together, but it was too late for that. The old Preston who'd endured so much for so long was afraid to ask, but the new hopeful Preston somehow found the courage. "You and Mrs. Payne really want to adopt me?"

"You heard us, huh?"

"Yes, sir."

Barrett stuck out his hand, and Preston grasped it and let

himself be helped to his feet. He dashed away the lingering water in his eyes.

"To answer your question? Yes. Very much."

Preston hated crying, especially in front of the marines, so he tried to stop, but his eyes kept filling up.

"It's okay. I'm a little misty myself."

And sure enough, Colonel Barrett Montgomery Payne, USM, Retired, had tears in his eyes. "Going to make it my mission to be the best dad ever."

Mrs. Payne called from inside. "Barrett, are you in the garage?"

"Yeah, honey. Just talking to Preston."

"Okay. Dinner's almost ready."

Preston was glad it was just the two of them talking. He knew how emotional and sentimental Mrs. Payne could be, and were she to step out and see what was going on, she'd start to cry, and then Preston would start to cry again, and they'd all be crying until Sunday, but this had to be the most moving experience of his life.

"I suppose I should ask you if you want to be adopted?"

"I'm crying like a four-year-old here. What do you think?"

The colonel's face showed a smile.

Preston met the steady gaze of the man who wanted to be his dad. "Can I call you something besides Colonel?"

"Up to you."

"Amari calls Trent Dad, but I want you to have your own name. How about I call you Pop, or Pops?"

It was the colonel's turn to wipe at his welling eyes. "Either one is fine. Real fine."

As if they had been doing it for a lifetime, Preston's pop spread his arms wide, and Preston walked into the first real hug he'd ever experienced and it felt so damn good, he had to take in a deep breath because it filled up his heart so much. "Thanks, Pops," he murmured.

"No, thank you, son. You've given this old jar-head a purpose."

Preston stepped out of the embrace and extended his fist. "Semper Fi," he whispered.

Barrett touched his knuckles to his son's and nodded. "Semper Fi."

Later that evening, Preston sat on his bed in his silent room, reading and not minding that he had no electronics. He had family, and the surety of that almost made him start crying again, but he wiped at his eyes and bucked it up, as Tamar would say. He was having such an amazing life, he wanted to stand on the porch and shout his happiness to Alpha Centauri. A soft knock on his door made him look up from the book on meteor showers that he'd borrowed from school.

It was Mrs. Payne. "May I come in?"

"Sure."

"How are you feeling?"

"Still up in the clouds."

Her lips curved into a gentle smile. "I know we talked about the adoption at dinner, but I just wanted to tell you how blessed I am, having you in my life. I know young men don't like a lot of mushy talk, so I'll be brief, but as I told Barrett, I've been wishing and praying for you since the day I found out I couldn't have children of my own. You are more than I ever dreamed, Preston. Way more."

"You can sit if you want."

She took a seat in the old armchair. "Remember the time I caught you reading the W. E. B. Dubois biography in the middle of the night?"

He smiled. "I do." It was during his first summer with them. "I knew then that you were a very special child."

"I knew you were okay too, because one, you didn't laugh at me for reading something like that, and two, you didn't make me put the book up, or say, go to bed."

"I was too impressed." She quieted for a moment, then added softly, "And I want to thank you for helping Barrett, too. He's been drifting since we moved here, and now I believe he's found an anchor in you."

Preston didn't know what to say. "I think he and I are going to be tight."

"I think so, too. I have a question."

"Shoot." It was a response he'd learned from the seniors in Henry Adams.

"The court will want to know what you want your legal name to be once the adoption is finalized. Do you have any idea?"

"Should I change it?"

"That's up to you."

He thought about it for a moment. "How about Preston Mays Payne."

There was approval in her eyes. "I like that."

"Since I met that Crenshaw lady, I think I want to keep my biological dad's name out of respect."

"That's a wonderful sentiment. Who knows, maybe one day you'll get to meet his family. Even though you never knew Lawrence Mays, I believe they'd be proud that you chose to honor him by keeping his name."

He agreed, and studied the woman who'd been nothing but kind to him since the first day they met. "Now I have a question for you."

"Shoot," she replied, and they both grinned.

"Can I call you Mom?"

"Oh, Preston." Tears filled her eyes. "That would be so wonderful."

After sharing a strong heartfelt hug and a few more tears, she left his room, and he was once again alone. At that moment, it occurred to him that the kid soon to be Preston Mays Payne would never be alone ever again, emotionally or otherwise, and for him that meant more than anything in the world.

The last piece of the puzzle was Leah. He'd blown it this afternoon, but next time he'd get it right. His life was on a roll, and he wanted her to be a part of it.

CHAPTER
17

Over at the rec, the Friday-night moviegoers were arriving and finding seats. Jack chose one at the end of a row on the far side of the auditorium and sat down to wait. He had no idea if Rocky would show, but he'd saved her a seat beside him, just in case. Inviting her to join him wasn't something he'd planned—the words just sort of rolled out—but he got the sense that she was dropping her guard, and that gave him hope.

He was still wearing the sling. The docs said he could discard it in a couple days, and he was happy about that; he needed to start looking for a new vehicle to replace the one totaled in the crash. Henry Adams wasn't a big place geographically, so he'd had no trouble getting around, but he was going to need wheels at some point. Who knew, maybe he'd even look at a truck, since that seemed to be the unwritten requirement about what was appropriate to drive.

He surveyed the people entering. Eli, Crystal, and the other kids were at home on lockdown, but he spotted Trent and Lily, Bernadine and Mal, and the Paynes. Marie Jefferson and Genevieve Curry came in, waved his way, and took seats down front. He'd positioned himself about three-quarters of the way up, so he'd be able to keep an eye on the two doors and not miss Rocky's entrance.

As the arrivals became a steady flow, the buzz of visiting and conversing filled the space. For Jack it had become a familiar sound and made him appreciate more and more how special a place Henry Adams was. Life was so easy and simple that this is what the community did on Friday night. They gathered, gossiped, caught up on the lives of their friends and neighbors, and then sat down as one to enjoy the movies. After living in L.A., he thought he'd stepped into an alternate universe on his first Friday night in town last year. It amazed him that they all knew each other. In L.A., he was lucky to know the neighbors living on either side, but here they were all related, or attended school together. They were godparents and godchildren, fathers and daughters, mothers and sons. The idea that they'd been doing this for generations was what blew him away the most, and now his and Eli's lives were a part of this living history as well. The enormity of that was staggering.

He saw parents and children that he didn't recognize, and guessed they were from neighboring communities like Franklin. More and more outsiders were showing up every week to take advantage of the no-frills, laid-back entertainment.

Apparently the members of the press and the FUFAs had nothing to do on a Friday night either. Some of the crews had left for the weekend, but those still in town were drifting in, carrying their popcorn and drinks and looking around for seats to claim for themselves and their colleagues. It was going to be a packed house, and he was glad he'd gotten in early.

Trent made his way over to where he was sitting and asked, "You busy tomorrow?"

"I'm going with Rocky in the morning to pick up a bike, but I'm guessing it won't take all day. Why?"

"Really? This like a date?" Trent didn't bother hiding his grin.

"She says no."

"Sounds like one to me."

Jack shrugged. "All I know is she invited me, and I said yes."

"Okay. The reason I'm asking is, I'm hoping we can get together and figure out what we want to sing for the Idol contest."

"What time?"

"How about four? At the garage."

"If I can't make it, I'll call you."

"Good enough. Did she say what kind of bike?"

"No."

"Knowing her, it's probably a motorcycle. She used to ride one when we were younger."

"Okay. I didn't know that."

They both saw Tamar up on the stage, ready to begin her role as the evening's mistress of ceremonies.

"Okay, Jack. Have a good time, and I'll see you tomorrow afternoon."

He quickly headed back to his seat beside his wife. Jack turned to check the doors again. No Rocky. Disappointed, he focused his attention on Tamar.

She began the night festivities by referencing the two-page surveys everyone had been handed upon entering the auditorium. She then turned the announcement over to Gary Clark.

"I need them back ASAP," he said, standing at his seat

in the middle of the room. "If you can't complete it tonight, bring it tomorrow to the groundbreaking. Mal says you can drop them off at the Dog, too. The surveys are very important if we want to open our own grocery store." He thanked everyone and sat down again next to his daughters.

Up on the stage, Tamar added, "Don't make me have to pay you a visit."

Laughter followed that.

"Okay. That's it for housekeeping. We're showing *The Princess and the Frog* and *All About Eve*."

She left the stage, the house lights went down, and the movie began.

Jack hadn't seen Disney's newest princess movie, and frankly, he wasn't sure he wanted to, but he did want to see Bette Davis work her magic in the second feature, so he sat back. About fifteen minutes in, he heard a whisper beside him in the dark. "Did you save me a seat?"

Surprise jerked him straight up. "Yes."

He scrambled to his feet to allow Rocky to pass.

"Thanks," she whispered.

He was grateful for the darkness, because he was grinning like a fool.

She leaned over close enough for him to smell a light perfume. "Sorry I'm late. Couldn't get the stupid FUFAs to leave so I could lock up, then I had to run home and take a shower."

"Glad you made it."

"Me, too."

After that, they focused on the screen, and Jack was in heaven. About five minutes later, she leaned close and whispered, "Would you like to go for a drink after the movie?"

Somehow managing not to jump up and shout hallelujah, he replied, "Sure."

When the movies were over, Bernadine left the auditorium with Mal's arm around her waist. *All About Eve* had been as wonderful as she remembered. Bette Davis was a fabulous actress.

They were among the last group of moviegoers to exit, and as they stepped out into the chilly blustery night and headed for the solar-illuminated parking lot a few yards away, Mal stopped suddenly and tensed.

"What's the matter?"

"Smell that?"

Bernadine did; then, as a gust of wind blew by, the scent became more pronounced.

People were flowing around them on the way to their vehicles, and Mal yelled out, "Gasoline! Don't start your rides!"

The wind grabbed his words, but those people closest apparently understood and stopped. Some people could be seen at the far end of the lot who obviously couldn't hear him because of the distance, but a few people were coming back at a run.

Trent ran up. "Do you smell that gas?"

"Yeah, I'm trying to get people to hold off starting up until we figure out where it's coming from."

The first explosion rocked the surroundings. One minute they'd been talking, and the next minute they were on the ground. A second explosion quickly followed. Red and orange flames filled the middle of the lot and rose into an undulating wall that sent fiery feelers rushing toward them over the surface of the lot.

"Run!" Mal bellowed. He grabbed Bernadine's hand, pulled her stumbling to her feet, and together they joined the panicked race back to the building. Behind them blast after blast reverberated against the night, shaking the ground so forcefully she almost went down again. Some of the older people were knocked off their feet, but friends and neighbors rushed to their aid to get them moving again. Thick black smoke burned their eyes and throats.

Scraps of flaming, spinning metal began showering down like rain, adding to the terror. Hands went up to shield heads, only to be burned. Chunks of white-hot debris slammed into shoulders and crashed into backs. Screams rang out. People fell and were helped up. She noticed Bing limping along slowly with his arm around Clay, supporting his weight.

Mal saw them too. The building was just up ahead, so Bernadine pushed him toward his friend. "Go! I'll be okay!"

He ran to assist them, and she covered the last few feet while frantically looking around for anyone else needing help. Her thoughts flew to the kids at home and prayed they were safe.

Trent, Gary, and Barrett ran by her, loaded down with fire extinguishers, but she wasn't sure that would make a difference. She turned to see. The entire lot was engulfed in walls of dancing flames. People were still running by her, jostling her as they passed, and all she could do was stare transfixed at the most surreal scene she'd ever witnessed. Camera crews were running toward the blaze.

Trent and his crew were spraying wide arcs of foam in an effort to keep the fire from jumping to the grass and eating its way up to the building. Her fear was that there would be more explosions from gas tanks igniting and they might be hurt, but she left them to their grim task, covered the last few feet to safety, and dragged herself inside.

The auditorium's interior was in chaos. Injured and dazed people were everywhere. Down by the stage Rocky was tearing open a packaged case of bottled water while Jack, with his arm in a sling, did his best to get the bottles passed out to the people lining up. Tamar was on a bullhorn, giving directions to keep the badly injured in the lobby and announcing that ambulances were on the way. Lily was on her phone. Her face and hair were streaked with black smoke. Men Bernadine knew to be reporters were carrying stacked Red Cross–type cots up the aisles to the lobby to accommodate the injured until the ambulances arrived. The water, cots, and blankets Marie and Genevieve were handing out were from the emergency supplies kept on site in case of a blizzard or tornado. No one had imagined they'd be needed for something like this.

Bernadine finally shook off the shock of the nightmarish last few minutes and hurried down the center aisle to help. Rushing in behind her were Dr. Reg Garland, carrying his doctor's bag, and Reverend Paula Grant, wearing her clerical collar.

In the end, thirty-five people were injured. Three of them had to be airlifted to Wichita to be treated for severe burns. A Franklin couple, Mike and Peggy Sanderson, who'd come to the movies to celebrate their thirtieth wedding anniversary, died when their truck caught fire.

Afterward, the weary locals and the first responders gathered at the Dog. Rocky opened up the kitchen and made coffee and sandwiches. The teens, along with Zoey and Devon, had ridden to the rec on their bikes, and after making sure their parents were okay, they were put to work in the kitchen.

Reg Garland and Reverend Grant looked dead on their feet from their ministrations to body and soul. Bernadine was sick from the death and destruction. She'd never imagined something so horrific happening in her town. Sheriff Dalton had arrived at the rec with some of the first responders. The parking lot was still too hot to do any preliminary forensics, he told her, but he admitted that a fire of such size and ferocity didn't usually happen by chance. He'd return in the morning along with ATF agents to try and get to the bottom of things.

She took the cup of coffee Mal placed in front of her. "Thanks."

He was wearing the same grim look he'd been wearing all evening, a look mirrored on the faces of everyone sitting in the Dog. "Clay just called from the hospital. Bing's leg's broken. He'll stay there overnight, and Clay will bring him home in the morning."

"Did he fall?" Lily asked, seated beside Trent, who reeked of smoke and extinguisher foam.

Mal shook his head. "He got hit by a flying truck door during the first explosion. He's lucky to still be with us."

"Who would do this?" She knew no one had an answer, but felt the need to express the question anyway. Al Stillwell instantly came to mind. Could he be so angry that he'd want to hurt people he didn't even know? She understood him wanting to take revenge on her, but the Franklin couple who'd lost their lives had no connection to the lawsuit whatsoever, yet their family would be holding a funeral in the next few days. What had happened to her idyllic little piece of paradise? She supposed the ills of society were destined to catch up with them sooner or later, but parts of her wanted to hire regiments of marines and SWAT teams with dogs to keep her people safe.

Greer Parker walked over to the booth where she was seated and said somberly, "We filmed some of the fire. If law enforcement wants to view the footage, have them contact me."

"I will."

"So sorry about all this, Ms. Brown. Not what you expect to happen in a town like this."

Bernadine agreed.

When everyone realized there was nothing more any of them could do, people started to head to their vehicles for the ride home, but some realized belatedly that they no longer had a vehicle. Marie had lost her old Pontiac. Mal's Ford had been parked at the Dog, and Trent's at the garage, so theirs had been spared. Lily's hadn't, and neither had Gary Clark's. Bernadine lost Baby, too.

Those without transportation were offered rides home with those who did. Once that was sorted out, Reverend Paula asked, "Bernadine, what about the groundbreaking tomorrow? Are we on or off?"

Bernadine looked around at the kids, Sheila and Barrett, Rocky and Jack, and everyone else waiting to hear her response. "We're on. If we hide under the covers, whoever started that fire wins, and I refuse!"

Applause, yells, and shouts of encouragement greeted her announcement, letting her know she'd made the right choice.

Reverend Paula smiled tiredly. "Then I'll see everybody at eleven o clock."

Rocky gave Jack, Eli, and Eli's bike a ride home. While Eli grabbed his bike out of the bed, unlocked the door, and went inside, Jack sat silently. Rocky looked over. "You okay, Professor?"

"Who would do this?"

She shrugged. "I don't know. It's a shame those people had to die. I hope Dalton finds whoever did it and puts them away before they do something else. I can't imagine how that poor family must feel. Reverend Grant said she heard the explosions out at Tamar's."

Rocky wanted to somehow banish the bleakness she saw in his eyes.

"Are you still going to get your bike?"

"Yes. You heard Bernadine, we're not running scared, so I'll be here at six."

"Then I'll be ready. We'll have to take rain checks on that drink."

"I know, but I'm glad we were there to help."

Mal dropped Bernadine and Crystal off at home. Inside the house, Crystal asked, "You sure you're okay?"

"I am. I'm just sad about the people who died."

"Me, too."

"Thanks for helping out in the kitchen."

"No problem. At first I thought the booms were thunder, then Doc Reg knocked on the door and said there was a fire. We could see it from the porch. He left Devon and Zoey with me and told us to stay put, but when we heard more of those big booms, Eli came over and said he was going to see what was happening, so we got everybody and rode in. Are we going to be in trouble?"

Bernadine hugged her close. "No, sweetie. You all did what you thought best, and no one can yell at you for that. Plus Rocky and Mal were glad for the help."

"I hope they catch the person."

"Me, too. Now I'm going up to shower, and then to bed. You should do the same."

Crystal gave her another hug. "I'm glad you're okay," she said fiercely.

"Me, too."

Lying in bed, Bernadine stared unseeing into the darkness while the memories of the fire played in her head. Now that it was all over, the terror and helplessness that had been holding her in its grip since the initial blast dissipated was replaced by righteous anger. How dare someone do this! How dare cost a couple their life just for coming to see a movie in celebration of their anniversary! If she had to offer every dime she had as a reward for information, she would. The arsonist was not going to get away with this! Whoever it was would be found, prosecuted, and locked up if it took the rest of her life.

CHAPTER
18

Early the following morning, Rocky left her trailer and walked out to her truck. The sun was just rising, and it tinted the dawn sky with pinks and gold. She shivered a bit in the chilly air. Even though it was late April, spring was still having difficulty giving winter the final boot, and as a result the temperature was in the mid-forties. Glad for the warmth of her old black leather jacket, she got into her truck and started it up.

Hoping her engine didn't disturb Tamar, the CNN guys, or Reverend Paula after the rough night they'd all had, she backed down the gravel drive that led out to July Road and used it to get to Main. Passing the Dog, she saw the lights on, indicating that Mal and Brian, the part-time cook who filled in for Siz on the weekends, were on their jobs. A minute later she drove by the rec and slowed to take in all the activity. A line of cop cruisers and unmarked cars were parked out front. Men and women in jackets emblazoned with local and national acronyms were all over the site, carrying clipboards and talking on phones. She saw Trent talking with a group of them, and Bernadine too. In the light of day the aftereffects of the fire could be seen in the burned remains of truck and cars littering the lots and the half-melted streetlights, warped and deformed like a picture by Salvador Dalí. Shaking her head sadly at the madness, she drove on to Jack's.

Jack. She'd been looking forward to this all week. Their shared ride home from the hospital had been nice. The look of utter surprise on his face when she walked into the waiting room was one she'd remember for a long time. He didn't impress her as being someone who was caught flat-footed often, so she gave herself points. And yes, she was nervous, probably more than she'd been in quite some time, but she was determined to see this through, no matter how many times she had to keep telling the Doubting Thomas voices inside to shut up and take a seat.

She pulled into the James driveway at precisely 5:55. Jack exited his front door, pulling his jacket on over his shoulder while trying to hold on to a red plastic coffee cup with the hand in the sling. He seemed to be managing it okay, and she liked that he was on time.

When he got in, he brought with him the faint hint of a nice cologne and his smile. "Morning."

"Morning." She had another one of those moments where she found herself just staring at him. Snapping out of it, she backed down the driveway while he secured his seat belt.

"So, how are you?" he asked.

"I'm good. You?"

They were heading to the highway.

"Doing good, too."

On the plains of Kansas early-morning radio was dominated

by farm reports, so she had her iPod plugged in. David Sanborn's horn flowed sweetly. Traffic was light. Rocky didn't know what to say, so she let the music take over the silence.

"Thanks for the invite," he said to her.

"You're welcome."

"What kind of bike are we picking up?"

"Vincent Black Shadow."

She could tell by his furrowed brow that he didn't have a clue as to what that was. "It's okay, most people have no idea what it is either, but it's a motorcycle—a classic. My dad used to have one when I was growing up. I've been looking for one to either buy or restore for about a year now."

She merged onto the highway and blew by a few slower-moving trucks. Once the road ahead was clear, she set the cruise control and relaxed. She glanced his way. "Did you love your wife?"

"Madly."

She liked that. Men sometimes stumbled over that question, as if owning up to their feelings was against some kind of male code, but he'd answered without hesitation. "Was that too nosy?"

"No."

"How'd you meet?"

He sat back, and the dreamy look that came over his face seemed to match the feelings he'd proclaimed so unashamedly. "Met her at the campus bookstore, and from the moment I met her, I was in love. Did you love your husband?"

"Thought I did until I caught him in my underwear."

He spit out coffee and began coughing.

"There are napkins in the glove box."

Continuing to cough, he gave her a sideways look, then

wiped his mouth and used another napkin on the drops of coffee dotting the black console. "So that's what you meant on Saturday when you said you were afraid I'd wind up wearing your underwear. I've been thinking about that on and off all week."

" Needless to say, I wasn't happy."

"How'd he look?"

"Think Cletus in a bikini."

He was still smiling. "That must've been something."

"Oh, it was. So much something I made Trent drive me to the airport so I could leave town." She paused as she thought back and said in a soft tone, "Really thought Bob would be the one. Nope."

Rocky wasn't sure what telling him all this meant, but if they were going to be embarking on whatever this was they were doing, she wanted him to know the ins and outs of how life had shaped her—good and bad. She turned to see how he was taking all this and met eyes so filled with quiet interest, she had to look away or drive off the road.

"That your only marriage?"

"Yes. I don't seem to do well in relationships. Either the guy's crazy or I am. Nothing's ever worked out." Maybe because she'd never opened up this way before, and neither had the men.

She had the truck rolling. The cruise control was set at eighty-five mph—just the way she liked it, even though it was an invitation to a ticket. As they blew past a marked cruiser hiding in plain sight on the shoulder, she hoped the patrolman would let her fly on, but in her rearview mirror she saw him swing out and gun after her. "Damn."

He peered into his mirror. "How fast you going?"

"Eighty-five."

He stared with so much surprise, she chuckled, "It's one of the things Tamar and I have in common—a girl's need for speed."

Slowing the truck, she pulled onto the shoulder, rolled down her window, and said, "Can you hand me that red envelope out of the glove box, please?"

He complied.

Watching the trooper close the distance between his vehicle and hers, Rocky realized she knew him. The recognition made her relax somewhat. When he reached the window, she said, "Hey, Carl."

"Rocky?" He swept surprised eyes over her and then Jack.

"How've you been?" she asked.

"Been good. You on your way to a fire?"

"Nope. Going to Hays to pick up a bike."

"Who's he?"

"A friend."

The way Carl scrutinized him from beneath the circular brim of his hat made Jack think the cop would say more, but he didn't, shifting his attention back to Rocky.

"Let me have your license and registration."

She passed them to him. He gave Jack another glance before walking back to his cruiser to run her info through his onboard computer.

"You two know each other, I take it?"

"Yeah. Dated him for a while a few years back."

"Ah." Jack's brain instantly began asking all the questions the male brain does when confronted with a former boyfriend, but he had enough sense not to say anything out loud.

Carl returned and gave her back her license and registration. "Letting you off with a warning, Rock."

"Thanks."

"How long you had this truck?" he asked, checking it out approvingly.

Jack put the registration into the red envelope and closed the glove box.

"About a year."

"Heard you were back in town."

"Since you're looking at me, you heard right."

"Still a hard-ass wiseass."

"Always."

He smiled for the first time. "Okay, go get your bike, and slow down, would you, please? I don't want to scrape your hard-ass wiseass off the pavement."

"Thanks, Carl."

He tossed Jack a farewell nod and departed.

She merged back into the traffic and after a few minutes eased it back up to eighty-five. It didn't surprise him that she'd paid no attention to the trooper's parting request. "Why'd you two break up?"

"Found out he was married. I don't do home wrecking. Do you think Shakespeare's Kate was really a woman of color?"

The gears in Jack's brain jumped off the track. Had he missed something?

"*Taming of the Shrew*. Scene Two. Petrucchio says: Kate, like the hazel-twig is straight and slender, and as brown in hue as hazel-nuts."

Jack blinked. "Um?"

"Took a Shakespeare class at the community college a

few years back. I asked the professor about it, and you'd've thought I was playing the dozens with his mother, the way he looked."

Jack was still trying to get his brain to move. "What did he say?"

"Told me, Don't be ridiculous. Told him to read the passage, but he refused. I dropped the class." She glanced over. "So, what do you think?"

He thought he had yet to meet a more fascinating woman. "I think you amaze me, Rocky."

"Good. Not sure what men like you talk about when you're off the clock. Don't want to bore you."

"No chance of that."

She nodded as if pleased. Jack was still mulling over his fascination when they exited the highway and drove into Hays.

They pulled into what appeared to be a salvage yard, by the look of all the rusted cars and farm equipment strewn about. The truck halted in front of an old cinder-block building that had the words "Wellers Cars and Parts" across the front in letters so faded and weathered they were barely discernible. She gave the horn a quick toot. A few seconds later an old man in a pair of jeans and a long-sleeved denim shirt came out, leaning on a brown cane. He walked slowly over to her rolled-down window with a smile splitting his whiskered face. "Morning, Ms. Rock. How you?"

"Doing good, Freddy. This is my friend, Jack. Jack—Freddy Wellers."

"Pleased to meet you, Mr. Wellers."

The old man peered into the cab. "Same here, Jack. What do you do?"

The abrupt question caught him off guard. "I'm the teacher in Henry Adams."

Freddy scanned him silently with piercing blue eyes. Jack felt like a sixteen-year-old being scrutinized by his date's father.

"You treat her nice, you hear?"

"Yes, sir." He sent a hesitant glance Rocky's way. Her profile showed Sphinx-like amusement.

But to her credit and his relief, she pulled Weller's attention away by asking, "My Shadow ready?"

"Yep, and in better shape than I thought. Needs a lot of TLC, though. You sure you don't want me to do the work for you?"

"Positive. I got this. Jack's going to help."

Jack's lips parted in surprise. In spite of having had a biker roommate, he knew next to nothing about motorcycles. Freddy looked as doubtful as he felt.

"Bike's around back."

"Hop in."

He complied, and once he was settled, warned, "Drive slow, now. Don't want you running into nothing."

"Me?"

"Yeah you, Miss Lead Foot."

"Chicken," she tossed back teasingly.

"Cluck cluck."

She shot Jack a smile that made his insides feel like they'd been warmed by the sun. He was really enjoying being in her company.

The drive around the building took just a few seconds, and the sea of car parts as far as he could see caused his jaw to drop. Piles of tires, fenders, and flattened doors were stacked sky-high. As she made a turn that drove them deeper into the yard, he marveled at a small mountain range of old engines, transmissions, and busted windshields rising next to hundreds of mounded struts and blackened exhaust pipes that would never breathe again. There were tractor parts and ancient refrigerators along with washing machines, banged-up dryers, and stoves with no doors. He now understood why Freddy had cautioned Rocky to drive slow. If any of the stacks fell, it would take first responders years to recover their pancaked bodies.

Freddy must have seen the wonder on his face. "Pretty impressive, huh?" There was pride in his voice, as if he were showing off a field of diamonds.

"Definitely." What impressed him most was the sheer size of the operation. He felt as if he'd been transported to a hallowed graveyard where old car parts, tractors and discarded appliances went to die. "Is this all for sale?"

"Nah. Sometimes a restorer or a kid needs something for an old wreck they're working on, but most of it's scrap I'm saving."

Jack wanted to know why, but was too busy staring around. They passed another giant pile of truck doors, all green. He couldn't help but put his earlier thoughts into words. "I feel like I'm in the place where car parts go to die—sorta like the elephant graveyard."

The old man chuckled. "If there was a place like that, this would be it."

The truck finally stopped in front of a garage with five open bays. Jack wondered if the building was original property, or if it had been salvaged too. The area around it was yet another graveyard, this time of bicycles. Piles of handlebars, frames, bike tires, and rusted-through fenders were everywhere. Jack was so focused on taking it all in, he realized Rocky and Wellers were getting out of the truck. He hustled to join them.

Rocky was cognizant of only one thing, and that was the bike sitting in the shadows of the garage's bay. She'd been trying to get her hands on a Vincent for nearly a year, and the sight of it was so moving, she paused, taking in its shape and unique design before approaching it almost reverently. Seeing past its terrible physical condition and filled with awe, she ran a hand over the rusted bars, the torn and rotting leather seat with its stuffing exposed as if it were made of silk. It was in bad shape. Rust and age obscured the fine curved lines and the once-black engine that had given the formerly beautiful piece of high-powered machinery its name. She'd paid an incredible amount of money for the bike, but once it was back on the road, it would be priceless.

"What do you think?" Freddy asked her softly. His voice broke her mood and brought her back to reality. "Lot of work, but she'll be gorgeous when I'd done."

"Going to take a while."

"I know, but I don't care." And she didn't. Even if the restoration took a year, her dream of owning a Vincent had finally come true. What mattered more was that every minute spent working on it would bring back memories of her father and the Vincent he'd owned during her childhood. In her heart she already sensed him smiling down. "Let's get the paperwork done so I can take her home."

In the year Jack had known Rocky Dancer, he couldn't remember ever seeing her so pleased. To him the bike looked like a candidate for one of Mr. Wellers's graveyards, but she obviously knew more than he did.

In the office, he waited while the two went over the paperwork. Once everything was finalized, she wrote out a check and handed it over.

The scrap dealer's old eyes twinkled. "First check for fifty grand I ever held."

Jack swung to her in surprise and received another Sphinx-like smile. To say he was floored was an understatement. *Fifty grand!* The inevitable question that followed was: How does the manager of a diner write a check for that much cash? The longer he was around Rocky, the more questions he had.

With the bike loaded and chained down in the bed of the truck, they waved good-bye to Mr. Wellers and drove off.

"So what's so special about this bike?"

"Other than being the biker Holy Grail, the Shadows were all hand-built by a company called Vincent HRD. The bikes were supposedly inspired by the RAF fighters that flew over the factory during World War II. Less than two thousand were made and they were designed so they could be ridden and maintained by injured soldiers."

She went on to tell him how the clutch could be operated with only two fingers, and how for its time, the bike sported many breakthrough innovations. "My dad owned one back in the day. Took me for my first ride when I was like four."

"Four?"

"Yeah. He'd put me behind him on the seat and use a belt to strap me to him until I got big enough to hold on to him on my own. Loved it."

"Put a four-year-old on a bike these days, and CPS will be at the door."

"I know. Things were different back then, especially out here."

"That's amazing to me. And your mom was okay with it?"

Rocky looked over and wondered how to explain to him about her mother. "My mom committed suicide when I was nine." She hadn't meant to begin that way, but the words sort of tumbled out, and now it was too late to take them back.

"Oh, Rock," he whispered. "I'm so sorry."

She shrugged. "Me, too. Are you hungry? I am. How about we stop and get something?" The eyes she looked into were filled with pain and questions, but he didn't press her for more information, and she appreciated that.

"Sure."

She swung into the first fast-food place they happened upon, and while they ordered, her admission hung between them like a third person in the cab.

"That's what you meant the other night when you said growing up out here as a kid was hard."

"Yes." She drove the car to the pickup window and took the bags and cups of drinks the kid handed out. She asked him, "Are you in a hurry to get back?"

"I have to meet Trent at four."

She looked down at her watch. It was nine thirty. "Then how about we park and eat."

"That's fine."

They found a spot in a side lot away from the main door and ate and talked. She told him about her mother, and all the fights she'd gotten into in school because of the illness, and how heartbroken her father became after her mother's death.

"That had to be hard on you both."

"It was. Part of the reason why I am the way I am, I guess. Hoping I'm not scaring you off."

"No, Rock. If anything, it makes me want to hang out with you even more."

"Really? Why?"

"Because I don't think you tell every Joe Blow that walks into your life what you just shared with me. That you'd trust me with that—I don't know. It's hard to explain, but I want to know everything about you now."

"I'd like to know a lot more about you, too."

"Only way to do that is spend more time together. Will you let me take you out?"

"Sure." She looked over his way. "Happy now?"

"Extremely. How about you?"

"Ditto."

They stared at each other for a timeless moment, and then Rocky leaned over and they shared a first kiss. When they drew apart, he ran a finger slowly down her cheek. "That was nice."

"Ditto," she whispered. "I think we should have our first date right now."

"And what do you want to do?"

"Let's go look at trucks."

He laughed long and hard. "You are something, Rocky Dancer."

"Yes, I am. Are you game?"

"No man in his right mind would turn down an invitation like that, so yeah, I am. Let's go."

CHAPTER
19

Back in Henry Adams, Bernadine spent the early morning talking with ATF agents and representatives from state and county law enforcement. The preliminary forensics report left her quietly furious. Her truck had been the flashpoint. Baby had been soaked in gasoline, as had the asphalt directly surrounding it. From there the gas was splashed around in random circles, all the way to the edge of the far lot. Now, standing with Sheriff Dalton in what was left of said lot, he spoke while she listened tensely.

"The perp was apparently waiting in that tall grass over there. When people began leaving the building, he or she lit the tail end of the gas, and the flames worked their way across the asphalt surface until they hit the mother lode."

"Which was my truck."

He nodded. "Yours exploded first."

"So someone was out to kill me."

"Or screw with you. Not sure. All we know is that your truck was definitely targeted, so we're assuming the fire was aimed at you—for whatever purpose."

"Do you think it's tied to the calls?"

"Possibly. Probably."

"So your recommendation?"

"I'd get security cameras mounted on every building in town to start, and install a system in your subdivision."

"Big Brother comes to Henry Adams."

He didn't reply, but the grimness in his gaze matched her own. "I want to offer a reward, if it'll help."

"Can't hurt. How much are you thinking?"

"Two hundred and fifty thousand dollars."

He stiffened.

"If that's not enough, I'll throw in another two hundred and fifty thousand. I want this murderer caught, Will."

"I know—so do we. I'll get the paperwork started."

"Anything else I should know? What about the threatening calls I received?"

"They still haven't gotten to it yet. ATF's got their canines out in the field, trying to determine if the person left a trail. Other than that, that's all for right now."

"Okay. Keep me posted. If you need me for anything, I'll be at the Dog."

Tight-lipped, she walked around the yellow crime-scene tape and started up the street to the diner.

When she arrived, everyone looked up. A few eager reporters hastily grabbed their digital recorders and made a move to approach, but the glare she blasted their way froze them on the spot. They seemed to rethink the matter and sat down again.

She looked around the dining room and silently beckoned to the people she did want to speak with, and they followed her into Rocky's quiet office.

Once the door was closed behind them, she told them what the sheriff had shared with her about the investigation, and his recommendations. "Trent, I want you to find us a cutting-edge security system, and I don't care how much it costs. Lil, get a hold of the fire chief over in Franklin and tell him we need guidance on purchasing two fire trucks, and what we need to do to get the trained personnel to man them. There'll never be another fire in this town that we have to fight with fire extinguishers."

She saw nods of agreement. "As soon as the police are done with their investigation, I want that lot razed and redone. Same for the lights."

She turned to Reverend Paula. "Get in touch with the Sandersons' family and find out if they need any help in any way—whether it's funeral costs, college fund, whatever—and get back to me."

Marie was next. "Get yourself a new car and send me the bill. Lily, you too. Both of you need wheels today. Monday at the latest."

Before either could voice a protest, Bernadine turned to Mal. "Babe, I need you to get me the names of the sixteen people who lost their vehicles in the fire. Tell them I'll be adding ten grand to whatever they get from their insurance companies."

She looked around. "If anybody thinks of anything else we may need to address the fallout of this insanity, let me know. Now, I'm going back out there to have a quick press conference, and then breakfast."

That said, she left.

She was on point about the brevity of the press conference. The reporters sensed she was too angry to answer nonsensical questions such as "Did she want to give the arsonist a message?" so they stuck to basic information like the state of the injured, how many town residents had lost cars in the fire, and how soon she planned to rebuild the parking lot.

And when it was over, she sat with Mal and ordered breakfast and they left her alone so she could eat in peace.

But she couldn't escape the news reports on the Dog's multiple big-screen TVs. Right in the middle of her eggs came a shot of the fire blazing like a movie from hell. She understood last night's event was the news du jour and tomorrow something else would be at the top of the hour, but she didn't want to see it again. Without being asked, Mal got up, pointed the remote, and preempted the news with Mighty Mouse cartoons.

Diners laughed and cheered. After bowing at the waist, he returned to the booth and met her smile.

"Thank you."

"It's Saturday morning. We're supposed to be watching Mighty Mouse."

"I can always count on you to save the day."

"Pretty good at beating up cats, too. Just so you'll know."

She laughed, and it felt good.

Last night's tragedy had stolen some of the joy tied to the groundbreaking for the new Henry Adams African Episcopal Church, especially since it would be built in the open field adjacent to the rec center. One had only to look over and see the parking lot strewn with charred automotive remains and the swarm of law enforcement people still gathering evidence.

Thirty people showed up, however. Add to that the large number of media who'd seemingly given up on getting anything further out of Bernadine but were looking to cover something until she offered more, or until the Cletus hearing on Monday, and you had a good-size crowd.

The event was low-key. Reverend Paula opened with a prayer for the Sandersons and the people who had been injured. She next offered a few remarks about the importance of Spirit, and her hope that everyone in the area, regardless of religious affiliation, would look upon the church as home.

"This can be a church for Baptists or Catholics or AME. The liturgy may be different, but not the touch and presence of the Holy Spirit."

Her next words were drowned out by the passage of a noisy car caravan filled with sign-holding sillies in pig masks screaming, "Long live Cletus!," "Cletus rocks!," and other Cletus-based nonsense as they drove past.

The media instantly swung their cameras toward the cars. Some reporters ran to their rental cars to give chase, while others put on their anchor faces and began speaking into microphones to send breaking news about this latest development back to their individual home stations.

Bernadine sighed angrily at their lack of respect. The arched eyebrow of Reverend Paula and the irritation on the faces of everyone else seemed to mirror her feelings. She couldn't wait until the crazies left town.

Once the FUFAs were no longer in sight, Reverend Paula finished speaking, and everyone prepared for the ceremonial groundbreaking.

Trent was present in his role as mayor, so Sheila handed him and Reverend Grant each a shiny new spade with a beautiful blue silk ribbon wrapped around the handle. Lily, videotaping the ceremony for the Henry Adams Archive Project, moved into position. Reverend Paula, wearing brand-new black-and-silver cowgirl boots, pushed her spade into the earth. Beside her, Trent did the same. The first spades of dirt were turned, and a vigorous round of applause split the late-morning air. In spite of all the turmoil, Bernadine's heart swelled. This would be the first new house of worship erected in Henry Adams in decades, making it yet another milestone on the town's journey to recovery. The reality of that further brightened both her mood and the day.

Usually after such events they convened at the Dog for a good time, but out of respect, Trent suggested it be postponed. He offered instead the idea of a celebratory cookout next weekend after all the injured came home, the Sanderson funeral had been held, and the FUFA hoopla around Cletus's hearing was over, and everyone agreed.

As the groundbreaking broke up, Bernadine saw Lily separate herself from Marie and Genevieve and make her way through the thinning crowd to her side.

"Where are you headed?" Lily asked.

"Office. Want to get Paula caught up on what's been going on while she's been away, and wait around for Jim Edison. He's flying in this afternoon."

The attorney who'd handled the lawsuit against Leo's company would be representing Bernadine in the suit being brought against her by the city of Franklin. For the life of her, she still couldn't figure out how the Franklin powers that be expected to prevail with no evidence to support their claim, but she'd let him and Judge Davis sort it out on Monday. She and Edison were meeting to discuss strategy. With all that was going on, she was not happy about having to take the time to prepare for Mayor Wiggins and his silliness, but it couldn't be helped.

Lily looked at her watch. "Trent and I are supposed to pick

up the kids at the library in a few hours. I'll stop by the fire station and see if the chief's in, so I can get started on the trucks and all."

"Make sure you start looking for a car."

"Will do. Not being able to get around is not fun."

While Lily moved on, Bernadine waved good-bye to a few locals getting into their cars, then waited for Reverend Paula to finish her visiting. Once that was accomplished, they made the short walk up the street to the Power Plant.

In her office Bernadine gestured Paula to a seat, got coffee for both of them from the urn in the lobby, and after taking a seat at her desk, filled the reverend in on the past week's drama. She began with the visit of Preston's grandmother, then told her about the threatening calls, the Big Box mess with the city of Franklin, and the electronics lockdown earned by the kids. Only after did she relate the confrontations with Al and Odessa Stillwell.

Paula shook her head. "The devil's been a'dancing—as the old folks say."

"Up and down the street."

"Personally, I think trying to make amends with the Stillwells was the right thing to do, but we can't force people to accept our generosity, be it in spirit or in cash. And right now, the family is too angry and probably a bit scared, knowing what they're facing. Sometimes that makes people act in ways that aren't, shall we say, Christian. Jesus said love thy neighbor, not pull a shotgun on them."

Bernadine had been in dire need of a dose of the priest's up-front way of looking at life.

"Keep leading with your heart, Bernadine. Nothing wrong with that."

"You've helped me a lot."

"Then my job here is done," she said, smiling and getting to her feet. "I'm going home to catch up on my jet lag and finish my sermon for tomorrow's service."

"Thanks for listening."

"That's what I'm here for, and thanks for catching me up. Call me later, if you want."

A short while later, the lawyer Jim Edison arrived for their consultation on the Franklin lawsuit, and she gestured him to a chair.

"I saw the fire on the news. My condolences on the deaths."

She thanked him and got down to business. They spent the better part of an hour talking strategy. She was pleased that his evaluation of the suit mirrored hers—Franklin didn't have a leg to stand on.

When their conference concluded, he closed his laptop. "This will be a preliminary hearing, and it shouldn't rise to the level of a trial. Let's just hope the judge agrees."

"Judge Davis knows her stuff."

"I'll be counting on that." He stood. "I'm rooming at one of the hotels on 183 until after the hearing. If you need legal advice on any of this madness, give me a call."

Thankful for his offer, she watched him leave the office and turned to her computer to learn what she could about purchasing fire trucks.

At 4:00 P.M., Jack and Rocky rolled up to Trent's garage. They'd had such a good time on their first date looking at trucks that Jack had put a down payment on a sleek silver Chevy he planned to take possession of just as soon as he got rid of his sling. "Thanks for the help with the truck."

"No problem. Trucks, I know. Romance, not so much. You're going to have to be patient with me."

He liked her honesty. "I've plenty of that."

She leaned over and gave him a kiss.

"I had a great day, Professor."

"Me, too." He ran a slow finger down her cheek. "Talk to you later."

She drove away, and he walked inside.

"Hey, you made it," Trent said, smiling. Gary was with him.

"I did. Hey, Gary."

"Hey. Heard you and Rock went on a date."

"We did, and I even bought a truck."

Trent laughed. "What?"

"Silver Chevy. I'll pick it up soon as I can dump this sling."

"You know this makes you an official Henry Adams townie, right?"

"And I'm glad to be. So, what are we singing? Have you decided?"

Trent replied, "Thought we'd see who's got the strongest voice first and go from there. Sing something."

Jack paused to think about what song he'd do. With their eyes on him, he was admittedly a bit self-conscious, but he ignored that and began the opening lines to Bruce Springsteen's "My Hometown."

By the time he reached the bridge, both men looked impressed. He sang on, and when he was done and the last note faded away, they applauded.

Trent declared, "We have our lead singer, boys."

"Oh yeah," Gary said, chuckling and clapping.

"Hell of a voice, Mr. James."

Jack was embarrassed by the praise. "Thanks."

Trent said, "Now, let's find a song so we can win this Idol thing."

After a few minutes of back-and-forth, and viewing a bunch of old-school R&B male groups on YouTube via Trent's laptop, they narrowed it down.

"I say we go with the Temptations," Jack said.

The decision was unanimous. They decided on which song they'd do and, with help from the videos, began rehearsing.

CHAPTER
20

On Monday morning, Riley arrived at the courthouse and was pleased by all the activity going on out front. Chanting demonstrators carrying signs featuring Cletus's picture and slogans supporting his case marched up and down the sidewalk, while scores of media people took pictures and did interviews. Vans bearing the logos of news outlets from as far away as Lawrence were parked along the curb. Heather Quinn promised him FUFA would get Cletus some publicity, and damned if they hadn't. He'd paid particular attention to his attire for the hearing. His suit was cleaned and pressed, and he'd dusted off his fake red carnation and placed it in his lapel. In his mind the day would be a momentous one, and when it was over, he was certain he and his hog would be reunited and he'd need to look good on the national news.

After parking his truck in the lot, he got out. There stood Ms. Quinn, waiting for him, just as she'd said she'd be when they talked on the phone last night. He assumed the tall older woman with the short gray hair standing with her was the FUFA lawyer she'd also mentioned.

Quinn nodded a greeting. "Good morning, Mr. Curry. I want you to meet Pat Starks, our lawyer."

Riley shook her hand, and they exchanged a few pleasantries and began the walk to the courthouse. As they mounted the steps, they were swarmed by the press. Riley stopped to take questions, only to be pushed ahead by a strong hand he assumed belonged to the lawyer. "Mr. Curry has no comment at this time!" she announced crisply.

He glared at her over his shoulder. She glared right back, so he kept moving. As soon as the hearing was over, he planned on holding a press conference, whether she approved of him doing so or not.

The lobby was almost as crowded as it had been outside. There were no demonstrators marching around, but there were plenty of media folks, uniformed deputies, and a number of people lined up to take seats once the courtroom's doors were opened. He saw a contingent of Henry Adams people in the center of the line, chief among them his ex-wife Genevieve, who shot him a withering look, but he pretended not to know her and turned away. He assumed she'd be testifying on behalf of the county. He hoped she knew she had to tell the truth.

The doors opened a few minutes later, and everyone filed in. He took a seat at one of the tables up front with Heather and the unsmiling lawyer Starks, who leaned over and said, "Don't say anything unless you're directly asked, Mr. Curry."

Liking her less and less, he responded with a terse nod.

At the other table were the county people, and Dr. Keegan was with them. None of them said hello, so Riley didn't either and instead thought about the judge. Although he and Cletus had been on the lam at the time, he'd heard through the grapevine that the presiding judge for the hearing, Amy Davis, was the same judge who'd let Bernadine Brown's junior felons off the hook the night they carjacked Mal July's truck during their first summer in town. She'd also approved the legal adoptions of the little hoodlums by their bleeding-heart foster parents. Granted, none of that had anything to do with Cletus's case, but it made him think she might be more inclined to side against his hog because she obviously liked Ms. Brown and her people, and none of them liked Cletus. He was counting on Heather Quinn and the lawyer to make sure there was no judicial hanky-panky.

The court bailiff, a hefty woman in a brown uniform, made everyone stand, and Judge Davis entered the room. Davis took her seat, and those in attendance followed suit.

She looked around the packed courtroom. "Now, before we start these proceedings, let me say to the lawyers, since this is not a formal judicial hearing, I will allow some leeway, but I expect decorum from both sides at all times."

She then addressed the courtroom. "And anyone causing a ruckus will be escorted out. Am I clear?"

Everyone nodded, including the FUFAs wearing the pig masks and the ones sporting rubber hog noses.

"All right, the county may present its case for the euthanization of the hog owned by Mr. Curry."

"His name's Cletus, Your Honor," Riley called.

Snickers were heard.

"Thank you, Mr. Curry. Cletus," she said, amending herself.

The FUFA lawyer shot him a look of disbelief, but he ignored it.

The assistant prosecutor, a young man named Matt

Mingus, stood and laid out the facts surrounding the demise of Morton Prell. He referenced the coroner's report that found asphyxiation to be the cause of death. "Mr. Prell died from being crushed against the living room wall of the Currys' home by the hog. Here are pictures taken by the first respond-ers of how Mr. Prell looked when they entered the home."

"Did you give the defense copies of these?"

"Yes, Your Honor."

She viewed the three pictures of what Riley knew to be Cletus, lying against the wall with the dead Prell hanging over his back, limp as a rag doll. If the sight impacted the judge, it didn't show on her face.

Mr. Mingus continued. "The hog has a nasty temper, Your Honor, corroborated in the sworn statement of Mr. Curry's ex-wife, Mrs. Genevieve Curry."

He handed her the statement, and she looked out and said, "Mrs. Curry, stand, please."

As Genevieve complied, Riley's lip curled distastefully.

"This says the hog bit you. Was this often?"

"Yes, Your Honor. Very often."

"It was your perfume!" Riley cried, jumping to his feet in challenge.

Genevieve shouted back, "Say that to me one more time, Riley Curry, and I swear I'll hit you so hard, they'll find you in China!"

The cheers of her supporters were countered by FUFA boos, and the judge banged her gavel. "Quiet!"

You could hear a pin drop.

"Another outburst, and I'm clearing the courtroom."

When she seemed certain that everyone understood, she

turned her attention back to Genevieve. "Thank you, Ms. Curry. You may take your seat. Now, Mr. Mingus, why did the hog sit on Mr. Prell? Was it an accident?"

"He hit Cletus over the head with a chair leg," Riley told her before Mingus could reply. "And every sentient being has the right to defend itself when faced with violence."

He thought he saw a smile play at the edges of the judge's lips, but he felt pretty good having used the ten-dollar word.

"Is this true, Mr. Mingus?"

"We only have Mr. Curry's testimony. No one was there, Your Honor."

"I was there. Ask Mal July about the cuts on Cletus's head."

Judge Davis looked around until she spotted July. "Mr. July, is that true?"

It was easy to see that Mal stood reluctantly. "Yes, Your Honor. The hog had a series of wounds that were stitched up by the county vet after they transported him from the scene."

Davis asked Dr. Keegan, "Is that correct?"

"Yes, Your Honor." Keegan didn't look happy

The FUFA lawyer finally found an opening in which to say, "Your Honor, nasty temper or not, the hog was abused by Mr. Prell, and therefore entitled to defend itself."

Mingus argued, "The hog is a menace and a threat to public safety."

The judge asked, "Other than his penchant for biting, has the hog ever killed anyone before?"

"Not that the county is aware of," Mingus admitted.

"Mr. Curry?"

"No, ma'am, Your Honor. Never."

"Mr. Mingus, did you know about the stitches?"

"Yes, ma'am."

"Did you take them into consideration when you signed off on the euthanization documents?"

"No, ma'am. We didn't deem it necessary. He killed a man, Judge Davis."

"That's already been established, Mr. Mingus. But the court's issue is with the fairness of your decision."

Mingus didn't appear to have a response to that, and Riley wanted to cheer.

"Mr. Mingus, does the county have anything else to present before I render my verdict?"

Genevieve stood up and said angrily, "Judge Davis, because of Riley and that hog, I have no home! It was condemned. Where's the fairness in that!"

Judge Davis kept her face void of emotion. "The court would advise you to speak with a legal representative to explore your options, Ms. Curry."

Riley saw Genevieve plop down into her seat and fold her arms angrily. Again, he wanted to cheer, and stick his tongue out at her for good measure, but the bridge of his nose began to throb as if to remind him of what had happened the last time he did that, so he returned his attention to the judge.

"Does anyone have anything else?"

It appeared as if no one did, so she said, "My ruling is this: The county will surrender Cletus to Mr. Curry, and—"

The FUFAs began cheering. Riley jumped up and hugged Heather Quinn.

The judge was banging her gavel.

When silence returned, she finished. "On these conditions: The hog is forbidden to come in contact with the general public, and Mr. Curry, that means no community cookouts or parades or any other event where people gather. If you have to take Cletus anywhere, it has to be in your vehicle, and he must stay there. Any violations, and you will go to jail, Mr. Curry. Do you understand?"

"I do, Your Honor. Thank you!"

"You're welcome. The case of *The City of Franklin vs. Bernadine Brown* will begin in thirty minutes."

She banged the gavel to close the proceedings.

Riley was ecstatic. He thanked Heather Quinn once again, and all the FUFAs who'd supported him. As he stood there, receiving their congratulations, he saw Genevieve staring his way. He shot her a big grin and did stick out his tongue. She lunged but was restrained by Marie Jefferson. Riley grinned and let himself be swept out of the courtroom by the happy FUFAs.

Once they were outside on the steps, the press was waiting. Riley straightened his shoulders and took the first question.

Inside, Bernadine looked over at Mal, seated beside her. He shook his head before saying, "Guess Cletus isn't going to be on a spit after all."

"Guess not, but at least Judge Davis spared us from having to put up with him in town."

"Too bad the county didn't have a stronger case, but when you think about it, Judge Davis was right. You can't put an animal down for defending himself."

She sighed heavily. "Knowing Riley, he'll probably violate the no-contact order before the day's over. He's going to want to rub everyone's nose in it."

She saw Heather Quinn and the lawyer leaving the

courtroom. Quinn nodded her way, and Bernadine responded in kind. Although Bernadine wasn't happy with the court decision, she wished the young woman the best.

A few minutes later, Bernadine put Riley and his victory out of her mind, because it was her turn to stand before the judge. Edison joined her at the table Riley and his people had used previously, and she watched skeptically as Wiggins, his toupee, and the city of Franklin's attorney took their spot at the adjacent one.

Once Judge Davis was seated again, she glanced at the paperwork and said, "Mayor Wiggins, I don't have a copy of the contract you are referencing for this preliminary hearing."

Edison said, "Because there isn't one, Judge Davis."

She paused. "What do you mean, there isn't one?"

"Ms. Brown and the city of Franklin have never entered into any contracts of any kind."

"Then why are we here?"

"My client wishes the answer to that question as well."

She turned a steely eye to the city's attorney, a woman named Benson who looked extremely uncomfortable. "Your Honor, I tried to convince Mayor Wiggins that the city had no case, but he insisted—"

"Upon wasting the court's time?"

"Yes, ma'am."

Bernadine held on to her smile.

Judge Davis said, "Okay, Mayor Wiggins, why do you think the court should hear this so-called lawsuit?"

"It's about fairness, Your Honor. Ms. Brown, by refusing to aid the region in its quest to recover from the recent recession, is putting everyone in danger."

"How so?"

"A Big Box store would be a boost to our community, but she refuses to pay her share of the good-faith fees, so they are not going to build a store in Franklin."

Davis looked first at Bernadine and then back at Wiggins. "Now, let me get this straight. Did she previously agree to pay this share?"

"No," Edison responded before Wiggins could.

"Then, Mayor Wiggins, what do you want the court to do?"

"Make her pay. She has the money."

Judge Davis sat back for a moment and viewed Wiggins as if she couldn't believe the words coming out of his mouth. "You want me to make her pay?"

"Yes, for the good of the region."

His lawyer was looking off as if praying to be magically transported elsewhere.

"First of all, this is America, Mayor Wiggins, and no court in the land can *make* a person pay for something they're not contractually obligated to. Second, if you ever waste this court's time with something this ridiculous again, I will throw you in jail for contempt. Now, get out of my courtroom." She brought down her gavel, stood up, and left the bench without another word or a backward glance.

Edison glanced over at the smiling Bernadine. "Wish all my cases were this easy."

"Nice work, counselor."

"Thanks. I have to be in San Francisco in the morning for another client, so I'll be heading back to the airport."

"Safe travel."

He thanked her, shook hands with Mal, and was on his way.

The Franklin contingent left hastily. She hoped this would be the last confrontation with Wiggins, but knew that would be too good to be true. She looked out at all the Henry Adams citizens who'd accompanied her to show their support and said, "Let's go home."

On the ride back in Mal's truck, she said, "Hopefully things will get back to normal."

"Depends on how you describe normal. Personally, I'll just settle for all those pig masks getting the hell out of Dodge."

She would too. That and finding the person behind the fire in the rec parking lot.

Two days later, everyone in Henry Adams rode over to Franklin for the Sanderson funeral.

Although only a few people in town knew the couple personally, Bernadine felt it important that they go and pay their respects because of how and where they died. Standing beside Mal at the service, she looked around and saw everyone from Bing in his wheelchair and leg cast to the Henry Adams kids who'd been allowed out of school to attend. All were in their Sunday best, and it was her hope that the family appreciated the show of respect.

Later, after the trip to the cemetery, the mourners returned to the small Unitarian church for the traditional repast. Bernadine was pulled aside by Mike Sanderson's father.

"Ms. Brown, I want to thank you for coming."

"It was my way of showing how terrible we all feel, Mr. Sanderson."

"Thanks. Please call me Joel."

The father was tall and gray-haired, with lively green eyes. Having never met his son, she had no way of knowing if the two favored each other, but she sensed they did.

"Thanks also for your generous offer to pay for the twins'

last year in school. Mike and Peggy worked so hard to make sure their girls were able to attend college, but it's been a struggle the past year and a half, with Mike out of work."

"I'm glad to help." The deceased couple had twenty-year-old twin daughters, Megan and Marie. She'd met them earlier. "If there's anything else I can do to help to make the burden lighter, please don't hesitate to call."

He gave her a hug, his green eyes teary. "Thank you."

"My condolences," she said softly.

When he backed away, he wiped at his eyes. "I see my wife waving this way. She must have somebody over there she wants me to meet. So let me get going. Again, thanks for your generosity. You be blessed, Ms. Brown."

"You as well."

She was about to go seek out Mal and see if he was ready to head back to town when someone touched her arm.

"Ms. Brown?"

She turned to see a young woman she'd not met before. "Yes. Hello."

"Hi. I'm Freda Stillwell."

Bernadine stilled and prepared herself to be blasted by Freda's anger.

"I hear you'll be helping Megan and Marie with their tuition."

"Yes. Do you know the family well?"

"Mrs. Sanderson was my Girl Scout leader. I loved her a lot."

"My condolences."

"When my parents divorced. I spent a lot of time over at their house. Mrs. Sanderson helped me deal with a lot of stuff when my grandmother refused to let my mom take me with her when she and Dad split."

Bernadine found herself moved by the admission. "I offered to help with your tuition, too."

"I know. Gram told me, and she told me what she said. I'm sorry she was so nasty."

"You don't have to apologize."

"I feel like I do."

"Are you going to have to leave school?"

"Already have. At least for this semester, but I have a full-time job off campus, and I'm pretty sure I'll be able to get some money for the fall."

Bernadine felt infinitely better. "I'd never ask someone to go against their family, but if you want my help, just call me."

"Thanks, but I think I'm good. In fact, I know I am."

Bernadine found herself liking the young woman. "How's your dad?"

She shrugged. "He's gone to Oklahoma to see if he can find a job in the oil fields. I wouldn't worry about him."

Bernadine wasn't sure how she was supposed to take that. "Okay. Please keep in touch if you'd like."

She nodded. "Nice meeting you, Ms. Brown."

"Same here."

As Freda Stillwell made her way back across the crowded hall, Bernadine found herself thinking, How curious.

Riding back to town with Mal, she told him of her encounter with Freda and asked him for the story behind the custody fight.

"It was ugly. Al was never faithful, and Ann, his wife, had had it. She filed for the divorce, but Odessa threatened to tell the courts she was unfit."

"Was she?"

"Not that I know of, but then you don't always know the

real deal sometimes. Maybe Odessa had something on her, maybe not. Anyway, Ann left, and Freda stayed."

"That's sad."

"Yeah, it is. The family never mixed much. You didn't see them at picnics or anything like that, but when you did, Freda always looked sad. Felt real sorry for her."

"She said she'll have money for school in the fall."

"Good to know."

Bernadine thought so, too.

CHAPTER
21

As the last few weeks of April merged into the steady warmth of the month of May, things sort of quieted down in Henry Adams. Those who'd lost their vehicles in the parking lot fire scored new ones and were back on the road again. The security system was purchased and installed, but law enforcement still had no clue as to the arsonist's identity. Jack and Rocky were officially a couple, and now that his sling was gone, they were often tooling around in his new Chevy truck, christened the Silver Surfer by Eli. When they weren't tooling, they were working on the restoration of her Vincent Black Shadow over at Trent's garage. The We're So Slick Gang finished their papers and turned them in. Officially off lockdown, they were so grateful to have access to their electronics that they vowed to never put themselves in a position to be without them ever again.

The first thing Preston did on the day he was allowed to log back on was to check his e-mail. Waiting in the in-box was an unopened message from his grandmother, Lenore Crenshaw. Damn! He thought his parents and Ms. Bernadine had forbidden any further contact. Apparently the directive had gone in one ear and out the other. Knowing if he didn't open it, it would drive him crazy, he braced himself and clicked. It read simply: "Dr. Margaret Winthrop, NASA."

"What the hell's that supposed to mean?" he asked aloud.

He went downstairs and found his parents in the basement. They were dancing! The tango! He knew it was the tango because of the ballroom dancing contest he'd watched with his mom last winter on the public television station. He'd done it mainly to please her, and although he thought the whole thing dumb, and an activity only old people probably enjoyed, he'd filed it away in his brain because with Mr. James as his teacher, he never knew what the next assignment might be.

But there they were, doing all the leaning and posing and twirling around to the weird music that apparently went with the dance. His mom even had on some of the old-fashioned high-heeled shoes the ladies in the contest had worn. It was obvious they didn't know he was in the room, so he waited and watched, especially his pops. He wondered how and where he'd learned to dance. Preston was pretty sure it wasn't part of the marine boot-camp regimen. The colonel was posed up like a bullfighter and looked both strong and powerful going through the steps. His mom was snapping her head back and forth, and he liked the way she smiled up into the colonel's face, too. Her eyes sparkled with enjoyment.

The music ended, and Preston clapped and entered the room. They both looked surprised and then bowed.

"You guys are good. I never knew you liked to dance."

His mom nodded. "We haven't done it in a while, but I've missed it."

"So have I," his dad said, beaming down.

Preston got the impression that they'd gotten a lot closer lately, and he liked that.

"We're rehearsing for the Idol contest," she said.

That surprised him almost as much as seeing them dancing.

"And I think we can win. No one else is going to be doing the tango, far as I know."

Preston was pretty sure he was right. He couldn't imagine what the audience would think when they saw them, and being a teenager, he wondered whether he'd be embarrassed by their performance, but he told himself that them doing something together they enjoyed overrode any potential personal issues he might have. "Need your help with something. Do you know who Dr. Margaret Winthrop is?"

"She's your birth mother," his pops said, looking a bit wary. "Where'd you get the name?"

"My grandmother. There was an e-mail from her when I logged on just now. From the date, looks like she sent it right after she was kicked out of town."

His mom sighed angrily. "Why would she do that, knowing her daughter doesn't want contact? That's so cruel."

He thought so too, but then again, his grandmother had shown herself to be that way the day she visited. This was just another example. "Does she really work for NASA?"

"Yes. She's an astrophysicist."

His eyes widened.

His mom searched his face with serious eyes. "Please don't contact her, Preston. She doesn't want it, and I don't want you to be hurt, thinking you can change that."

Sadness rose inside to replace the elation. She was right, of course, but he wished she weren't. "Is it okay if look her up on the Net? I just want to know what she looks like."

His father said, "Sure, no harm in that, and wanting to know is natural."

"Thanks."

With concern in her voice, his mom asked, "Are you okay?"

"I guess, but like you said, sending me her name was real cruel."

They nodded understandingly.

"I'm going over to Amari's for about an hour for our Idol practice."

"How's the James Brown revue going?"

"Don't ask. Amari thinks Devon's insane, and I do too." Preston wasn't looking forward to the rehearsal or the competition. "Are you two still coming to watch the asteroid shower with our class in the morning?"

"Wouldn't miss it for the world. Thought we'd leave here around three thirty," the colonel said.

Everyone was meeting out at Tamar's because there were fewer lights there than anywhere else, especially now that the solar lights were all over town. "I'm going to bed soon as I get back. See you later. I liked the dancing."

Up in the room, Preston stared at the name he'd printed out. He wanted to Google it right then so badly, but James Brown and the other Flames were waiting. He went across the street, and Trent let him in. "They're in the basement. Just follow the sound of your boy fussing."

Preston hadn't any idea what that meant, but while going down the basement steps he heard, "Mom, I'm *not* wearing a wig!"

Entering the finished basement with its big-screen TV and

comfortable seating, Preston saw the mutiny on Amari's face, the determination on Devon's, and the humor on Eli's. Ms. Lily was saying, "One day you're going to need Devon's help with something, Amari."

"I'll bet it won't involve wearing a wig. Come on, Mom. Why are you encouraging this crap?"

"It isn't crap. Once you get into it, it's going to be fun. Promise."

"Bull—I mean, no, it's not!"

Ms. Lily shook her head and smiled.

Eli said, "Oh, stop whining and just put the thing on."

They finally noticed Preston standing there, and Amari asked, "Do you want to wear a wig?"

Wig! Nobody said anything about wearing wigs!

But Eli was in front of the mirror on the wall, putting his on and cracking up. "I look like Elvis."

Ms. Lily held out a black hairy thing for Preston to take that resembled something he'd seen on the heads of the old ladies riding the bus back in Milwaukee. He took it only because she was an adult and he had to, but he had no intentions of putting it on his own head.

Devon tugged his on, and Ms. Lily began styling it with a comb.

Eli, still enjoying his reflection in the mirror, looked puzzled for a moment. "How's that song go? Oh, yeah"—he sang out loudly—"Viva Las Vegas!"

Amari grumbled, "You don't look like Elvis. You just look ridiculous."

Preston thought he looked a lot like Fred Munster.

Trent came down, took one look at the boys, and immediately went back up the steps, laughing uproariously.

Amari yelled, "No fair laughing, Dad! This shit's not funny."

"Amari . . . ," his mom warned.

"It's not!"

Preston realized that if Amari surrendered, he'd have to as well, and suddenly his worries about being embarrassed by his parents doing the tango were superseded by the reality of his own public embarrassment. If he had known this was the cruise he'd signed on for, he would've cashed in his ticket and let the ship sail without him.

In the end, Amari donned his wig, and Preston did the same.

Eli laughed. "Now we all look like Eddie Murphy in *Dreamgirls*."

"Shut up!" Amari snapped.

Preston hadn't gone anywhere near the mirror and had no intentions of doing so. He already knew how wack he looked.

Devon was beaming under his wig, however. Pretending he had a microphone in his hand, he bent over and sang, "Please, please, don't go." He then did a few of James Brown's swift-footed moves and grinned.

Amari looked like he wanted to make him eat the imaginary mic, and Preston wasn't far behind.

Devon asked, "Is Ms. Genevieve through making my cape?"

"Almost," his mom replied. "Okay, Eli. Your turn."

While Preston looked on, Ms. Lily took the comb and scissors to Eli's black wig. Preston had no idea where she'd gotten the fake hair, but he wished he knew, so he could return his. When she was done with all the cutting and the curling iron, Eli had a pompadour that the old guy Little Richard would have been proud of. Eli went back to the mirror and grinned from ear to ear. He picked up his phone and passed it to Preston.

"Here, take a picture. I want to send it to my dad."

Preston couldn't imagine why Eli was so into this madness, but he took the pic and gave the phone back.

It was Amari's turn to get styled next, and he wore an angry face the entire time his mom worked on him. Once he had his pompadour, he got up and sat down heavily on the couch.

"You're looking good, Amari," Devon said.

"Get away from me," Amari snarled.

Preston was last and endured the process without comment. The wig was hot, however. He felt like he was wearing a blanket on his head.

"All done, Brain. Go look."

"I'd rather not. Can I take it off now?"

"Hold on a minute."

She retrieved three wig stands from the table and passed them out. "Put them on here when you're not wearing them."

Preston immediately raised his hands to his and was told, "But don't snatch them off. Be gentle."

So he gently removed the stupid thing from his head and set it on the faceless wig stand. They were supposed to be rehearsing too, but he'd had enough trauma for one evening. "Okay. We have to get up early to see the asteroids, so I'm going home and going to bed."

Devon protested, "But we're supposed to practice."

Amari removed his wig and started for the stairs. Preston was sure Amari was going to respond with a certain two-word phrase Preston thought highly appropriate considering the hell Devon was putting them through, but Amari didn't respond, probably because he didn't want to go back on lockdown.

"But Mom!" Devon whined like the brat he could sometimes be as Amari disappeared.

"Give it a rest, Dev," Ms. Lily replied. "You have a whole month and a half before the contest. There's plenty of time to rehearse. Leave your brother alone for now."

He was pleased to hear her tell Devon to step back. Now if she could just be convinced to tell him to forget about the whole thing, he and Amari would be happy, but he knew that wasn't happening.

He said his good-byes. Carrying his pompadour on the wig stand, he left the July house to return to the sanity of his own.

Back upstairs in his room, he Googled his birth mother's title and name, and a lot of links popped up. For the next hour he read everything he could about the famous astrophysicist who'd given him up for adoption, and when he was done, he was quite impressed. She was a very well-known scientist. After all the searching, reading, and clicking on links, he hadn't found a picture of her, so he still didn't know what she looked like; he did find the phone number of her office, however. He wrote it down and went to bed.

The very sleepy Bernadine couldn't believe she'd agreed to get up before the crack of dawn to go and sit in an open field and watch a meteor shower, but she had. Although she wanted to go back to bed, a part of her was excited. This would be her first time participating in such an event, and from what she'd been hearing from her friends and neighbors, they'd never done anything like this either. The gathering was another example of Jack James's topical teaching; they were all so lucky to have him as the community's teacher.

She tiptoed around getting dressed because Crystal was

still asleep and she didn't want to wake her. The town's oldest princess refused to get up at such an ungodly hour, extra credit or not, and Bernadine didn't force the issue. There were going to be a lot of more important things the two of them would butt heads over before she grew up and went out into life on her own, so Bernadine refused to sweat the small stuff.

Dressed, she went downstairs and got coffee and a bowl of cereal. As soon as she was done eating, and the caffeine kicked in, she called Mal to let him know she was ready to be picked up.

While waiting, she tried not to think about the work waiting for her at the office, but it took her over anyway. The fire trucks were on order. When Lily initially spoke with the Franklin fire chief, he'd agreed to help them out, but when Bernadine called him a few days later, he told her Mayor Wiggins had threatened to fire him if he did. The memory made her shake her head again, but instead of sending a hit man after Piggly Wiggly, she'd contacted the fire department over in Lawrence, and so far they'd been very forthcoming and generous in offering suggestions and answering the dozens of questions she and her people had about putting together a department for Henry Adams. She'd be calling their chief later today with more questions about building a structure to house the two trucks she'd purchased.

The police were done with the rec's parking lot, and replacement had already begun. New lights were also on order, scheduled to arrive by week's end. That there was still a murdering arsonist on the loose was disturbing. Sheriff Dalton said the person might be holed up somewhere, content to gloat over the terror and never strike again, or planning a second act. She didn't like either scenario, but liked the latter the least. Her reward for information leading to the arrest and conviction of the person responsible, widely publicized, had resulted in a few tips, but so far none were of any substance.

A short toot of a horn signaled Mal's arrival, so she put all that away for now and left the house in anticipation of having a good time.

And a good time was had by all. The predawn air was quite chilly, so Rocky had coffee on hand for the adults and hot chocolate for the children.

"Can you believe all these people?" she asked Mal, keeping her voice low. All around them people were engaged in hushed conversations, as if not wanting to disturb the darkness.

"This is something," he replied, glancing around.

Everywhere one looked, flashlights and small lanterns spotlighted people seated on blankets, air mattresses, and lawn chairs. There were couples both old and young, families with little kids, off to the side a whole section of the Dog's college-age waitstaff with their friends.

Mal cracked, "I hope they know Tamar won't be letting them use her bathroom."

She chuckled and quieted along with everyone else as Jack stood in the glow of a flashlight and began an explanation of what they'd all be seeing.

When he was done, the lights were doused, and all eyes were trained on the sky.

The shower began rather slowly, but soon the gathering began seeing ten and fifteen streaks of light every few min-utes, and as the spectacle gained speed and oohs and ahhs could be heard, she wondered how many wishes were being made on all the falling stars. She offered up a few wish-filled prayers of her own for those she loved, and for all the children around the world eking out lives under the boot of poverty, wars, and abuse.

As the day moved closer to dawn, there were fewer and fewer sightings, the signal for everyone to pack up and head home. They could now all say they'd witnessed a meteor shower, particularly the one known as Eta Aquarid.

While everyone out at Tamar's drifted off to work, the Dog, and in some cases back to bed, Riley Curry was up making breakfast for himself and Cletus. He was so happy to have his hog back home where he belonged, he'd let Cletus sleep inside on the floor beside Riley's bed. That privilege lasted only long enough for Riley to get out of bed one morning a few days later and step barefooted into one of Cletus's surprises, so from that night forward the hog slept outside in the hog house Eustasia had commissioned for Cletus and Chocolate to occupy. It was equipped with a sleeping area, a large sunken tub filled with mud for wallowing, and a wall-size high-def television that showed the Animal Planet twenty-four hours a day, every day.

And that's was what Cletus was watching when Riley entered, carrying a huge dog bowl filled with rice cereal and milk. While Cletus ate noisily, Riley reflected on all the good things that had come out of the trial. For one, the media requests had gone through the roof in the days following Cletus's release. Major newspapers and weekly magazines of all kinds and from all over the world competed to be the first to show Cletus on their cover. Thanks to a tip from one of the people in Heather Quinn's office, he knew what to charge for the privilege and had amassed a sizable amount of money as a result. Then there were the letters from the schoolchildren, both national and international, asking for autographed pictures of Cletus in his camouflage gear and Ray-Bans. With the aid of the money paid to him by the media outlets, he'd brought in a professional photographer to take pics of his hog in various outfits. He also found an ink stamp featuring a hog's hoofprint on the Internet and used it to "sign" the pictures before sending them out.

Cletus was quite the sensation, and in Riley's opinion well worthy of all the fuss and acclaim. The only place Cletus wasn't a celebrity was in his hometown of Henry Adams. No one had come by to congratulate Riley on the court victory. He'd tried to call Eustasia down in Texas to let her know how proud Cletus looked, strutting out of the county pen when Riley came to take him home again, but the maid said Eustasia wasn't taking any calls. A man of lesser confidence might have been upset by the lack of charity, but not Riley; the phone call he'd received yesterday was going to make him and his hog the envy of everyone around. Just as soon as Cletus was done eating, he was going to put him in the bed of the new red truck he'd purchased and drive to the Dog for some breakfast of his own. While there, he planned to make the announcement that would make them all wish they'd treated him better, especially old hateful Genevieve.

Upon entering the Dog, Riley heard the loud music and saw Mal July behind the counter at the cash register. July looked up suspiciously. "What can I do for you, Riley?"

"I came for breakfast."

"Sure. Follow me."

As Riley was taken to one of the empty center tables, the other diners gave him the eye. He saw Bernadine Brown sitting with Lily July, the laughing junior felons in a booth in the back, and Trent July seated with the teacher and the loser Gary Clark. He also noticed Genevieve seated with Marie Jefferson at a booth on the far side of the room. She glowered at him as always, but even though he ignored her, he was glad she was there to hear his grand announcement straight from the horse's mouth.

As he looked over the menu, he hoped someone would come over and chitchat or ask how Cletus was enjoying being back home, but no one did, so he gave the waitress his order and waited for his food to come.

It arrived a short while later, and with Genevieve's hostile eyes watching his every move, he ate his breakfast. When he was done, he stood up and tapped his knife on his water glass to get everyone's attention. Because of the music, it took a second or two for them to look his way. Luckily, the song on the jukebox ended just at that moment, so he said, "I'd like to make an announcement."

He saw Mal July watching him with narrowed eyes, so Riley asked, "Can you stop the music for just a moment, Mal?"

A few boos were heard, and it was obvious that July didn't want to comply with the request, but he did and the diner was silent. Glad to see that everyone was now focused on him, especially Genevieve, he said, "This town won't have me and Cletus to kick around for a while. We—"

Cheers and applause filled the room before he could complete what he planned to say. "Would you let me finish!" he yelled.

Laughter followed his outburst, and the room went quiet again until someone shouted, "Hurry up, Riley. We don't have all day!"

He gathered himself again. "I got a call yesterday from a major Hollywood producer who wants to put Cletus in films."

Mal asked, "Is that it?"

A voice yelled, "Turn the box back on, Mal!"

This was not going the way Riley envisioned. He'd been expecting awe and envy, not disinterest, and certainly not disdain. In an attempt to regain his momentum, he added, "And Cletus is going to make me the richest man in Kansas!"

Genevieve countered drily, "And when that happens, make sure you use some of that money to hire you a top-notch lawyer, because I'm suing you for embezzlement, mental anguish, destruction of property, and anything else I can think of."

More cheers erupted. The music came back on, and an angry Riley snatched up his bill and went to the cash register to pay it. Storming back to where he'd parked his truck, he started it up and drove away. He got the last word, he figured; he hadn't left a tip.

CHAPTER
22

After breakfast, Preston, Leah, and Amari left the Dog and walked down Main to spend the day at the rec. Because they were on school break, they were going to shoot some hoops, play chess, and maybe watch a Mummy marathon on the big screen in the auditorium. On the way, they talked about the awesome meteor shower and then Mr. Curry's announcement.

"Who would be stupid enough to put that dumb pig in a movie?" Amari asked.

Preston certainly didn't know. "Especially since Mr. Curry acts like he's a few fries short of a Happy Meal."

"I sort of feel sorry for him, though," Leah confessed.

"Why?" Preston asked, surprised.

"He doesn't have anybody but Cletus."

Amari asked, "Do you know what he let that pig do to Ms. Genevieve's house? I don't feel sorry for him one bit."

"I don't either," Preston added. "The first summer we moved here, he kept calling us members of the FFA."

"What's the FFA?" Leah asked.

"Future Felons of America."

"Oh."

"Man's a nut job, and so is his killer hog," Amari said, summing things up.

When they reached the rec, they checked in with Tamar and Marie and then went down to the gym.

"Got something I need to talk to you two about," Preston said once they were inside.

Amari asked, "The colonel acting dumb again?"

They took seats on the bleachers.

"No, it's my birth mom."

For the next few minutes, he told them the story of how he learned her name and what he found out about her on the Net.

"And she's a NASA astrophysicist? Wow, that's sweet," Leah gushed.

"I really want to contact her."

Amari shook his head. "You can't, man. No contact means no contact."

Preston had prepared himself to hear that, but it wasn't what he wanted to hear. "I have her office phone number, too," he revealed for the first time.

"Brain, you're just going to get your feelings hurt. Just leave it alone, okay?" Amari pleaded.

In his mind, Preston knew that, but in his heart . . . "Okay. I just wanted to get your opinions."

Amari said, "Which means, you're going to get in touch with her anyway, aren't you?"

Surprised by how well Amari knew him, he confessed quietly, "Yes."

The serious concern on Leah's face made the feelings he had for her fill his chest. She looked as if she didn't want him to be hurt either.

Amari gazed out over the empty gym for a moment and then looked into Preston's eyes. "Then go for it, and I hope it works out for you. I really do."

Preston sensed Amari was thinking about his own situation, and the no-contact message his birth mom had sent to him via Griffin July last fall. Although Amari was a master at hiding his true feelings, Preston knew he was still hurting inside. "I'll let you know how it turns out. Let's go get the balls."

That night around 1:00 A.M., Preston picked up his phone. Punching in the numbers to Dr. Winthrop's office, he waited for the call to go through. He'd chosen this particular time because he was sure to get her answering machine. He didn't want to bother her, but he did want to leave a message, and once he finished saying what he wanted to say, he'd never contact her again.

The machine came on, and for a moment he was so nervous and tongue-tied, he hung up. It was like the mess he'd made out of trying to talk to Leah about being his girl all over again. Taking in a deep breath to calm himself, he gathered his courage and dialed the number again. When the machine kicked in, he waited for the beep and said, "Hi, Dr. Winthrop, my name's Preston Mays. I know you don't want to hear from me, but I just wanted to leave you a message, and I promise I'll never bother you again. I'm not mad at you for not keeping me. I'm having a real good life. My parents love me a lot, and I love them." He could feel emotions starting to rise inside, so he kept talking. "I love physics too, and one day when I'm older I'm going to make you and my parents very proud."

He cleared his throat around the tears. "I'm going to be officially adopted soon, but I'm not changing my name. Even though I never met my birth dad, I plan to be Preston Mays Payne out of respect." Plowing on, he whispered, "And thanks for having me—otherwise, I wouldn't be here."

He ended the call, dragged his hands over his wet eyes, and burrowed into the bedding to go to sleep.

Miles away in Florida, Dr. Winthrop was working late. When she walked into her office and saw the light flashing on the answering machine, she hit the button and sat down at her desk to go over the notes she'd made for the briefing to-morrow. But as the caller introduced himself, she froze. Staring at the machine, she listened in shock. When the voice of her son faded away and the office was once again still, she realized there were tears running down her cheeks. With a shaking hand she replayed the message, and this time, when it ended, she put her head in her hands and wept from both pain and joy.

A few days later, a large package arrived at the Payne household via FedEx. It was addressed to Preston. While his parents looked on curiously, an equally curious Preston opened it. The hardware packaged inside left him stunned. "It's a telescope!"

There was also an envelope with his name on it. "Did you buy me this?" he asked, opening the note, but when he saw the NASA letterhead, he started to shake.

His pops asked, "You okay?"

He showed them the letterhead, and his mom's hand flew to her mouth.

"I know I wasn't supposed to call her, but I left a message on her answering machine. I didn't think she'd do this."

"What's the note say?"

He read it aloud, "Dear Preston. Every budding astrophysicist needs good equipment. Dr. M. Winthrop." It was short and sweet and way more than he ever dreamed he'd get as a response to his call. "Is it okay if I keep it?"

"Of course," the colonel told him. "It was sent in good faith and should be accepted in the same way. Do you agree, Sheila?"

"Yes." She walked over and peered down at the pieces. "Are you going to be able to put it together?"

"I'm going to call Leah to help me. She has a telescope at home."

The colonel nodded. "Then go ahead. You're probably going to want to use it as soon as it gets dark."

The elated Preston looked at his parents. "Are you mad at me for calling her?"

"Water under the bridge, son, and it turned out well. Can't be upset with that."

He was thankful for their understanding. "I told her I had a family that I loved a lot."

His mom said, "And we love you a lot."

"I told her that, too."

His dad grinned and said, "Call Leah."

Leah's dad dropped her off a short while later, and the colonel promised to bring her home after dark.

As they moved the box out onto the deck and viewed all the pieces, Leah said excitedly, "This piece is top-of-the-line, boyfriend."

Preston's head shot up in response to that last word. "What?"

"Nothing."

"You sure?"

He nodded. "Let me go get my laptop so we can download the manual and the registration form."

Upstairs in his room, he picked up the laptop and prayed his feelings for Leah didn't make him say something stupid.

Even with Leah's knowledgeable help, it took them almost two hours to put the scope together and get it properly mounted on the tripod that came with it. He was impressed by Leah's mechanical knowledge and the ease with which she handled the screwdrivers and ratchet set. When it was finally done, they both stood back and looked at it with pride.

"We have ignition, Houston," she said, smiling.

Preston was so happy he felt like he might burst. He had his first, very own telescope, and it had been sent by his famous scientist birth mom. How awesome was that! Equally as awesome was the fact that Leah'd helped him put it together, and every time he used it, he'd think of her. He was going to name the telescope after her, too, but planned to keep that to himself. He didn't want her to think he was dumb. "Thanks, Leah. I'd be still trying to put it together if you hadn't helped."

"You're welcome. We make a pretty good team."

"Yeah, we do. The best."

She was looking at him, and he was looking at her. He could feel the words he'd been wanting to say to her for weeks start to bubble up.

She spoke first. "I have a question for you."

"Shoot."

"Why do I feel like there's something you've been wanting to ask me?"

He froze, and his brain did the same. "Um."

She turned away and leaned on the deck rail and gazed out at the open field. "Never mind. I'm probably just imagining it. Sorry."

"No. You're right," he hastily replied.

She faced him again. "Am I?"

"Yeah. It's like this. I want to ask you if you'd be my girl, but I've never asked anyone before, so I don't know what I'm supposed to say or how."

To his surprise, she gave him a smile. "It's not like I've had a whole lot of practice being asked, so that makes us even, I think."

Emboldened by her confession, he said, "I like you a lot, Leah."

"I like you a lot, too, Preston."

He wanted to jump up on the top rail and let the world know how happy he was. "So, can we be boyfriend and girl-friend?"

"Just as soon as you talk to my dad, we can."

"Your dad?" he croaked.

"Yeah. He told me any boys that want to be more than friends have to come talk to him about it first."

"Why?"

She shrugged. "One of those old-school things, I think. He said, any boy who was serious about me should have enough courage to do that."

Preston doubted he'd able to spell *courage*, let alone find enough to talk to Mr. Clark about his feelings for Leah. Not that Mr. Clark wasn't a good guy, but this whole thing had become way more complicated than he'd ever envisioned. She was waiting for him to make a decision, though. "Okay. I'll talk to your dad."

"Good."

His mom appeared at the screen door. "You two ready for dinner?"

He said they were, but his stomach was suddenly all knotted up at the prospect of talking to Leah's dad and he doubted he'd be able to eat a thing, but he did because she'd made her off-the-hook spaghetti.

After dinner, he and Leah cleaned up the kitchen, and when they were done, he said to her, "I need to talk to my pops for just a minute."

"That's fine. I'll be out here, looking at the manual."

His parents were in the living room, watching the evening news. "Pops, can I talk to you about something real quick?"

"Sure. What's up?"

"Um . . . alone. No offense, Mom, but it's guy stuff."

"No offense taken. How about I go keep Leah company until you two are done?"

"Thanks, Mom. She's out on the deck."

After her departure, Preston gave his dad a quick rundown on the situation.

The colonel's initial response was, "Good for Gary. I like that."

"I don't. I'm scared to death."

"Just be yourself, and answer any questions he has as truthfully as you can."

"That's all?"

"Yes. Gary knows you're a good kid. I'm sure he'll be pleased that Leah's going to be with someone as levelheaded and smart as she is. I know I would be, were she my daughter."

"Then do you mind waiting around after we take her home, so I can to talk to him tonight?"

"Not a bit, and I'll be pulling for you."

"Thanks."

"No problem."

Preston and Leah had a great evening. Their excitement over the telescope quadrupled as they took close-up looks at the night sky. "The moon looks so close I feel like I could reach out and touch it," he told her, looking into the eyepiece.

"That's an awesome telescope. The one we have at home, Dad picked up at a flea market. It's in good shape, but it's Jurassic compared to yours."

For the next hour they took turns peering at the moon and the nearby constellations and being amazed. And then it was time for her to go home. He didn't want her to go, though. He'd really enjoyed having her over and wished she could visit all the time.

"Thanks for letting me come over," she said as she opened the screen so he could carry the telescope inside.

"Thanks for helping me put it together." He set the tripod down in the kitchen. Later, he'd take it up to his bedroom. "Well, let's go so I can talk to your dad."

On the ride, they were so busy being excited about the astronomy books they wanted to get and how tight the telescope was, Preston forgot all about his talk with her father. But as soon as the colonel pulled up into the Clark driveway, the knots took over again.

They got out, and while Leah headed to the door, his pops said, "Good luck, and by the way, the first rule of impressing a girl's father is to escort his daughter to the door."

Damn! "Leah, hold up. Thanks!" he said hastily and hurried to catch up to her before she reached the porch.

He was at her side when she opened the door and stepped in.

Her father was up on a ladder, changing a lightbulb in the fixture in the front hall. "You two have a good time?" he asked as he reattached the glass globe by tightening the small screws.

"We did," Leah said, holding on to the ladder until he finished and climbed down. "His telescope is so sweet. The view is oh my goodness."

Her dad chuckled. "Thanks for having her over, Preston, and thank Barrett for me for bringing her home."

"I will. Um, can I talk to you about something before I leave?"

He folded the ladder and set it against the wall. "Sure, what is it?"

Leah said, "Bye, Preston," and hurried up the stairs and out of sight.

Her father viewed her hasty departure curiously before turning his attention back to Preston.

"Um, sir."

Mr. Clark raised an eyebrow, but Preston did his best to ignore it. "I—really—"

Mr. Clark crossed his arms over his chest. "You really what?"

Preston gathered his courage and said firmly, "I'd really like to ask Leah to be my girlfriend, but she said I had to talk to you about it first."

Preston saw the surprise that flashed in Mr. Clark's eyes and then the scrutiny that followed. "How old are you, Preston?"

"Fourteen, almost fifteen."

"Leah can't date until she's sixteen."

"I understand, but I can't drive until I'm sixteen, so it's not like I can take her anywhere, sir."

He thought Mr. Clark smiled, but he couldn't be sure.

"I admire your courage, Preston, and your character. Let me talk to Leah first, and then I'll let you know."

Preston hadn't envisioned this part about having to wait, either, but his only option was to say, "Okay, thanks. Good night."

"Good night."

Preston forced himself not to look toward the stairs that led to the second floor as he made his exit.

When he got back into the truck, he fell back against the seat from trauma and disappointment.

His father backed down the drive and steered the truck in the direction of home. "How'd it go?"

"He said he had to talk to Leah and let me know," he answered gloomily.

"At least he didn't tell you flat-out no."

"I guess."

"Gary's just being a good dad. If you have a daughter, you'll probably do the same thing."

"No, I won't, because I'm going to remember how it felt to be under the spotlight."

His father chuckled, "And I'm going to remind you of this conversation if and when you do have a daughter, so count on it."

When they got home, Preston carried the telescope upstairs and set it in his bedroom by the door that led out to his small deck. He was still amazed that he'd received the awesome gift, and he wondered if he'd hear from his birth mom again. He also wondered how long it might take Mr. Clark to say yes or no, but he supposed his pops was right, Mr. Clark hadn't said no right off the bat. Taking out his phone, he sent

Amari a text inviting him over; five minutes later, Amari walked in the door.

"Hey, Brain, what's up?"

He told him first about Leah and having to talk to her father.

Amari shook his head. "Nope. If I have to go through all that, I'm not having a girlfriend. I didn't know you had to talk to a girl's father first."

"I didn't either. Pops said it's an old-school thing."

"Was that the big news you sent the text to me about?"

"Yes, but I got some other big news. See my new telescope?"

"Oh, wow. That is tight."

Amari walked over and checked it out. "Your parents got this for you?"

"No. My birth mom." In that moment, Preston wasn't sure he should have shared that. Amari went still, and had the oddest look on his face.

"Your birth mom?"

"Yeah. I just wanted you to see it. Didn't mean to make you sad and stuff about your own mom."

Amari waved him off. "I'm good. I think it's awesome that contacting her worked out. Now come show me how this thing works."

Before they could begin, Preston's phone sounded. He checked the message. It was from Leah, and all it said was: "YES!!!"

Amari looked at his smiling face. "What?"

"Leah's dad said yes!"

"Way to go, Brain!"

They exchanged a high five.

Amari cracked, "Next thing you know, you're going to be booking the Dog for your wedding reception."

Preston rolled his eyes and laughed. "Yeah, right." But he felt good.

Bernadine had had a long day, and now, driving home from her last meeting—an update at Tamar's on how to best schedule the rehearsal times at the school's kiva and the rec auditorium for the people in the Idol contest who wanted access—she was glad the day was done. The evening's meeting was one of the few pre-Idol work sessions she'd had to attend; Tamar, Sheila, and their crew had everything in order, and she thanked heaven for them. Their efficiency freed her to concentrate on more pressing issues, like arranging for Gary Clark to pay calls on some of the region's large food distributors next week and going over the final blueprints for their firehouse. She and Trent decided on a volunteer fire department for the present, but that involved getting the volunteers recruited and then trained.

It was a nice night, and the starry sky she saw through her windshield reminded her of the asteroid viewing a few days ago. Jack said there'd been lots of interest in having a similar event, so he'd be holding another during the summer.

There hadn't been another vehicle in sight on the long, deserted stretch between Tamar's and the Dog, but now she spotted lights coming up behind her. In case the other car was in a hurry, she pulled closer to the shoulder to let it pass, but instead of going by the vehicle rammed her. Her head rocked back, and a split second later she was scrambling to keep her truck on the road. She was struck again and she hit the sync on her dash and screamed, "Mal! Some idiot—"

Hit again, she cried out in panic and fear as the truck went barreling down into the ditch, clipped the tall grass, bounced as it hit a low spot, flipped, came down on its cab, and skidded a few yards to a stop. The last thing she remembered was hearing Mal's voice yelling, "Baby girl! What's wrong! Bernadine!"

Bernadine opened her eyes, but she was so groggy it was a chore to keep them open. She was in a dimly lit room but didn't know where or why. Then she saw Mal and Crystal standing beside her. She wanted to ask what was going on, but her eyes fluttered closed again, and she drifted back into the black.

When she surfaced again, she had no idea how much time had passed, but she saw Mal asleep in a chair and Crystal watching her from another. She tried to call her, but her throat was so dry it was difficult to form the words.

Crys walked over and gently stroked her forehead. Bernadine could tell she'd been crying. A straw touched her lips, and she drew on it until cool water flooded her mouth and throat. "Where am I?" Her voice sounded raspy.

"Hospital. You were in an accident."

Suddenly Mal was standing there too. "Hey, you," he called softly. "Welcome back."

Her foggy brain was still processing the word *accident* when suddenly it all came flooding back. "Somebody ran me off the road."

Crystal had tears running down her cheeks. "Sheriff Will is looking for them."

"Are you okay?" Bernadine asked her daughter. She dearly wanted to soothe the fear and sadness in her eyes, but she could barely move.

"I'm okay," Crystal replied reassuringly, and gently stroked Bernadine's forehead again.

Mal said, "All those blessings you've been passing out paid off. Doc said there's not a scratch on you. You have some bumps and bruises, and your neck and back are going to be pretty sore for a while, but you'll be able to go home maybe as early as tomorrow. They want to keep you around for observation just to make sure, though."

Some of her anxiety diminished. "How's my truck?"

"Pretty much totaled," he told her.

"So I have to buy *another* truck?"

"Looks that way, but you were lucky. Trent and I found you just a few minutes after you crashed. It could've caught fire, anything, especially if you'd been out on the highway or some other place far away from home."

"Was the other truck still there?"

He shook his head. "But there were was glass and pieces of the truck all over the road. It sustained a lot of damage. Dalton's put a notice to all the body shops in the county, so if that truck shows up, he'll know."

Bernadine realized she was even more tired than she'd been earlier.

Seemingly sensing this, Crystal said, "Go back to sleep. OG and I will be here with you until they let us take you home." Crys bent and hugged her as best she could, and the kiss she placed on Bernadine's cheek eased her back into oblivion.

CHAPTER 23

Bernadine's accident was the talk of the town, and when she was released from the hospital a few days after the crash, she came home to a house so packed with flowers that her living room looked like a florist shop. She was sore and bruised all over, but not so much that the outpouring of goodwill the flowers represented didn't have an impact.

"Wow!" she whispered as Mal helped her ease down onto the sofa. There were roses and lilies and vases of colorful snapdragons standing next to others holding daisies, zinnias, and gorgeous blooms she didn't know the names of.

A smiling Crystal said, "There's a bunch in your bedroom, too. I started running out of places to put them."

"I can see why." Her back was aching something fierce, but she ignored it as best she could for the moment. She was just grateful to be home and in one piece. She'd take another pain pill in a little while.

Mal said, "How do you feel about visitors? Lots of people wanted me to let them know when you got home."

"Give me a few hours to get situated, and then you can open the floodgates."

There was a knock on the door. "I'll get it," Crystal said.

In the small moment that she was gone, Mal said, "You scared this brother to death. Glad you weren't hurt any worse than you were."

"Me, too. Thanks for finding me. Sometime soon, I want to hear the details."

Crystal returned with Sheriff Will Dalton, who asked, "How are you, Bernadine?"

"I've been better, Will. You?"

"It's been a pretty good morning. Got a tip on the arsonist and your accident."

She sat up as straight as the pain would allow. "Did it pan out?"

"Took the suspect in a little while ago."

"Who?"

"Dessa Stillwell."

Bernadine was stunned. "Really."

"Freda Stillwell came to the office this morning. She had some gasoline-soaked clothes in a bag. Said her grandmother came home the night of the fire reeking of gasoline, but she didn't put two and two together until she saw the newspaper article about the fire the next morning."

"Poor Freda."

"Not poor anymore. Two hundred and fifty thousand dollars buys a lot."

Bernadine nodded and remembered her conversation with the girl the day of the Sanderson funeral about her financial plans for the upcoming school year. She was willing to bet Freda had already decided to turn her grandmother in for the reward money. "She told me she was real close to Mrs. Sanderson."

"Told me the same thing. Might have been what initially cemented her decision."

Mal said, "That, and that she and Dessa never got along. Dessa ran Bernadine off the road, too?"

He nodded. "Freda said when Dessa came home, Freda asked her about all the damage to the truck, and Dessa said she'd hit a deer, but when her grandmother parked the truck in the barn and began stacking hay bales around it like she was hiding it, Freda wanted to know why. Dessa told her to get back in the house and mind her own business. When she heard about your accident, she figured out why her grandmother was trying to hide the truck. That's when she called my office. The deputies executing the search warrant on the place this morning found a voice enhancer too, so the mystery about the threatening calls is probably solved."

Bernadine hoped he was right. "I wonder why she didn't call you right after the funeral?"

"She said she had to find the clothes her grandmother was wearing the night of the fire. Took her some time. She found them in a crawl space at the top of one of the barns."

Bernadine sighed and shook her head sadly. What a convoluted and sad tale. She wondered if Freda had been waiting all her life for some way to pay her grandmother back for not letting the girl go with her mom when her parents split up. "So, what about Al Stillwell? Was he involved?"

"Not that we can tell so far. He's in Oklahoma, and we verified that he was working the night of the fire, and the night you crashed."

"Thanks for letting me know, Will."

"Glad we can finally put this mess to bed. Now I can concentrate on practicing for the Idol competition."

Bernadine laughed. "What?"

"Yes, ma'am. Planning to win, too. Wife's already spent the five hundred dollar first prize."

Mal asked, grinning, "And what are you doing?"

"I'm not telling you, July. It's a secret, but it's no secret who's going to be taking home that money."

Crystal shook her head and chuckled. "You old people are a mess."

Later that evening, seemingly everyone within fifty miles had stopped by to wish Bernadine well. She was particularly happy to see Roni, who'd finally returned home from her whirlwind worldwide tour. Reverend Paula came by to pray with her, and when the last group of visitors finally departed, Bernadine hobbled into the downstairs guest room, downed some pain meds, and crawled into bed. But as she lay there, she thought about Freda and her grandmother. On one hand, her money would offer Freda a tremendous future, but on the other hand, her money and the lawyer it paid to handle the lawsuit had contributed to what Dessa felt was no future, and Bernadine wondered if she'd ever rid herself of her feeling of guilt.

By the end of May, Bernadine was all healed up and back in her office, working full-time. Jack bought Eli an old car so that he and Crystal could attend a series of weekend art classes at the Fort Hays University, which freed Jack up on those same weekends to help Rocky with the motorcycle. Preston heard nothing further from his birth mother or grandmother, but at his mom's suggestion he sent Dr. Winthrop a handwritten thank-you note for the kick-ass telescope. He continued to

hold hope that they'd meet face-to-face one day in the future.
And according to the rumors, Riley and Cletus had flown to
Hollywood.

And all over town people were practicing for Henry Adams
Idol. Some contestants, like Jack and the Mad Dads—the name
Amari gave them—practiced publicly at the kiva under the
contest's music director, Roni. Others, like the Paynes, were
practicing secretly, hoping that the element of surprise would
boost their chance of taking home the big prize. Devon's re-
hearsals were better too, mainly because Trent quietly bribed
Amari and Preston with a twenty-dollar bill to "encourage"
them to play along.

On a late Monday afternoon in the middle of June, Bernadine looked up from her desk to see Tamar enter her office.
Trailing in the matriarch's wake was the leather-clad, oh-so-
handsome bad boy Diego July.

Tamar said, "He's here to talk to Crystal."

"She's down at the college in Hays, checking out an art
exhibit. Hello, Diego."

"Hi, Ms. Brown.

"I'll send her a text."

Bernadine couldn't read Tamar's mood, but she sensed
Tamar wanted the matter between Crys and Diego resolved as
quickly as possible and Bernadine did, too.

When Crystal read the text from Ms. Bernadine on her phone,
she blinked and read it again. Diego? At her office? Goose
bumps flew up her back. She looked around for Eli and saw
him over by a canvas, talking to a couple of kids from Franklin High. She hastily gathered up her tote and the brochures
she'd picked up when they entered the exhibit, and hurried

over. "Excuse me, but Eli, you have to take me to the Power Plant. Now."

He looked up from his conversation. "Be ready to go in just a minute."

Ignoring the irritation on the faces of the kids he'd been talking with, she countered insistently, "We have to go now. Ms. Bernadine wants me at her office, and it's an emergency. Come on!" She grabbed him by the arm.

He told the kids, "Guess I'm going now."

While she pulled him along, he dug into his pocket for his car keys. "Your mom okay? She's not hurt again, is she?"

"No, no. Diego's here, and—"

"Diego?" Eli asked flatly, and came to an abrupt stop. "I'm driving you back to see him?"

"Yes, and don't trip. Car's over there."

"I know where I parked."

During the ride back to town, she pulled down the mirror to check her hair and makeup. She ignored the way Eli rolled his eyes . . .

"So you think he's here to ask Ms. Bernadine for your hand."

"Stop hating."

"Then stop being so damned dumb!"

"Just drive."

"Don't worry. Getting your dumb butt to Diego as soon as possible."

"You're just jealous."

"Of a jerk who never finished high school? You doing meth now?"

Crystal wanted to punch him out. How many times was he going to throw Diego's being a dropout in her face?

When they arrived at the Power Plant, she got out, stormed to the door, and didn't look back.

And there he was. When she entered, Diego stood up, and the smile on his superfine face made her heart beat like it was going to burst through her layered tees. "Hey, Diego."

"Hey, Crystal."

She tore her eyes away from him and settled them on the inscrutable faces of Ms. Bernadine and Tamar.

"Thanks for being so quick," Ms. Bernadine said, showing a small smile.

She nodded at Tamar. "Eli brought me back."

"Diego has something to talk to you about. Tamar and I'll be in Lily's office, so you two can have some privacy."

"Okay, thanks." She couldn't believe she was actually going to get to talk to him alone, but Tamar and Ms. Bernadine slipped out.

Once they were gone, she sat down, and he did the same.

"How you been?" he asked.

"I'm good. How about you?"

"Good."

Crystal felt like a kid on Christmas morning.

"I hear you and the boys were put on lockdown because of what you told Ms. Brown about me."

"Yeah, I'm sorry if I got you in trouble."

"You know I'm too old for you, right?"

Crys looked down at her hands. "I went with a guy twenty-one before."

"Then he needed his ass kicked. You're still a kid. Besides, you're not that girl anymore. How long have you been off the street?"

"Almost three years now."

"You don't want to go back out there, not even with me."

"How do you know?"

"Just by looking at you. You're a princess now, Crystal. Perfect hair, makeup, clothes. You told me in the e-mails that you'd been to Spain, and that you and Ms. Brown fly around on her jet. Nobody I knows does that. I'll bet you even know what kind of wine to pick at those fancy eating places."

"Sometimes." She wasn't allowed to drink, but she'd been to many upscale restaurants with Ms. Bernadine and her girls.

"I'll admit, the first time I saw you, you knocked me to my knees, and because you were working at the Dog, I thought you were a college girl, but when Trent told me your real age, I knew I had to back off."

She kept her eyes focused on the ring she was twisting on her finger.

"Crys, look. If I made you think that we could be more than friends for now, I'm sorry. I thought you knew we were just kicking it. No way would I have wanted you to run away from home. And if you want to know the truth, I'm not looking for any kind of a serious relationship. Things might be different later on, but right now, I'm a July. It's all about me, and the more ladies the better. You don't want to get caught up in that."

His bluntness made her feel stupid. It also hurt. Playing it off, she waved her hand. "Don't worry about it. I'm good. Sorry Tamar made you come."

"She thought it was important to get this straightened out, and so did I."

"Okay. Thanks."

"Still friends?"

"Sure."

"Crys?"

She met his eyes and hoped he didn't see the tears stinging them.

"You may be young, but you are so way out of my league. Maybe one day we'll be more even."

"Not if you don't go back to school, we won't be."

He laughed. "See? Way out of my league."

Crys still felt young and silly, but a part of her was glad they'd had this talk. "Thanks, Diego."

"Any time." He stood up, and she followed suit.

He walked over and placed a kiss on her forehead. "Stay sweet, baby girl. Tell Tamar I'm gone, would you?"

"I will."

Flashing her a smile, he strode out of the office.

Once he was gone, she wiped the tears from her eyes and took out her phone. She didn't want to see anyone, so she sent Ms. Bernadine a text saying she and Diego were done and that he was gone and she was going home.

When she stepped outside, Eli was still parked by the curb. He leaned over and opened the passenger door. She got in.

"You okay?"

She didn't reply.

"You want to talk?"

Her voice came out in a whisper. "No. Just take me home."

Eli started up the car and did as she'd asked.

When he pulled up into her driveway, Crystal sat silently before confessing. "You were right."

"About what?"

"Diego. He told me I was too young for him."

When Eli didn't respond, she looked over. "You aren't going to laugh and say, Told you so?"

"Friends don't do that."

She dropped back into silence.

"I'm going to ask Samantha to go out with me."

She stared. "Samantha from school?"

"Yeah. Been talking to her off and on for the past few weeks. When she's away from Megan, she's kinda cool."

Crystal wondered why her life seemed to be falling apart. "Why're you telling me?"

"Just wanted you to know, I guess. That friend thing again."

"Okay. Thanks for the ride. I'll see you later."

She got out, and he backed down the driveway and drove the short distance across the street to his house. She entered her silent house and immediately ran up the stairs to her room. Closing the door, she sat on her bed and cried. Nobody told her growing up would be so complicated, or that being a princess would make her feel like she was living in a cage. She wanted out, for at least a little while, but didn't know how that was going to be possible.

Back at Bernadine's office, she and Tamar sat in Lily's office in silence. Bernadine had purposefully turned on the com on her desk before leaving with Tamar because she wanted to hear what Diego said to her daughter, and as the mom, she had a right to be nosy.

Tamar said, "Sorry Crystal's hurting, but I'm glad the so-called relationship turned out to be not what she thought."

Bernadine agreed. Her heart ached for Crystal, but not the way it would've had she really taken it in her head to run away from home. "Thanks, Tamar."

"You're welcome."

When Bernadine got home from work, Crystal was sitting out on the deck. "Hey, Crys."

"Hey."

"How'd it go with Diego?"

She shrugged. "He said he was too old for me, and that he hadn't been hitting on me. I feel so stupid."

"You shouldn't."

"Well, I do, and I feel like I can't breathe. I like my life here, but I miss my old one."

Bernadine sat down in one of the empty chairs at the table. "And what do you miss?"

"You want the truth?"

"Always."

"Being able to go and do what I want, when I want. I miss the streets and the noise and the people. I can't tell you the last time I smelled a McDonald's."

Bernadine showed a small smile. "Out here is definitely different."

"Sucks sometimes."

"So, what do you want to do?"

"I don't know. Diego said I'm not the same girl I used to be. He called me a princess because I get to fly on jets."

"Regular kids don't get those kinds of perks. So, do you want to be the old Crystal?"

"Sometimes, yeah, I do. She was fly."

"And the new Crys isn't?"

"I'm still fly, but I'm rich-girl fly—there's a difference."

"Ah."

"It's hard to explain."

"I understand. Growing up is hard."

"Tell me about it."

"But we all hope to reach a point in our life where we're comfortable in our skin, and for some us it takes a while.

You've been plopped down in a whole new world, Crys—no one expects you to find your footing right away."

"It's been three years, and the old me is still inside, wanting to get out."

"She's always going to be inside. We can't just turn off our past like a light switch."

"I guess."

"On the next school break we can fly down to Dallas or New Orleans and let you smell a McDonald's, if you want."

Crys smiled. "Maybe."

"And you can always go and talk to Reverend Paula if you need helping figuring stuff out, too. One of the blessings of being here is you have a large extended family willing to help out any way they can."

"I know. Maybe I will talk to the Rev."

Bernadine stood. "Whatever you do, just know that I love you, and I'm here for you."

"Thanks, Mom."

"I'm going to go change clothes. Who's cooking tonight, you or me?"

"I'll cook. It'll give me something else to think about."

Bernadine moved around the table and planted a kiss on her cheek. "Hang in there, sweetie."

Crys hugged her tight. "I will."

On her way up to her bedroom, Bernadine was glad they'd had the talk, but she felt something looming on the horizon, like the smell of rain before a thunderstorm.

CHAPTER
24

The Fourth of July dawned sunny and bright. The cookout at Tamar's began with breakfast and ended early that afternoon so that everyone could head over to the rec's auditorium for the Idol contest.

When Bernadine entered the auditorium, it was already filling up. She spotted Reg Garland, seated by himself. "Can I sit with you?"

"Sure. I think we may be the only two people in the county not performing."

"You may be right."

In spite of his smile, she sensed sadness. She wondered if he and Roni were doing better as a couple now that Roni had been home for a while, but it would be out-and-out rude to ask something so personal, so she didn't and watched the people entering instead.

For the next half an hour people filed in. Twenty minutes before the curtain was due to rise, a quick look-around showed that all 125 seats were filled. The air in the room was electric.

At precisely eight o clock, Sheila came out onstage. "Welcome to the first Henry Adams Idol competition."

Thunderous applause greeted her words, and she smiled. "We have some great acts for your enjoyment this evening, so sit back, have fun, and if you feel the urge to stand up and shake a tail feather, that's all right, too."

Laughter greeted that.

"First up, we have Five-O! Let's give them a hand!"

The curtain lifted and there stood Sheriff Will Dalton, of all people, wearing a long rocker's wig over his buzz cut and holding a guitar! With him were three other guitarists and a guy behind a huge drum set. She stared wide-eyed at Reg, who was grinning ear to ear. Before she could put her shock into words, Will hit some chords on his guitar and began rocking the house with "Brown Sugar" by the Rolling Stones. And to her delight they were good, damn good. Will not only sang but played lead, lighting up that guitar with a solo that had people on their feet shaking tail feathers and everything else. She then understood what he meant about winning the competition. The next people up were going to have to grow wings and fly around the room to beat the performance of Five-O.

When the band hit the last note, the frenzied audience went nuts.

Next up was a little girl who appeared to be no older than ten. She was cute, and though she had a terrible voice and even worse dance moves, she was trying. Bernadine leaned over to Reg. "What's she singing?"

"Katy Perry."

Bernadine wanted to ask who that was, but rather than put her ignorance on display, she sat back and let the girl's performance help her recover from being rocked half to death by Will Dalton and his band Five-O.

The little girl finally finished and made her exit to a round of polite applause.

The house lights went down for a minute, and when the curtain rose, this time there were three girls standing in a spotlight with their backs to the audience, arms extended. They too were wearing fake hair, but their costumes were glitzy-looking ball gowns like Diana Ross and the Supremes wore in the 1960s. It was easy for Bernadine to figure out that the girls on the outside were Crystal and Leah, and that the shorty in the middle was Zoey. The lights slowly came back up, and the small orchestra behind them was revealed for the first time. She stared at Reg.

"My wife the music director never does anything halfway. The musicians'll be onstage for the rest of the competition."

Bernadine was about to ask him how come she knew nothing about any of this when the musicians began, and Zoey, holding the mike, whipped her head toward the audience and belted out like the diva that she was, "What you want, baby I got! What you need—"

Bernadine's mouth dropped. Aretha! Sure enough, with Crystal and Leah singing backup, Zoey tore up the place, prancing and posing and singing her little butt off. She sounded like Teena Marie's Mini-Me, and the folks in the audience were on their feet, singing and dancing and clapping in time with the song and the jamming musicians.

Zoey was in her element, and she appeared to be having a ball. Crystal and Leah didn't miss a step in their moves, and went through their routine grinning giddily.

When they were done, the appreciative applause was deafening, and a smiling Sheila walked back out to center stage. "That was the group Girlfriends! Let's give them another hand."

The audience didn't have to be asked twice.

Once they quieted, Sheila said into her mic, "And now, doing another Motor City favorite—"You Got to Earn It," by the Temptations—Jack and the Mad Dads!"

Bernadine stared. *Who?*

Out walked Jack, Trent, and Gary. Jack stood in front of the floor mic, and Trent and Gary flanked him on the left and right. They were dressed in black suits and white sneaks. Bernadine was so blown away, her hand covered her mouth in delight.

The drummer started the rhythm. The bass guitar followed, and when the rest of the small orchestra took up their parts, Jack took the mic and crooned, "To get stones from a rock, you got to break it . . . ," and Gary and Trent sang, "Yeah yeah yeah."

Jack's falsetto was nothing compared to Eddie Kendricks's original, but in Henry Adams it was enough to make the women start screaming, especially Rocky, who was on her feet. The Mad Dads worked their way through the easy-paced R&B classic, and once again folks were on their feet, dancing, clapping, and singing. Bernadine looked around the partying audience and cracked up at the sight of four old white guys doing the Temptation walk in the center aisle.

At the music's bridge, the Dads did a series of Temptation steps that brought down the house. They then repositioned themselves, and Jack pulled the mic free and crooned on. When they were done, they bowed in unison, and the audience screamed themselves hoarse.

Bernadine said to Reg, "These folk are trying to put me back in the hospital!"

Reg rolled his eyes in response.

Mal came out next. He sat on the stool he'd carried out with him and sang the Otis Redding classic "Sitting on the Dock of the Bay." He was good—not spectacular, but he appeared to be having fun, and that was all that mattered.

Next up, to her surprise, was Clay Dobbs, who walked out to center stage dressed in a fine looking cream-colored, western-styled suit and a matching wide-brimmed Stetson. He was carrying a big brown guitar. He positioned himself on the edge of the stool Mal used, and his opening series of twang-filled notes made even Bernadine jump to her feet as he sang, "The thrill is gone . . ."

His voice was outstanding, and his skilled guitar playing awesome. Once again the audience added their voices, and soon the lyrics to the old B.B. King classic rose to fill the space. He sang effortlessly and flawlessly. He was so good that were she in charge, he'd be the night's winner.

When he finished, he stood, bowed, and walked smoothly back into the wings.

Lily and Trent walked on and sang "Reunited," by Peaches and Herb. Their voices blended well, and Bernadine thought their choice of song was very sweet and appropriate, considering all love had taken them through.

Reverend Grant came out next and did a cover of the lovely Yolanda Adams gospel tune "I'm Gonna Be Ready." She had a good strong alto voice, and Bernadine could hear a few people in the seats behind hers singing along.

Following her was an elementary school student from Franklin, who played "Flight of the Bumblebee" on his violin.

He was pretty good, not good enough to win, but the audience gave him a rousing standing ovation.

The stage lights went down, and Tamar walked out. "Next, Colonel Barrett Montgomery Payne and his wife, Sheila, in the tango!"

A spotlight came on, and there they were, posed like a couple in a ballroom competition. Bernadine couldn't believe her eyes!

The sultry music began, and the Paynes began their strut. Barrett steered Sheila through the steps, pausing every now and then so she could snap her head back and forth. It was obvious that they knew what they were doing. They moved as one, leaning against each other and then backing away—the crowd loved it.

The stunned Bernadine glanced over at Reg, and he laughed and shouted over the mayhem, "Amazing, right?"

"Yes!"

The routine was about five minutes long, but she could've watched them for an hour or more. Skill and finesse could be seen in every move. When they ended the mesmerizing performance, they bowed, exited to roof-raising applause, and Bernadine finally closed her mouth. Who knew!

There was a short break while the musicians and the audience tried to catch their breath, and then Sheila walked out again. "Okay, our last act of the evening,"

A drumroll sounded, and over it Sheila yelled, "The hardest-working entertainers in the state of Kansas. Devon W. July and the Flames!"

And out they came, Amari, Preston, Eli, and Devon. The audience went wild upon seeing the shiny black pompadours on their heads. Devon had on a suit, but his Flames were wearing black tees, jeans, and sneaks.

The musicians started a bluesy number, and Devon grabbed the mic and pleaded, "Please, please don't go." Behind him, the Flames moved slowly to the left and right, answering with the same sung phrase. Devon kept pleading as he and the boys covered the old James Brown tune. And soon Devon was singing and spinning and moonwalking and dropping to his knees, begging the mythical woman to please don't go.

Folks in the audience were screaming.

Then the song slowed as if ending, and the begging Devon was hunched over and pleading into the mic while the Flames kept up their slow-moving chant. Still bent over as if he were dying from his broken heart, he began moving offstage, singing all the while. That's when Eli draped the cape over Devon's back, just like in the old James Brown Revue, and Bernadine leaped to her feet along with everyone else in the audience. And just like Brown, Devon kept the cape on for a few seconds, thrust it off, and went into a dizzying dance routine. He snatched the mic up and pleaded again, "Baby, please don't go."

Even the musicians were on their feet as they played away. The cape was draped over his back three more times, and three more times, Devon shook it off, whirled the dance moves that did James Brown proud, and added a series of splits.

It was apparent to everyone watching that Devon belonged on the stage. His performance was wild, funny, and most of all sensational. When he and the Flames finally slowed and walked their way back into the wings, the applause and cheers went on endlessly.

Bernadine finally fell back into her seat, feeling as if she'd run a marathon.

Reggie asked, "So who's the winner?"

"Everybody was good, but I'm putting my money on Clay."

He said, "I'm going with the Paynes."

The judges, Roni and Siz, were polled while the audience waited expectantly. A few minutes later, Sheila walked back out to announce the results. "In fourth place, and the winner of one hundred dollars: Devon and the Flames!"

Applause.

"In third place, and the winner of two hundred and fifty dollars: Clay Dobbs."

Louder applause.

"Our second-place prize of three hundred dollars goes to Five-O!"

Insane applause.

And then she grinned. "In first place, and the grand prize winner of five hundred dollars, drumroll, please—"

The drummer obliged.

"The Paynes!"

The musicians struck up the tango music again, and a smiling Barrett ran out onstage, took his wife by the hand, and they tangoed like nobody's business. The screaming crowd jumped to their feet and gave the winners their due.

On the ride home with Mal, Bernadine couldn't believe how exhausted she was. All the clapping, screaming, shaking, and singing had left her limp. "That was fun. Sorry you didn't win."

"It's okay. Glad Clay won something, though."

"How long has he been playing guitar?"

"Since we were probably seven or eight."

"Wow. He was excellent. And how long has Will been playing? His group was good, too."

"He shouldn't've even been allowed to enter."

"Why not?"

"Because he used to play with one of those old rock groups back in the day. For all intents and purposes he's a professional."

She smiled, leaned over, and hooked her arm in his.

He said to her, "Got something for you in the glove box."

"And it is?"

"You have to open the box and see."

Wondering what this wonderful man was up to now, she did as he asked and withdrew a small blue velvet box. She opened it and was awed by the sight of a small faceted sapphire, centered on a gold chain. "Mal, this is beautiful."

"You like it?"

"I do. Are we celebrating something?"

"Yes. Me and you. I'm calling it a Promise Necklace."

She looked over at him in confusion. "And what's that mean?" She lifted the delicate chain free of the box.

"Means, since we decided to not decide on marrying, I promise to love you like no other, in sickness and health and in sunshine and rain."

"Oh, Mal."

"Not done."

She chuckled softly, and her heart was full. "Sorry, go on."

"I promise to be there when you need me, and stay out of your way when you don't. I promise to be upfront and honest, dependable, understanding, and to make sure you stop turning the world every now and then long enough to smell the roses."

"Anything else?"

"Not that I can think of."

"That's some pretty powerful promising."

"I have a pretty powerful woman."

She leaned over and kissed him on the cheek. "I love you."

"And that's a good thing."

That night, as she lay in bed thinking back on the day, she was once again very thankful to be living in her little town on the plains. Her foster kids were thriving, their parents too. She'd found love in the arms of a man who could make her laugh and send her heart soaring all in the same moment. She was building a church and a grocery store and a fire station. There were a few things nibbling on the edge of her contentment, however, the most important being Crystal. She sensed something not right with the daughter of her heart, and she wasn't sure how it might manifest itself, but she planned to keep loving her no matter what the future held.

She also planned to get a full night's sleep; tomorrow was another day in Henry Adams, and she needed to be ready.

FROM

**BEVERLY
JENKINS**

AND

**WILLIAM
MORROW**

Discussion Questions

1. How did the title *A Wish and a Prayer* resonate through the story?

2. Will the relationship between Jack and Rocky flourish or flounder?

3. Do you think Bernadine's guilt over the Stillwell family will affect her future philanthropy endeavors?

4. What did you think of Bernadine's and Mal's decision not to formalize their relationship?

5. Discuss Preston's story line. How did you feel about it?

6. Should a child's Internet activities be monitored by a parent or guardian?

7. Did Cletus have the right to defend himself, and did you agree or disagree with Judge Davis's decision in the case?

8. Have you or your family ever participated in a night-sky-watching activity?

9. Do you believe Dr. Margaret Winthrop and her mother, Lenore Crenshaw, will ever reconcile?

10. Discuss what you'd like to see happen next in Henry Adams.

Author's Note

A Wish and a Prayer is the fourth trip to Henry Adams, Kansas. As in the previous installments, there were moments of joy, tears, and wishes coming true. I found Preston's story particularly satisfying because many foster kids never get a permanent loving family or make contact with their birth parents. He did both and can now continue to pursue his dream of becoming a renowned astrophysicist like his birth mom, and his hero, Dr. Neil deGrasse Tyson, without worrying about having to adjust to a new home in the future.

The previous three books have spawned many questions from readers—chief among them: Will Mal and Bernadine finally get together? And Will Rocky ever give poor Jack the time of day? I hope those burning questions have been answered to your satisfaction.

Bernadine's wealth caused some issues in this story. Whether her guilt over the Stillwell family will affect her future philanthropical endeavors is unclear.

The idea of the Idol competition was sparked by a conversation I had with my mother-in-law. She lives in a small town on the western side of Michigan. Her community has been holding its version of *American Idol* for a few years now and I thought it would be a hoot for Henry Adams to have its own. Who knew the Paynes could tango, or that Sheriff Will Dalton could rock the house? I had a ball with the competition and I hope you in the audience had fun, too.

As always, questions remain. Will Cletus really find fame in Hollywood? Will Reg and Roni find love again? Will Crystal break Bernadine's heart by running away? And how much more whitewash can Marie Jefferson's fence stand? Stay tuned. The answers to these questions and more may be revealed in the next visit to Henry Adams. Until then, be a Blessing to a child near you.

See you next time,
B.